Darker Than Desire
A Dark, Spicy Romance with an FTM Trans Male Hero and Deadly Obsession
Lucinda Wicked

Copyright © 2025 by Lucinda Wicked

All rights reserved. No part of this publication may be reproduced, stored or transmitted in any form or by any means, electronic, mechanical, photocopying, recording, scanning, or otherwise without written permission from the publisher. It is illegal to copy this book, post it to a website, or distribute it by any other means without permission.

This novel is entirely a work of fiction. The names, characters and incidents portrayed in it are the work of the author's imagination. Any resemblance to actual persons, living or dead, events or localities is entirely coincidental.

Lucinda Wicked asserts the moral right to be identified as the author of this work.

Lucinda Wicked has no responsibility for the persistence or accuracy of URLs for external or third-party Internet Websites referred to in this publication and does not guarantee that any content on such Websites is, or will remain, accurate or appropriate.

Designations used by companies to distinguish their products are often claimed as trademarks. All brand names and product names used in this book and on its cover are trade names, service marks, trademarks and registered trademarks of their respective owners. The publishers and the book are not associated with any product or vendor mentioned in this book. None of the companies referenced within the book have endorsed the book.

Edited by: The Celestial Coven

Advisors: W. Davis

Cover Art by: Getcovers.com

First edition

Contents

Dedication	V
Preface	VI
Acknowledgments	VIII
Triggers:	IX
Shadows of Obsession Playlist	XI
Prologue	1
Chapter 1	8
Chapter 2	15
Chapter 3	23
Chapter 4	32
Chapter 5	41
Chapter 6	49
Chapter 7	56
Chapter 8	64
Chapter 9	73
Chapter 10	77
Chapter 11	84
Chapter 12	93
Chapter 13	103
Chapter 14	113
Chapter 15	127

Chapter 16	133
Chapter 17	138
Chapter 18	142
Chapter 19	147
Chapter 20	153
Chapter 21	160
Chapter 22	171
Chapter 23	178
Chapter 24	186
Chapter 25	193
Epilogue	201
Endnotes	208
Afterword	209
About the Author	211
Also by Lucinda Wicked	212

To my real-life Talon,

If fate brought us together, it's because the world needed a little more chaos. Thank you for always supporting my mayhem and being my partner in crime.

Preface

IN THE SHADOWS OF chaos, where trust is a rare currency and survival is never guaranteed, **Darker Than Desire** was born—a story of resilience, redemption, and the unyielding power of love. At its heart is Talon Hayes, a man whose life has been defined by battles both external and internal. Former military turned ghost in the underworld, Talon navigates a treacherous world with precision and ferocity, but the scars he carries run deeper than his skin.

Talon is more than a soldier, more than a protector. He is a trans man, and his journey of self-discovery, survival, and finding a sense of belonging is woven into every chapter of this story. This book is about honoring his identity without defining him solely by it—showcasing his strength, vulnerability, and complexity as a fully realized character. Talon's experiences as a transgender man, from navigating relationships to confronting the world's expectations, are integral to his character but not his sole battle. His journey is one of many layers, where the intersections of identity, trauma, and love create a tapestry as raw and intricate as the world he inhabits.

Writing Talon's story has been a deeply personal journey. As an author, I believe representation matters—not just for those who rarely see themselves reflected in stories, but also for those who seek to understand lives different from their own. Talon's struggles and triumphs as a trans man are treated with the respect and nuance they deserve, woven seamlessly into the narrative alongside the high stakes, tension, and romance that drive the plot.

This book isn't just about danger, betrayal, and love—it's about finding light in the darkest corners of life, about fighting for who you are and who you love. It's about accepting the scars that shape us, while refusing to let them define our futures.

For readers who share some of Talon's experiences, I hope you find in him a reflection of strength, perseverance, and possibility. For those who don't, I invite you to walk beside him, to see his world through his eyes, and to embrace the complexity that makes him whole.

Talon's story is one of survival and self-acceptance, of daring to reach for connection even when it feels impossible. It's not an easy journey, but it's one worth taking. Because even in the deepest shadows, there's always the possibility of finding light—and love.

With all my gratitude and heart,

Lucinda Wicked

Acknowledgments

To my real-life Talon—this book wouldn't exist without you. From the very first idea to the final chapter, your guidance, insight, and unwavering support have been a cornerstone of this story. You've been my sounding board, my cheerleader, and my co-conspirator in crafting a world where Talon Hayes and Havoc could thrive. You didn't just help me write these characters—you breathed life into them, giving them a depth and authenticity I couldn't have achieved alone.

Thank you for sharing your voice, your experiences, and your heart with me throughout this journey. Your input made Talon's story not just more genuine, but more powerful. You helped me navigate the challenges of representing a trans man with honesty and respect, and your feedback was invaluable in creating a character as layered and complex as Talon. I hope this story reflects the care, thought, and love you poured into it alongside me.

More than anything, thank you for being my friend. For believing in me when I doubted myself, for pushing me to keep going when I felt stuck, and for reminding me why we tell stories in the first place. This book is as much yours as it is mine, and I couldn't be prouder to have shared this journey with you.

Here's to Talon and Havoc—and here's to you.

With endless gratitude,

Lucinda Wicked

Triggers:

Dear Reader,

Before delving into the realms of 'Darker Than Desire,' we believe it is essential to provide you with insights into the sensitive and potentially triggering content woven into the fabric of this narrative. Your emotional well-being is of utmost importance, and we wish to empower you to make an informed decision about whether to proceed.

Within the pages of this tale, you may encounter intense and challenging themes. Brace yourself for vivid depictions of:

- Blood and injury
- Body dysmorphia
- Breath play
- Death
- Dirty talk
- Emotional manipulation
- Grief and loss
- Gun violence
- Intense arguments and conflict
- Internalized transphobia
- Kidnapping

- Knife play

- Marking (biting, scratching)

- Mentions of war and combat

- Obsessive behavior

- Power imbalances

- PTSD

- Rough sex

- Self-doubt and insecurity

- Torture

- Touch-me-not dynamics

- Toxic relationships

- Trauma from past abuse

- Violence

- Voyeurism

Reader discretion is advised, and we encourage those who may be sensitive to these themes to approach the story with caution or seek additional information before proceeding. While our aim is to craft an engaging narrative, your well-being remains our priority.

Thank you for your understanding.

Lucinda Wicked

Shadows of Obsession Playlist

<u>Spotify</u>

Ordinary - Alex Warren Take Me to Church - Hozier

Creep - Radiohead

Love Runs Out- OneRepublic

Demons- Imagine Dragons

Control- Halsey

Paint It, Black- The Rolling Stones

Arsonist's Lullabye- Hozier

Everybody Wants To Rule The World - From "The Hunger Games: Catching Fire" - Lorde

Way down We Go- KALEO

Monster STARSET Before You Leave Me - Alex Warren

Do I Wanna Know?- Arctic Monkeys

Take What You Want (feat. Ozzy Osbourne & Travis Scott)- Post Malone, Ozzy Osbourne, Travis Scott

Madness- Muse

No Rest for the Wicked- Lykke Li

Seven Nation Army- The White Stripes

Bring Me To Life- Evanescence

UnsteadyX- Ambassadors

Devil's Backbone- The Civil Wars

Tears Don't Fall- Bullet For My Valentine

Hurricane- Thirty Seconds To Mars

Surrender- Natalie Taylor

Dead Man Walking- Jelly Roll

Wicked Game- Chris Isaak

War Of Hearts- Ruelle

Shadow on the Sun- Audioslave

Control- Zoe Wees

Rescue Me- OneRepublic

Running Up That Hill- Placebo

Prologue

THE DESERT AIR WAS dry and electric, the kind of night where every shadow felt sharper, every sound amplified. Talon crouched behind a crumbled wall, Havoc by his side. The Belgian Malinois was a shadow himself, silent and steady, ears perked and eyes locked on their target—a heavily fortified compound just ahead.

"You good, buddy?" Talon whispered, his voice barely audible over the faint hum of cicadas. Havoc gave a low rumble of acknowledgment, his tail flicking once. Talon allowed himself a ghost of a smile, the kind that faded as quickly as it came. They'd done this a hundred times before: reconnaissance, infiltration, extraction. Routine. But tonight felt different, and that gnawed at his gut.

Through his earpiece, the commander's voice crackled. "Hayes, move to position Bravo. You've got five minutes."

"Roger that," Talon replied. He gave Havoc the signal—a subtle hand gesture—and the dog moved seamlessly into a low stalk. Together, they crept along the outer perimeter, their movements practiced and precise.

They reached the first checkpoint without incident. Talon's fingers ghosted over the cool metal of his rifle, his body humming with adrenaline. From his vantage point, he could see guards patrolling the compound, their movements erratic. Something was off.

"Team Alpha in position," another voice said through the comms.

"Bravo here," Talon murmured, pressing himself against the shadows. "Awaiting orders."

The response was immediate. "Proceed with caution. Intel suggests an increase in hostiles. Secure the asset and get out."

Havoc gave a low growl, almost imperceptible, but Talon felt it like a warning bell. He placed a calming hand on the dog's neck. "Easy, boy."

They moved forward, navigating through the maze-like compound. Havoc's nose worked overtime, sniffing out traps and signaling clear paths. Talon's trust in him was absolute. Havoc had saved his life more times than he could count, and tonight would be no different—he hoped.

They reached the central building, their target inside. Talon crouched by the door, Havoc by his heel, both waiting for the signal to breach. The countdown in his head began. Three. Two—

The explosion came out of nowhere.

A deafening roar ripped through the night, throwing Talon and Havoc back. His vision blurred, ears ringing as he struggled to process what had just happened. The compound was in chaos, alarms blaring, shouts echoing from all directions. Talon pushed himself up, wincing at the sharp pain in his side.

"Mayday, mayday! Bravo compromised!" he shouted into his comms, but all he got was static. The line was dead.

Havoc barked sharply, drawing Talon's attention. The dog was on high alert, his body tense and ready for action. Through the haze, Talon saw them—figures moving toward them, weapons raised.

"Shit," Talon muttered. He swung his rifle up, taking aim as the first hostile came into view. The firefight was brutal and fast. Talon moved on instinct, taking down one, then another, but there were too many. Havoc launched himself at an attacker, his teeth sinking into flesh with a ferocity that made Talon's chest tighten with both pride and fear.

"Havoc, fall back!" Talon yelled, his voice raw. The dog obeyed, retreating to his side, blood on his muzzle. Talon grabbed a flashbang from his belt, tossing it toward the advancing enemies. The explosion of light and sound bought them a few precious seconds.

"We're not dying here," Talon growled, more to himself than Havoc. He pushed through the pain, leading them toward the extraction point. But every step felt heavier, his vision swimming. He realized with grim certainty that he was losing too much blood.

As they neared the edge of the compound, another explosion rocked the ground beneath them. Talon was thrown forward, landing hard. His weapon skittered out of reach, and he barely had time to react as a shadow loomed over him. The enemy raised their weapon, and Talon's heart lurched.

Havoc moved like a blur, leaping between Talon and the attacker. The sound of the gunshot was deafening. Havoc yelped, but he didn't falter, his jaws locking around the assailant's arm, bringing them down.

"No!" Talon roared, dragging himself up despite the searing pain. He grabbed his sidearm, firing a clean shot at the attacker before collapsing next to Havoc. The dog's breaths were shallow, his blood pooling beneath him.

Talon pressed a trembling hand to Havoc's neck. "Stay with me, buddy. Don't you dare leave me." His vision darkened as adrenaline gave way to exhaustion.

The last thing he remembered was the sound of approaching helicopters and the feel of Havoc's warm body against his side.

Talon woke in a sterile hospital room, his body screaming in protest as he shifted. The memories flooded back in painful detail. His hand flew to the scar running across his torso, a cruel reminder of his failure. Havoc—

"He's alive," a voice said, pulling Talon from his spiraling thoughts. A woman in fatigues stood at the foot of his bed, her expression unreadable. "Your dog's tough. He'll pull through."

Relief was short-lived. The next words cut deeper than any wound. "As for you, Hayes, your actions compromised the mission. You're being discharged—dishonorably."

Talon's heart sank. "You're kidding. I—"

"Save it," she interrupted. "This isn't up for debate. Pack your things. You leave tomorrow."

Left alone, Talon stared at the ceiling, his mind racing. The betrayal stung worse than the pain in his body. He'd given everything, and it still wasn't enough.

In the corner of the room, Havoc rested in a crate, his bandages stark against his fur. Talon reached out, his fingers brushing the cold metal. "Guess it's just you and me now, buddy."

Havoc opened one eye, his tail thumping weakly. And in that moment, Talon made a vow. If the system didn't want him, he'd make his own rules. The shadows would become his home, and anyone who crossed him would regret it.

The world had turned its back on him. Now, it was his turn.

Talon stared at the horizon as he stepped out of the base for the last time, the duffel bag heavy on his shoulder. Havoc limped slightly beside him, a permanent reminder of the night everything changed. The early morning light painted the sky in shades of orange and red, the promise of a new day that felt hollow.

The first few weeks were a blur of aimless wandering, his mind clouded with anger and betrayal. He sought out old contacts, those who operated in the shadows, people who thrived where law and morality were distant concepts. It wasn't long before Talon found himself entrenched in their world, doing the only thing he was still good at: fighting, surviving, and hunting.

The bond with Havoc became his anchor. Every time the nightmares came, dragging him back to that night, it was Havoc's steady presence that brought him back to reality. The dog's loyalty reminded Talon of a time when he still believed in something greater than himself.

But the shadows were not forgiving. Talon learned quickly that trust was a currency too expensive to spend. Every mission, every deal was a tightrope walk between survival and destruction. And though he built a reputation as someone not to cross, the cost weighed heavily.

Months passed, and the pain in his body eased, but the scars inside festered. Talon became a ghost, moving from one job to the next, his name whispered among those who feared him. Havoc, ever by his side, became his only confidant in a world of shifting loyalties.

One night, as he sat in the dim light of a small apartment he barely called home, Talon found himself staring at the dog's calm gaze. "They think they broke me," he said aloud, his voice hoarse from disuse. "But we're still here, aren't we?" Havoc's ears perked up, and he gave a single wag of his tail, as if agreeing.

Talon leaned back, the weight of the world pressing down but no longer crushing him. "One day, we'll show them," he murmured. "We'll show them all."

The darkness outside the window reflected his resolve. The world had taught him to expect nothing but betrayal, but he had Havoc, and that was enough for now. Enough to keep going, enough to stay alive. Until it wasn't.

As weeks turned into months, Talon began to take on riskier jobs. Each mission etched itself into his body, the scars piling up as reminders of battles won and nearly lost. Havoc, ever faithful, stayed by his side, his own wounds healing slower than Talon would have liked. Yet, the dog's resilience mirrored Talon's own, a silent pact to keep moving forward no matter the cost.

There were moments of stillness that caught Talon off guard. Nights when the adrenaline faded and the silence of his apartment threatened to swallow him whole. On those nights, he would sit on the floor, Havoc resting his head on Talon's lap. "You're the only thing that makes sense anymore," Talon would mutter, his voice a mix of bitterness and gratitude. Havoc's quiet presence was his only solace in a world that felt increasingly empty.

The jobs became darker, the lines Talon once refused to cross blurring until they disappeared entirely. He stopped questioning the morality of his actions, focusing solely on survival. It wasn't about loyalty or honor anymore; it was about proving to himself that he could endure. That he could be more than what they tried to reduce him to.

Yet, in the back of his mind, a small voice whispered doubts. Was this all there was? A cycle of violence and revenge, with no end in sight? The thought would linger, only to be silenced by the next mission, the next fight. Talon told himself it didn't matter. As long as he and Havoc were alive, nothing else did.

One night, after a particularly brutal job, Talon found himself staring at his reflection in a cracked mirror. The man who stared back was a stranger—harder, colder, and more broken than he'd ever imagined. Havoc's soft whine broke the silence, and Talon turned, the dog's steady gaze grounding him in a way nothing else could. "We'll get through this," Talon whispered, though he wasn't sure if he believed it.

The world outside his apartment remained unchanged, a constant reminder of the battles yet to come. But as Talon sat with Havoc by his side, he allowed himself one fleeting moment of hope. Maybe, just maybe, there was still a way to find meaning in the darkness. To reclaim something he thought he'd lost forever.

That fleeting hope was often eclipsed by the demands of survival. On one mission, deep in a seedy port city, Talon found himself surrounded by double-crossers—mercenaries who thought they could take him out for an easy bounty. Blood stained the alleyway when it was over, but the encounter left Talon shaken. Not from the fight itself, but because Havoc had been hurt shielding him. Again.

Talon knelt beside Havoc that night in the back of a stolen truck, his hands shaking as he patched the dog's wounds. "I don't deserve you," he murmured. Havoc responded with a faint wag of his tail, his trust unwavering even in the worst moments. That trust only deepened Talon's guilt.

The next morning, Talon stared at the horizon, the rising sun casting light on a battered world he could barely recognize. For the first time in years, he let himself think about the future—not just surviving, but something more. Something better. But the weight of his past hung heavy, and he knew redemption wasn't something he could just take. It had to be earned.

The resolve settled in his chest like an immovable stone. He couldn't undo the scars on his soul or the harm he'd caused, but he could try to be better—for Havoc, if not for himself. It wouldn't be easy, and it wouldn't happen overnight. But for the first time in years, the idea of change didn't feel impossible.

Havoc, by his side as always, gave him a reason to try.

Chapter 1

The warehouse loomed like a forgotten sentinel, its corrugated metal walls painted in the muted glow of flickering streetlights. Inside, the air hung heavy with the stench of rust and oil, mingling with the faint tang of mildew. Shadows stretched long and jagged across the floor, broken only by the rhythmic sweep of headlights from passing cars. Somewhere in the distance, the wail of a siren cut through the night—a reminder of the chaos beyond these walls.

Talon Hayes stood at the center of it all, a solitary figure amidst the desolation. Dressed in dark tactical gear that spoke more of function than form, he exuded a quiet authority. His sharp gaze swept the room, cataloging every creak and whisper, every flicker of movement. Beside him, Havoc sat, his grizzled muzzle betraying his years, though his posture remained tense, muscles coiled like a spring. The retired K9's ears flicked at the faintest sound, his loyalty to Talon unwavering.

The soft click of Talon's boots on the concrete echoed faintly as he paced, his mind as sharp as the shadows that danced across the walls. Every detail in the warehouse was a potential threat—from the loose chains swaying in the rafters to the oily sheen of a puddle beneath a flickering overhead light. His fingers brushed against the grip of his sidearm, a familiar weight that grounded him in moments like these. Trust was a luxury he couldn't afford—especially not tonight.

The buyers arrived in a black SUV that growled its way into the warehouse, headlights piercing the dim gloom. Four men emerged, their faces shrouded in shadows and suspicion. Talon didn't flinch, betraying not a single ounce of uncertainty. Instead, he nodded curtly—a signal for them to approach.

"Where's the merchandise?" the leader demanded, his voice low and gravelly, matching the rough edges of his leather jacket.

Talon reached into a nondescript duffel bag at his feet, revealing the weapons within. "Everything you asked for. Payment first."

For a moment, silence hung between them, taut as a drawn wire. The leader smirked, motioning to one of his men, who handed over a briefcase. Talon's trained eye caught the man's hesitation—the slight tremor in his hand, the bead of sweat tracing a line down his temple. Something was wrong.

The exchange began smoothly enough. But then, the faintest click of a safety being disengaged reached Talon's ears—just enough to confirm his suspicions. Havoc growled low, a warning, as Talon shifted his weight imperceptibly, his hand drifting toward the holster at his hip.

The buyer's betrayal came swiftly, the man lunging for a weapon hidden beneath his jacket. Chaos erupted as gunfire echoed through the cavernous space, each shot a crack of lightning in the darkness. Talon moved like a ghost, every step calculated, his aim unerring. He neutralized the threats with clinical efficiency, his expression as cold and unyielding as steel.

A ricochet sang past his head, shattering a stack of crates behind him. Havoc lunged, teeth bared, driving one of the attackers to the ground. Talon's heart pounded in rhythm with the chaos, but his breathing remained steady. Panic was a foe he had long since mastered.

When the last echo of gunfire faded, Talon stood among the wreckage, his chest rising and falling in measured breaths. The four men lay scattered—groaning or silent. Havoc padded to his side, muzzle streaked with grime but tail wagging faintly, proud of their survival.

Talon crouched briefly by the leader, now clutching a bleeding shoulder. "You made a mistake," he said evenly, voice devoid of malice but weighted with finality. "Don't make another."

Without waiting for a response, Talon retrieved the briefcase, a grim sense of satisfaction settling over him. It was over—for now.

As he exited the warehouse, the cold night air bit at his skin, offering a fleeting sense of clarity. Havoc pressed close to his leg, a silent comfort. Talon's fingers brushed absently over his chest, adjusting the binder beneath his shirt—a small, grounding ritual. The scars beneath it ached faintly, memories of battles fought on multiple fronts, both external and internal.

The weight of his past lingered like the smoke still curling from his pistol. The faces of those he'd lost flashed briefly in his mind: a brother-in-arms, a childhood friend, a lover. Ghosts that had long since taken up residence in the quiet moments of his life, whispering reminders of his failings.

He paused by a shattered window of the warehouse, staring out at the city beyond. The skyline glimmered with promise, but for Talon, it only reflected the cracks within. His reflection in the glass caught his eye. He studied the man staring back—hardened, weary, but still standing. There was power in that, even if it felt hollow some days.

He moved through the darkened streets with purpose, Havoc keeping stride beside him. The city was a different kind of battlefield, one where enemies didn't wear uniforms and allies were few and far between. He'd learned to navigate it the hard way, carving out a path one deal, one fight at a time.

As they walked, Talon's mind wandered back to the briefcase. Blood money, some would call it. For him, it was survival—currency to keep moving, to stay one step ahead of those who wanted him gone. It was also a means to an end, though what that end looked like, he wasn't sure anymore. Freedom, maybe. Or something quieter.

The distant hum of life surrounded him—the occasional rumble of a car, muffled conversations from alleyways, the sharp crack of glass under his boots. Each sound was a reminder of how far he'd come from the orderly precision of his military days. Chaos had become his home now, and he'd adapted, but a small part of him still yearned for structure—for peace.

By the time Talon reached his safe house, the first hints of dawn were creeping over the horizon, painting the sky in muted shades of gray and gold. Havoc settled on a worn blanket in the corner, his watchful eyes finally softening. Talon sank into a chair, the briefcase on the table before him. He stared at it for a long moment before opening it—the neatly stacked bills inside a stark contrast to the chaos it had cost.

He closed it again, leaning back and letting his eyes drift shut. Sleep wouldn't come easily, but he would take what rest he could. Tomorrow, the ghosts would still be there, waiting.

As he sat in the dim light of the safe house, Talon's gaze drifted to a faded photograph pinned to the wall. It was the only personal touch in an otherwise sparse room. The image showed a younger Talon, eyes brighter, standing alongside a group of soldiers. Their smiles were genuine, unburdened by the weight of the world they were yet to fully understand. His fingers traced the edges of the photo, stopping over the face of his closest friend, Alex—a name that still tasted of ash and regret.

A soft whine pulled him back to the present. Havoc had lifted his head, amber eyes watching Talon with quiet concern. "Can't sleep either, huh?" Talon murmured, offering a half-smile. Havoc padded over, resting his head on Talon's knee. The simple gesture eased some of the tension coiled within him.

Talon reached down, scratching behind Havoc's ears. "You know," he began, his voice barely above a whisper, "some days I wonder what it would be like to just... disappear. Leave all this behind." The dog's ears perked up as if considering the possibility himself. "But then, where would that leave us? Running forever?"

He stood, moving to the small kitchenette to pour himself a glass of water. The pipes groaned in protest as the tap sputtered to life. Taking a sip, he glanced out the window. The city was awakening, lights flickering on in apartment buildings, silhouettes moving behind curtains. Normal lives, he thought. Lives he could never touch.

His thoughts drifted to his family—people who knew him by a different name, a different face. The last conversation with his mother replayed sharp words and sharper silences in his mind. Acceptance had been too much to hope for. He'd stopped trying long ago, but the ache remained—a dull throb that flared in moments like this.

Returning to his chair, Talon pulled out a worn notebook from a hidden compartment beneath the table. Flipping it open, he scanned the list of names and numbers—contacts, debts, favors owed. It was his lifeline, a web of connections that kept him afloat in dangerous waters. But it was also a chain, each link binding him tighter to a world he wasn't sure he wanted to be part of anymore.

He closed the notebook with a sigh, rubbing his temples. "Maybe it's time for a change, Havoc," he said aloud. The dog tilted his head, ears twitching. "Don't give me that look," Talon chuckled softly. "I know it's risky, but staying the same might be worse."

The idea of leaving the city tugged at him—heading somewhere unknown, where his past couldn't catch up so easily. But the risks were immense. Enemies had long memories, and disappearing wasn't as simple as it sounded. Still, the thought of starting fresh held a certain allure.

A sudden buzz broke the silence. Talon tensed, reaching for his phone. A blocked number. He hesitated before answering. "Yes?"

A distorted voice crackled through the speaker. "Job went south tonight. Heard you were involved."

Talon's jaw tightened. "I handle my business. What do you want?"

"Information. Meet me at the usual place. One hour."

The line went dead before he could respond. He set the phone down, a cold knot forming in his stomach. Trouble was brewing, and it seemed he was already in the thick of it.

He looked at Havoc, whose eyes mirrored his own concern. "Looks like sleep will have to wait," he said, reaching for his gear. The ghosts of the past weren't just memories—they were shaping his future, whether he liked it or not.

As he prepared to leave, Talon caught sight of himself in a cracked mirror by the door. Dark circles framed his eyes, and a faint stubble shadowed his jawline. Adjusting his binder once more, he took a deep breath. The physical armor was easy to don, but the emotional armor felt heavier with each passing day.

Stepping back into the night, the city enveloped him like a shroud. The streets were quieter now, the early morning hours casting everything in a surreal hush. Havoc moved silently beside him, ever vigilant. Talon couldn't shake the feeling that he was walking into a storm—one that had been gathering for a long time.

They navigated through alleyways and side streets, avoiding the main roads, where patrol cars occasionally prowled. The meeting point was a dilapidated pier overlooking the river, where secrets were as deep as the waters below. As they approached, the silhouette of a lone figure became visible against the faint glow of the horizon.

"You're early," the figure remarked as Talon drew near.

"Didn't have much else to do," Talon replied coolly. Havoc sat at his side, eyes fixed on the stranger.

The man stepped forward, the dim light revealing a face etched with scars and weariness. "Things are changing," he said. "There's a target on your back after tonight."

Talon's eyes narrowed. "There always is. What's different now?"

"New players in town. They don't like freelancers operating on their turf. The ones you dealt with—they were small-time but connected."

A muscle in Talon's jaw tensed. "Why warn me?"

The man shrugged. "Consider it a professional courtesy. You've done me a solid before."

"Noted." Talon shifted his weight. "Is that all?"

"One more thing." The man's gaze flicked to Havoc before returning to Talon. "They're not just after you. Anyone close to you is a potential target."

Talon felt a chill run down his spine. "I don't have anyone close."

"Maybe not anymore," the man conceded. "But be careful all the same."

Without another word, the man melted back into the shadows, leaving Talon alone with his thoughts. He stared out over the water, the ripples distorting the reflection of the city lights. The idea of leaving had been a distant dream moments ago; now, it felt like a necessity.

"We can't stay here," he murmured to Havoc. The dog looked up at him, tail wagging ever so slightly as if in agreement.

As dawn broke, washing the sky with hues of pink and gold, Talon made a silent vow. He would confront whatever was coming head-on, but on his own terms. The ghosts of his past had dictated his life for too long. It was time to take control—to forge a new path, no matter how uncertain it might be.

Chapter 2

HE DISAPPEARED INTO THE night, unaware that sharp eyes were tracking his every move from the shadows.

The docks were quiet, but the quiet didn't fool Aurora Ben-Yosef. It was the kind of silence that smothered sounds, the kind you had to listen through to catch what was hidden beneath. Her boots crunched softly against gravel as she slipped between rusted shipping containers, her every movement precise. She was a shadow in the chaos of the industrial sprawl, invisible to anyone who might be watching.

Aurora paused at the corner of a container, pulling her hood tighter around her face. The glow from a streetlamp barely reached her, but she didn't take chances. Her hand hovered near the taser concealed in her jacket pocket as she scanned the area. The smuggling ring, she'd been tracking for weeks, was supposed to meet here tonight—an arms deal, if her sources were right. She wasn't about to miss her chance to gather evidence.

She reached into her backpack, pulling out a small, improvised surveillance drone. The device wasn't top-of-the-line, but it worked well enough for someone who built it in their kitchen. With a practiced hand, she launched it into the air, watching the feed on her phone as the drone buzzed silently above the docks. The camera panned over the rows of containers and warehouses, revealing a grimy SUV parked in the shadows and the faint outlines of men inside.

Aurora's lips pressed into a thin line. They were here, just as she'd suspected. She adjusted her phone's brightness and zoomed in on the vehicle, snapping a few pictures of the license plate. The next step would be closer surveillance. Her pulse quickened, but she forced herself to breathe steadily. She'd prepared for this—mapped the layout, noted every possible escape route, and even tucked a fake ID in her back pocket, just in case.

She crouched lower and slipped her phone into her jacket. Her curly black hair cropped short, framed her face, but she tucked any stray strands beneath her hood. The shadows were her friend here, and she wouldn't risk breaking their trust. Her hazel eyes darted to a figure moving in the distance. A man—tall, broad-shouldered—was walking away from the warehouse, a dog at his side.

Aurora's heart skipped a beat. She recognized him immediately. Talon Hayes. The name was scrawled in red ink across the top of one of her notes. Her contacts had described him as dangerous, calculating, and not someone to approach lightly. But here he was, alone and seemingly vulnerable, slipping into the night as though he hadn't just walked out of an illegal arms deal.

She didn't hesitate. Stepping out from her hiding spot, Aurora quickened her pace, careful to stay far enough behind to avoid detection. Her eyes stayed trained on him, her mind racing. She wasn't sure whether to confront him or keep tracking him, but either way, she couldn't let him disappear. Not when he might be the key to cracking this case wide open.

"Hey!" she called, her voice low but firm.

Talon stopped mid-stride, his head tilting slightly. The dog beside him growled a low, rumbling sound that sent a shiver down Aurora's spine. Slowly, Talon turned, his piercing gaze locking onto her. His expression was unreadable, but his posture screamed warning.

"What do you want?" His voice was gravelly, calm, and entirely unwelcoming.

Aurora didn't falter. "You just walked out of a crime scene. I think we should talk."

Talon's eyes narrowed. He shifted his weight, his hand brushing the edge of his jacket. Aurora didn't miss the subtle movement toward what was likely a concealed weapon. "I don't know who you are," he said coolly, "but you've got the wrong guy."

"Funny," she shot back, her voice steady despite her pounding heart. "Your name's come up a few times in my investigation. Talon Hayes, right? Or should I call you the Phantom?"

His jaw tightened, and for a moment, neither of them moved. The tension crackled between them, sharp and electric. Havoc, the dog, barked once, breaking the silence, but it didn't ease the moment. If anything, it made it worse.

"You shouldn't be here," Talon finally said, his voice dropping an octave. "Whatever you're looking for, you won't find it."

"I'm looking for answers," Aurora said, standing her ground. "And from the looks of things, you might have some."

Talon took a step closer, his imposing frame casting a shadow over her. "You're making a mistake," he warned. "Walk away now, and I'll forget this happened."

Aurora clenched her fists. "Not happening."

Before either could make another move, the distinct sound of tires screeching shattered the standoff. Aurora spun toward the source of the noise as a black van tore into the lot, headlights cutting through the darkness. Men armed with rifles spilled out, shouting orders and spreading out like wolves on the hunt.

"Friends of yours?" Aurora asked, her voice tinged with sarcasm.

Talon's eyes darted to the van, then back to Aurora. "No. Get down."

Before she could argue, Talon grabbed her arm and pulled her behind a stack of crates. Bullets peppered the metal containers, the sound deafening as the attackers opened fire. Havoc growled, pressing close to Talon, his ears pinned back.

Aurora's heart thundered in her chest as she fumbled for her taser. "Who the hell are they?"

"Third-party," Talon muttered, peeking out from their cover. "Probably after the deal—or me."

"Great," Aurora hissed. "Now what?"

Talon didn't answer immediately. Instead, he assessed the situation with a practiced calm that sent a chill through her. He nodded toward a gap between the containers. "We move. Stay close and keep your head down."

Aurora hesitated for a fraction of a second before nodding. She wasn't thrilled about taking orders, especially from him, but staying put wasn't an option. Together, they darted through the maze of containers, Havoc leading the way. Bullets whizzed past, some so close Aurora could feel the heat as they skimmed by.

They ducked into a narrow alley between two warehouses, the shouts of their attackers growing fainter. Talon pressed his back against the wall, his chest heaving as he scanned their surroundings. "We can't stay here," he said. "They'll fan out."

Aurora leaned against the opposite wall, clutching her taser like it was a lifeline. "You seem awfully calm for someone being hunted."

"This isn't my first ambush," Talon replied dryly. "You?"

She glared at him. "I don't usually get shot at during stakeouts."

He almost smirked but caught himself. "Welcome to my world."

The sound of footsteps cut their conversation short. Talon motioned for silence, his hand on Havoc's collar to keep the dog still. Aurora held her breath as shadows passed by the alley entrance, the attackers just inches from spotting them.

When the footsteps receded, Talon turned to Aurora. "We split up from here. You go back to wherever you came from and stay out of this."

Aurora straightened, her glare returning full force. "Not a chance. I've got just as much reason to see this through as you do."

Talon's jaw tightened. "You're going to get yourself killed."

"Maybe," she shot back. "But at least I'll be doing something that matters."

For a moment, Talon said nothing, his expression unreadable. Then he sighed, shaking his head. "Stubborn."

"You have no idea."

The distant hum of an engine reminded them they weren't out of danger yet. Talon motioned for her to follow, leading her through another series of alleyways and out onto a deserted street. A battered sedan sat parked at the curb, its windows cracked and its paint peeling.

"Get in," Talon said, unlocking the door.

Aurora raised an eyebrow. "Seriously?"

"Unless you want to stick around and meet them again."

With a reluctant sigh, she slid into the passenger seat. Havoc jumped into the back, his tail wagging as though the chaos hadn't fazed him. Talon started the car, and they sped off into the night, the attackers' shouts fading into the distance.

For a while, the only sound was the hum of the engine and Aurora's steady breathing as she calmed herself. Finally, she turned to Talon. "So, what's your plan?"

"Survive," he replied curtly.

Aurora crossed her arms. "Not exactly reassuring."

Talon glanced at her, his expression softening just slightly. "You want answers? Stick around. But you might not like what you find."

As the city lights blurred past, Aurora couldn't help but wonder if she'd just made the worst mistake of her life—or the best decision she'd ever make.

The city's outskirts blurred into shadowy shapes as Talon drove, his hands steady on the wheel. Havoc had settled into the backseat, his head resting on his paws, though his ears occasionally twitched at the sound of passing cars. Aurora sat stiffly in the passenger seat, her arms crossed and her gaze fixed out the window, but she couldn't help stealing glances at Talon.

"So," she said finally, breaking the silence. "Is this how you usually spend your nights? Arms deals, ambushes, dragging strangers into your mess?"

Talon smirked faintly, his eyes never leaving the road. "Not strangers. You're the one who decided to follow me."

"You were leaving a crime scene," she shot back. "What did you expect me to do? Walk away?"

"Yes," Talon said simply. "You're in way over your head."

Aurora bristled. "You don't know anything about me."

"I know enough," Talon replied, his voice calm but firm. "You're determined, reckless, and probably too smart for your own good. But you don't belong in this world."

Aurora opened her mouth to argue but stopped herself. He wasn't entirely wrong, but that didn't mean she was about to back down. "You think you're so different?" she countered. "What makes you the expert on who belongs here?"

Talon didn't answer right away. His grip on the steering wheel tightened slightly, and his gaze darkened. "Experience," he said finally, his voice quieter. "Trust me, this life doesn't end well for anyone."

Aurora frowned, sensing the weight behind his words but unsure how to respond. Instead, she leaned back in her seat, her eyes scanning the darkened streets as they sped past. "Where are we going?" she asked after a moment.

Talon glanced at her, his expression guarded. "Somewhere safe. For now."

"Safe?" Aurora repeated with a hint of skepticism. "That doesn't sound very specific."

"You'll live," he replied flatly, turning the car onto a side road that led toward an industrial district. The area was eerily quiet, with only the faint hum of machinery in the distance breaking the stillness.

Talon parked the car in a secluded lot near an abandoned factory. He turned off the engine and sat in silence for a moment, his fingers drumming lightly on the steering wheel. "Stay here," he said finally, opening the door. "I'll be back."

"Wait—what?" Aurora protested, unbuckling her seat belt. "You're not just leaving me here."

Talon paused, half out of the car, and looked at her. "You wanted answers. Fine. But those answers come with risks, and I'm not dragging you any deeper until I know what we're dealing with."

Aurora's jaw tightened, her frustration clear. "I can handle myself."

Talon arched an eyebrow. "Prove it by staying put." Without waiting for her response, he stepped out of the car, Havoc following close behind.

Aurora watched him disappear into the shadows, her mind racing. She hated being sidelined, especially when she felt so close to uncovering something big. But despite her annoyance, she couldn't deny the tension in the air—the sense that this wasn't a situation she fully understood.

Minutes ticked by, and Aurora's patience wore thin. She debated going after him, but her gut told her to wait, even if she didn't like it. Her fingers drummed against her thigh as she scanned the area, her instincts on high alert. Something about this place felt off.

Just as she was about to reach for her phone, a shadow moved outside the car. Aurora tensed, her hand slipping to her taser. The shadow grew closer, resolving into Talon's silhouette. He opened the driver's side door, sliding back into the seat with a grim expression.

"We've got a problem," he said without preamble, starting the car again. Havoc jumped into the back, his ears perked.

"Care to elaborate?" Aurora asked, her voice sharp.

Talon's gaze flicked to her briefly before returning to the road. "Those guys at the docks? They weren't freelancers. They were sent by someone bigger."

Aurora frowned. "Bigger, how?"

"Organized," Talon said, his tone clipped. "And they're not just after me anymore. They've got eyes on anyone sniffing around their operations—including you."

Aurora felt a chill run down her spine but masked it with a defiant glare. "So, what now? You're just going to run?"

Talon's jaw clenched. "No. But I need to know exactly who I'm dealing with before I make a move. And if you're smart, you'll walk away now."

Aurora leaned forward, her soft curves pressing against the table as she held her ground. "I told you, I'm not walking away."

Talon's lips twitched, almost into a smirk. "Stubborn," he muttered under his breath. "Fine. But don't say I didn't warn you."

The car fell silent again as they navigated the empty streets, the weight of the situation pressing down on both of them. Aurora wasn't sure what she'd just gotten herself into, but one thing was certain—she wasn't turning back now. Aurora's chest heaved as they sped away, her pulse hammering in her ears. The city blurred past, neon lights streaking against the windshield. She dared a glance behind them—nothing but darkness. But something still felt off.

"Drive faster," she muttered, not taking her eyes off the rearview mirror.

Talon didn't answer, but his grip on the wheel tightened, knuckles bone-white.

Chapter 3

Aurora's chest heaved as they sped away, her pulse hammering in her ears. The city blurred past, neon lights streaking against the windshield. She dared a glance behind them—nothing but darkness. But something still felt off.

The quiet inside the car felt wrong. Too sudden, too forced—like the city itself was holding its breath.

Aurora kept checking behind them, waiting for the flash of headlights that never came. Talon didn't speak, didn't flinch. His hands stayed locked on the wheel, his jaw like carved stone.

Finally, he exhaled, low and sharp. "We're clear. For now." The night roared to life around them as Talon's battered sedan tore down the narrow street, headlights bouncing off the crumbling brick walls of the industrial district. The third-party attackers weren't far behind—another black van and two motorcycles weaving through the maze-like streets with ruthless determination. Gunfire echoed in the distance, the sharp cracks growing louder as the pursuers closed the gap.

Aurora clung to the passenger seat, her curves pressing into the leather as she stole a glance out the back window. "They're gaining on us!" she shouted over the growl of the engine.

"I noticed," Talon said dryly, his focus razor-sharp as he swerved onto another side street. Havoc, in the backseat, let out a low growl, his ears pinned back in warning.

A motorcycle screeched up alongside the car, the rider leveling a handgun at them. Before Aurora could react, Talon jerked the wheel hard, slamming the sedan into the bike. The rider was thrown off, skidding across the pavement as the motorcycle flipped and crashed into a dumpster.

"That's one," Talon muttered, his tone cold and controlled.

"Are you always this calm when people are trying to kill you?" Aurora snapped, her heart pounding in her chest.

"Only when I'm busy," Talon shot back.

Another barrage of bullets shattered the back window, spraying glass across the seats. Havoc barked sharply, and Aurora ducked instinctively, shielding her head. "This is insane!" she yelled, fumbling for her taser even though she knew it was useless in this situation.

Talon spared her a glance. "Stay down. Let me handle this."

Aurora didn't respond, her mind racing for a solution. Her eyes landed on the glove compartment. Without thinking, she reached over and popped it open, pulling out a compact but powerful handgun. "Guessing you don't mind if I borrow this?"

"Just don't shoot me," Talon growled, accelerating as another motorcycle closed in.

Aurora leaned out the passenger window, the wind whipping at her face. She steadied her stance, shifting her weight in a way that felt powerful, aimed, and fired. The shot wasn't perfect, but it was enough to clip the motorcycle's tire. The rider lost control, veering into a parked car and crashing in a shower of sparks.

Talon glanced at her, his expression unreadable. "Not bad."

"Thanks," Aurora said, her voice tight. "I'm not exactly a novice."

Before Talon could respond, the van loomed into view in the rearview mirror. Its headlights were blinding, and the sound of its engine filled the air like a predator closing in for the kill. The driver leaned out of the window, an automatic rifle in hand, and opened fire.

Talon swerved hard, narrowly avoiding the spray of bullets. "They're not letting up," he muttered, his frustration evident.

"What gave it away?" Aurora snapped, gripping the gun tightly. "We can't keep running like this."

"Then what do you suggest?" Talon demanded, his tone sharp. "You seem to have all the answers."

Aurora glared at him but said nothing. She glanced at the approaching van, then at the maze of side streets ahead. Her mind worked quickly, piecing together an idea. "Turn left up ahead," she said suddenly.

"What?" Talon barked.

"Just do it!"

With a growl of annoyance, Talon yanked the wheel left; the tires screeched as the car veered into a narrow alley. The van tried to follow but clipped the corner of a building, sending it spinning out of control. It slammed into a pile of debris, and for a brief moment, the world went quiet.

Talon slowed the car, his eyes darting to the rearview mirror. "Nice move," he admitted begrudgingly.

Aurora exhaled shakily, her heart still racing. "Thanks. Now what?"

"Now we disappear," Talon said, his voice grim. "For now."

He navigated the sedan through a series of winding streets, finally pulling into the shadowed entrance of an abandoned parking garage. The car's engine clicked as it cooled, and the silence was a stark contrast to the chaos of moments ago.

Aurora leaned back in her seat, her adrenaline slowly fading. "That was close," she said softly, her voice trembling slightly despite her best efforts to stay composed.

Talon didn't respond immediately. Instead, he got out of the car, motioning for Havoc to follow. "Stay here," he said to Aurora, his tone leaving no room for argument.

She ignored him, climbing out of the car as well. "Not a chance," she said firmly. "I'm not just going to sit around while you figure out our next move."

Talon's gaze flicked to her, irritation flashing in his eyes. "This isn't a team effort."

"It is now," Aurora shot back, crossing her arms. "Whether you like it or not."

Talon sighed, running a hand through his hair. "You're impossible."

"And you're stuck with me," Aurora said, a faint smirk tugging at her lips despite the tension.

Before Talon could retort, his phone buzzed in his pocket. He pulled it out, his expression darkening as he read the message on the screen. "Damn it," he muttered under his breath.

"What is it?" Aurora asked, her brow furrowing.

"They know who you are," Talon said grimly, his voice low. "And they're not just after you anymore."

Aurora's stomach dropped. "What do you mean?"

Talon met her gaze, his eyes hard. "Your family. They've got your family in their sights."

Aurora's breath caught in her throat. "No," she whispered, shaking her head. "They don't even know—"

"They know enough," Talon interrupted. "And if we don't move fast, they'll make their move."

Aurora's mind raced, panic threatening to overwhelm her. Her parents and her younger sister had nothing to do with this. They didn't even know the full extent of her investigation. The thought of them being dragged into this nightmare made her blood run cold.

"What do we do?" she asked, her voice trembling.

Talon's expression softened just slightly, the hardened edges giving way to something almost empathetic. "We stop them," he said simply. "But you're going to have to trust me."

Aurora hesitated, the weight of the situation pressing down on her. She didn't trust easily, and Talon was far from someone she'd choose as an ally. But right now, she didn't have a choice.

"Fine," she said finally, her voice steady despite the fear clawing at her chest. "What's the plan?"

Talon glanced at her, a faint glimmer of respect in his eyes. "We start by finding out who's pulling the strings. And then we end this—for good."

As they climbed back into the car, Aurora couldn't shake the feeling that this was only the beginning. The stakes had never been higher, and the lines between ally and enemy were starting to blur. But one thing was clear: their fates were now tied together, for better or worse.

The silence in the parking garage was suffocating, broken only by the faint sound of dripping water somewhere in the distance. Aurora sat rigid in her seat, her mind spinning. Her family was supposed to be safe, far removed from the dangerous work she'd taken on. The thought of them being dragged into this sent a chill down her spine.

"We need to move," Talon said, his voice cutting through the stillness. He glanced at her, his expression unreadable. "They'll act fast if they think it gives them leverage."

Aurora clenched her fists. "How do they even know about my family? I've been careful. I don't—"

"You're dealing with professionals," Talon interrupted, his tone firm but not unkind. "They don't need much to put the pieces together. A name, a phone number—they can work with that."

She hated how calm he sounded, as if this was just another day in his life. But then again, it probably was. "We can't let anything happen to them," she said, her voice trembling.

"We won't," Talon replied. "But you need to focus. Panic won't help anyone."

Aurora took a shaky breath, forcing herself to nod. She wasn't used to taking orders, especially not from someone like Talon, but right now, she didn't have the luxury of arguing. "What's the first step?" she asked.

"We start by figuring out where they'll strike," Talon said, his eyes scanning the darkness outside the car. "They'll try to leverage your family to flush you out, but they won't act until they're sure it'll work."

Aurora frowned. "So they're watching them? Waiting?"

"Most likely," Talon confirmed. "And if they think you're onto them, they'll escalate."

The thought of strangers watching her family's every move made her stomach churn. "We need to get to them," she said, her voice firmer now. "Warn them. Get them somewhere safe."

Talon hesitated, his gaze flicking to her. "That's risky. If we go to them now, we could lead the attackers right to their door."

Aurora glared at him. "So what? We just leave them out there as bait?"

"No," Talon said sharply. "But if we're going to protect them, we need to be smart about it. Charging in blind is how people get hurt."

The weight of his words settled over her, but she refused to let it paralyze her. "Fine," she said through gritted teeth. "What do you suggest?"

Talon leaned back in his seat, his mind clearly working through the options. "We draw them out," he said finally. "Make them come to us."

Aurora blinked. "And how do we do that?"

Talon's lips twitched into a faint, humorless smile. "We give them exactly what they want—us."

The plan didn't sit well with Aurora, but as Talon laid it out, she had to admit it was their best option. They would stage a meeting at a neutral location, somewhere public enough to minimize the risk of outright violence but secluded enough to give them room to maneuver. The attackers would be forced to reveal themselves, and with any luck, they could take them down before things spiraled further.

The idea of using herself as bait made Aurora's skin crawl, but she couldn't deny the logic. "And my family?" she asked. "What happens to them while we're playing this game?"

"They won't be alone," Talon said. "I've got a contact who can keep an eye on them, make sure they're safe until this is over."

Aurora's eyes narrowed. "And I'm supposed to trust this contact?"

"You're trusting me, aren't you?" Talon countered, his tone dry. "Like it or not, we're in this together now."

Aurora didn't respond. Instead, she stared out the window, her thoughts a storm of worry and determination. She didn't like relying on anyone, least of all someone like Talon, but she didn't see another way forward.

As they prepared to leave the parking garage, Talon's phone buzzed again. He checked the screen, his expression darkening. "They're on the move," he said. "We don't have much time."

"Then let's go," Aurora said, her voice steady despite the fear simmering beneath the surface.

They drove in tense silence, the city lights casting fleeting shadows across their faces. Talon's grip on the wheel was firm, his focus unshakable, while Aurora sat poised, ready for whatever came next. Havoc, sensing the tension, lay alert in the backseat, his eyes scanning the streets as though he, too, was part of the plan.

They arrived at the meeting spot—a desolate construction site on the outskirts of the city. Tall cranes loomed overhead, their skeletal frames casting eerie shapes in the moonlight. Piles of concrete and rebar littered the ground, creating a maze of potential cover.

"This is where you want to make your stand?" Aurora asked, her skepticism clear.

Talon nodded. "It's defensible. Lots of places to hide, and we can see them coming."

She didn't argue, though her nerves were on edge. As they got out of the car, Talon handed her a small earpiece. "We'll stay in contact. Stick to the plan."

Aurora slid the earpiece into place, her fingers brushing against her short hair. "I've got it," she said, her voice firm.

Talon and Havoc disappeared into the shadows, leaving Aurora to take her position near the center of the site. The weight of the gun in her hand was both reassuring and unsettling. She hated feeling exposed, but if this was the only way to protect her family, she would see it through.

Minutes passed like hours as Aurora waited, her senses on high alert. The sound of an approaching vehicle broke the stillness, its headlights cutting through the darkness. She tensed, her heart hammering in her chest as the black van from earlier rolled to a stop a few yards away.

Men emerged from the van, their movements calculated and predatory. Aurora counted five of them, all armed, their eyes scanning the site for any sign of a trap. She forced herself to stay calm, knowing Talon was nearby, watching.

"Where is he?" one of the men barked, his voice echoing through the site. "We know you're working with him. Tell us where he is, and maybe we'll let you walk away."

Aurora stepped forward, her grip on the gun tightening. "I'm right here," she said, her voice steady despite the fear clawing at her throat.

The men laughed, their confidence infuriating. "Brave," the leader said, smirking. "But stupid. You're outnumbered, and you've got no backup."

Aurora's lips curled into a faint smile. "Who said I'm alone?"

At that moment, Talon struck. Emerging from the shadows, he moved with precision, taking down the nearest man with a swift, calculated blow. Havoc leaped into action, tackling another attacker to the ground with a feral growl.

The fight erupted in an instant, bullets flying and shouts ringing out. Aurora darted for cover, firing off a shot that grazed one of the attackers' arms. She ducked behind a stack of concrete, her heart racing as she tried to keep track of Talon and Havoc in the chaos.

Talon was relentless, his movements fluid and efficient. He disarmed one attacker, using the man's own weapon against him before turning to face the next threat. Havoc stayed close, his fierce loyalty evident in every calculated move. Though it should bring some form of comfort that Aurora had him on her side, the violence that bled from his very breath unsettled her.

Aurora wasn't idle. She fired at another attacker, forcing him to take cover. Her training kicked in, and her fear was replaced by a sharp focus. For a moment, she even found herself impressed by how seamlessly she and Talon seemed to work together.

The fight ended as quickly as it began. The attackers lay incapacitated, their weapons scattered across the ground. Talon stood at the center of it all, his chest heaving as he scanned the area for any remaining threats. Havoc trotted to his side, his tail wagging slightly despite the tension.

Aurora emerged from her cover, her hands trembling as the adrenaline began to wear off. "That... was intense," she said, her voice shaking slightly.

Talon glanced at her, his expression softening just a fraction. "You held your own," he said simply. There was something behind Talon's eyes that she couldn't quite place.

She almost smiled but caught herself. "Thanks. You weren't so bad yourself."

Talon's phone buzzed again, and he checked it with a frown. "It's not over," he said, his voice grim. "They've regrouped."

Aurora felt the weight of his words, but she refused to let it crush her. "Then we keep going," she said, her determination clear. "Whatever it takes."

Talon studied her for a moment before nodding. "Whatever it takes."

Chapter 4

Talon exhaled sharply. 'We move now. Before they catch up.'

The sedan bumped along the dirt road, the engine humming steadily as the dense forest swallowed them whole. The headlights cut through the darkness, illuminating narrow trees that loomed like silent sentinels. Aurora winced, gripping her plush waist as the car jolted over a deep rut.

"You're bleeding through your jacket," Talon said flatly, his eyes fixed on the winding path ahead.

"It's nothing," Aurora muttered, though the sharp pain in her ribs told a different story. Each breath brought her a flash of pain that burned.

Talon's lips tightened, but he didn't argue. Instead, he pressed the gas pedal harder, urging the car up the final incline before the road leveled out into a clearing. A small cabin came into view, its weathered wooden exterior blending seamlessly with the surroundings.

"This is it?" Aurora asked, her voice tinged with disbelief.

Talon ignored the tone. "It's safe," he said simply, parking the car and cutting the engine. "That's all that matters."

Havoc leaped out as soon as the door opened, sniffing the air and wagging his tail as he padded toward the cabin. Talon rounded the car, opening Aurora's door before she could protest. "Come on," he said gruffly, extending a hand to help her out. His grip was firm, as he steadied her fuller frame.

Aurora hesitated, her pride warring with the pain shooting through her side. Finally, she accepted his hand, gritting her teeth as she climbed out of the car. The world swayed slightly, and Talon steadied her with a firm grip on her arm.

"You're stubborn," he muttered, guiding her toward the cabin.

"You're bossy," she shot back, though her words lacked bite.

Talon didn't respond. He unlocked the door and ushered her inside, flicking on a dim overhead light that cast a warm glow on the small space. The interior was stark and utilitarian, with minimal furniture and bare walls. A worn couch sat in the corner near a wood-burning stove, and a small kitchen was tucked into the far side of the room.

"Sit," Talon ordered, nodding toward the couch.

Aurora opened her mouth to argue but thought better of it. She sank onto the couch with a wince, leaning back as Talon disappeared into a side room. Havoc trotted over, resting his head on her knee and staring up at her with curious eyes.

"Well, at least one of you has manners," Aurora murmured, scratching behind the dog's ears.

Talon returned a moment later with a first aid kit in hand. He knelt in front of her, his expression unreadable as he set the kit down and began inspecting her jacket. "You're lucky it's just a graze," he said, pulling the fabric aside to reveal the wound beneath. "Could have been a lot worse."

Aurora felt her face heat up at the sudden exposure of her skin.

Aurora flinched as he dabbed antiseptic onto the cut. "You don't exactly have the softest touch, you know."

"This isn't about comfort," Talon replied, his tone clipped. "It's about keeping you alive."

Aurora rolled her eyes but didn't argue. She watched him work, noting the precision in his movements. There was something oddly reassuring about his no-nonsense demeanor, even if it grated on her nerves. She found herself oddly focusing on his fingers as he worked the thread and needle with precision.

"You've done this before," she said after a moment. Aurora couldn't stop herself from focusing on Talon's hands as he worked her wound.

Talon's gaze flicked to hers, then back to the wound. "Enough times."

His curt response only fueled her curiosity, but she decided against pressing him—at least for now. Instead, she let her eyes wander around the cabin, taking in its spartan design. There were no photos, no personal touches of a normal life or a normal man, just the bare essentials. It was a place meant for survival, not comfort. This thought brought a pang of sadness in Aurora's chest for him.

When he finished, Talon packed up the first aid kit and stood. "You should rest," he said, his tone brooking no argument. The sudden separation of skin-to-skin contact left a cold wave over her skin, and goosebumps erupted where the tips of his fingers were grazing her skin only moments before.

Aurora snorted. "Sure. Because that's exactly what I feel like doing after almost getting killed."

Talon's jaw tightened, but he didn't respond. He moved to the kitchen, filling a metal bowl with water and setting it on the floor for Havoc. The dog padded over, lapping it up enthusiastically.

Left to her own devices, Aurora shifted on the couch, her eyes wandering again. A stack of books sat on a nearby shelf, their spines worn and faded. She couldn't resist getting up and crossing the room to inspect them, ignoring the twinge in her side. Most were military manuals, but one caught her eye: a weathered copy of The Odyssey.

"Didn't peg you as a Homer fan," she said, holding up the book.

Talon glanced at her but said nothing, his expression unreadable.

Aurora smirked, setting the book back on the shelf. "You're just full of surprises, aren't you?"

The tension between them simmered, unspoken words hanging in the air like a charged wire. Havoc, sensing the mood, trotted back to Aurora and nudged her leg with his nose. She smiled faintly, scratching his ears again.

"At least someone here likes me," she muttered.

Talon leaned against the kitchen counter, his arms crossed. "Havoc doesn't trust easily," he said after a moment. "If he likes you, it means something." Talon's eyes watched the dog closely as if not believing the sight.

Aurora raised an eyebrow. "Are you saying I've earned your dog's seal of approval?"

"Maybe," Talon said, a faint smirk tugging at the corner of his mouth.

The rare hint of humor caught her off guard, and for a brief moment, the tension between them eased. But it didn't last long. Aurora's thoughts returned to the situation at hand, the danger looming over her family.

"We need to talk about our next move," she said, her tone serious.

Talon nodded, pushing off the counter and grabbing a map from a nearby drawer. He spread it out on the table, motioning for her to join him. "This is the area we're dealing with," he said, pointing to a cluster of markings. "If they're watching your family, they'll likely have a base of operations nearby."

Aurora studied the map, her brow furrowing. "And what about the smuggling ring? How does this all connect?"

Talon hesitated, his expression darkening. "It's bigger than just a ring," he said finally. "This is organized—international. Whoever's behind it has resources and reach."

Aurora's stomach tightened. "And you know this how?"

Talon's eyes met hers; the weight of his past was evident in his gaze. "Because I've dealt with them before."

The revelation sent a jolt through her, but before she could press him further, Havoc barked sharply, his ears perked toward the door. Talon's expression hardened instantly. He motioned for Aurora to stay back as he moved to the window. Talon placed himself between her and the door, which caught her attention.

"What is it?" Aurora whispered, her pulse quickening.

Talon didn't answer right away. He peered into the darkness, his hand drifting toward the holster at his side. "Stay here," he said finally, his voice low.

Aurora ignored him, grabbing the handgun he'd given her earlier. "If someone's out there, I'm not just sitting around."

Talon shot her a look but didn't argue. They moved toward the door together, their steps silent as they positioned themselves on either side. Havoc growled softly, his eyes fixed on the shadowed woods beyond the porch.

Talon opened the door slowly, his gun drawn. The cool night air rushed in, carrying the faint scent of pine and damp earth. The forest was silent, save for the occasional rustle of leaves in the breeze.

"See anything?" Aurora asked, her voice barely above a whisper.

Talon shook his head, his gaze sweeping the trees. "Nothing."

They stood there for a long moment, the tension coiling tighter with each passing second. Finally, Talon stepped back inside, locking the door behind him. "We're not alone out here," he said grimly. "Stay alert."

Aurora nodded, her grip on the gun tightening. She didn't like feeling hunted, but she wasn't about to let fear control her. If whoever was out there thought they could scare her off, they were sorely mistaken.

As the night wore on, Aurora found herself unable to sleep. She wandered the cabin, her thoughts swirling as she pieced together everything she'd learned so far. Her eyes landed on a locked chest tucked beneath the bookshelf. Curiosity got the better of her, and she knelt beside it, running her fingers over the worn wood.

"What are you doing?" Talon's voice cut through the silence, startling her.

Aurora glanced up, her cheeks flushing slightly. "Just... exploring," she said defensively.

Talon's eyes narrowed, but he didn't press her. "Get some rest," he said. "Tomorrow's going to be a long day."

Aurora stood, brushing off her hands. "Fine. But this isn't over."

As she settled back onto the couch, she couldn't shake the feeling that the chest held answers—answers that might explain the enigmatic man standing guard by the door. For now, though, she let it go. The mystery of Talon Hayes would have to wait.

Aurora stirred restlessly on the couch, her thoughts too loud to let her sleep. Every creak of the cabin's wooden frame or whisper of the wind through the trees outside kept her on edge. She glanced toward Talon, who sat at the table, sharpening a knife with a slow, methodical rhythm. His face was impassive, but the tension in his shoulders betrayed his alertness.

"You're not going to sleep either?" she asked, her voice cutting through the quiet.

Talon didn't look up. "Someone has to stay awake. Just in case."

Aurora sighed, sitting up despite the ache in her side. She instinctively shot a hand to her side where the stitches pulled at the sensitive skin. "You can't keep this up forever, you know."

"I've done worse," Talon replied evenly. "And I don't take chances when it comes to survival."

The weight of his words hung between them, and Aurora leaned back, studying him. There was a quiet intensity about Talon that she couldn't quite figure out—something that went beyond his tactical precision or his stoic demeanor. It was in the way he moved, the way he spoke, as though every decision carried the weight of something much heavier than the moment at hand. He moved like smoke — silently and deadly.

"Don't move too much," Talon shifted slightly and glanced down at Aurora's side, where her shirt was now dried with blood. Talon stood and closed the distance between them in only a couple of strides. "I don't wanna have to fix your stitches because you're being stubborn."

Aurora instinctively shrunk back into the couch., when Talon reached her. His hand shot out to steady her by her shoulder, and he lifted her shirt.

Talon clicked his tongue in frustration, "You slipped one of your stitches." Talon grabbed his kit that was still nearby and popped it open. Aurora felt her throat dry up from the thought of getting her stitches fixed.

She wasn't weak by any means, but she was human. That much, she would admit.

Talon pulled out his small thread scissors and snipped the small thread that held her red-tinted skin together. His fingers worked delicately, leaving the feeling of pain as something only in Aurora's imagination.

Aurora couldn't steady her heart. He was close. Too close. Aurora internally scolded herself for focusing on a small freckle that sat beautifully in Talon's eye.

Then everything seemed to stop when Talon's eyes met hers. He continued to work on her stitches, his eyes trained on hers.

"I'm sorry," Aurora's voice was barely above a whisper.

Talon didn't respond. He returned his gaze to her wound, and a harsh tug caused Aurora to gasp. Without thinking, she shot her hand to Talon's shirt, gripping it like it was her only saving grace from the pain.

Her breath was ragged, and her body felt weak. Underneath her touch, Talon's body felt rigid, every muscle was coiled like a spring like being touched by another human was his poison.

"From the way you handle confrontation," Talon snipped the thread and moved in closer to the wound to inspect it. "I never would've guessed that you were shaken by needles."

Talon didn't pull away. And Aurora didn't answer. It was taking everything in her to not faint from the pain. Aurora couldn't bring her gaze to Talon's, whose face was now only inches from hers.

"Aurora," Talon's hand shot out to her chin and focused her gaze on his. "Focus on me for now."

Aurora slowed her breathing, trying her best to find comfort in the cold soul in front of her. She should shrink back, push him away, and fix the wound herself like she had done so many times before this, but she didn't want to.

His gaze was cold, just like earlier, but his eyes were different. They held something behind them that Aurora couldn't quite place. Then, his eyes shot down to her lips. Only for a brief second. At first, Aurora thought she imagined it. But no matter how much she tried to convince herself that it didn't happen, it didn't change the fact that she wanted it to be true.

He was cold, hardened by the past he carried on his shoulders. Aurora knew that the military created two things well: war and soldiers who are only that: soldiers. It was obvious that Talon wasn't able to reclaim his human side, at least not fully.

Talon cleared his throat and suddenly placed distance between them. His hand gently wrapped around Aurora's wrist like it were glass, and he would break it by just breathing too harshly.

A moment passed, then two, and his fingers began to warm her wrist. And just when she began to savor the comfort that the connection brought, it was ripped away as Talon stood.

"Get some rest," Talon averted his gaze and cleared his throat once more. "We have a long day tomorrow."

"What about you?"

"What about me?" Talon turned fully away now, but not before stealing a glance at Aurora's exposed skin.

With a heated face, Aurora shot her hands up and pulled the cloth down to cover herself.

"You need rest, too. You can't just ignore sleep."

"I can if I need to."

"You talk like someone who's used to being alone," she said softly.

Talon paused, his hand stilling over the blade. For a moment, it looked like he might answer, but he shook his head instead, returning to his task. "Alone is safer," he said finally, his tone leaving no room for debate.

Aurora didn't respond right away. She got up, moving toward the locked chest she'd noticed earlier. "What's in here?" she asked, crouching down and running her fingers over the worn edges.

Talon's eyes snapped up, his expression sharp. "Don't."

The single word carried enough weight to freeze her in place. She looked over her shoulder at him, her curiosity sparking into defiance. "You said I should rest. Looking around helps me think."

"That's not just looking around," Talon said, standing. He crossed the room in a few swift strides, stopping in front of her. "It's personal."

Aurora raised an eyebrow. "Personal? So you do have secrets."

Talon's jaw clenched, his gaze hard. "Everyone has secrets. The smart ones know when to leave them alone."

Aurora held his stare for a moment before stepping back, raising her hands in mock surrender. "Fine. I'll let it go. For now."

Talon watched her closely, his guarded expression returning. He didn't say anything as she returned to the couch, but the tension between them was palpable. Whatever was in that chest, it was clearly something he wasn't ready to share.

As she laid down, Aurora couldn't help but feel like she'd touched a nerve—one that might explain the puzzle of Talon Hayes. And while she respected his boundaries, she knew herself well enough to admit that she wouldn't stop digging. Not when she was so close to uncovering the truth.

Chapter 5

THE MORNING CREPT INTO the cabin with a slow, reluctant light, casting long shadows across the wooden floor. Aurora stirred on the couch, her body aching but her mind already alert. She blinked up at the ceiling, momentarily disoriented, before the events of the last 24 hours came rushing back.

The sound of a rhythmic scraping broke the silence. She turned her head toward the source and found Talon sitting near the wood-burning stove, sharpening the blade of a small axe. Havoc lay at his feet, his head resting on his paws, but his ears twitching at every faint sound from outside.

Aurora sat up carefully, trying not to aggravate her injuries. "Do you ever stop working?" she asked, her voice hoarse from sleep.

Talon didn't look up. "Not when there's work to be done."

Aurora rolled her eyes, swinging her legs over the side of the couch. "You know, normal people take breaks."

"Normal people don't survive situations like this," Talon replied evenly, the scrape of the blade against the sharpening stone punctuating his words.

There was a pause as Aurora studied him. He seemed almost peaceful in this moment, his movements deliberate and his focus unwavering. It was a stark contrast to the calculated ruthlessness she'd seen the night before. "You're different when you're not being chased or shot at," she said.

Talon stopped sharpening the blade, his eyes flicking to hers. "What's that supposed to mean?" There was a small flame behind his eyes. One she had noticed before but couldn't place. It was brighter now.

"It means you almost seem... human," Aurora said with a faint smirk, though her tone lacked malice.

Talon exhaled sharply, setting the axe aside. "Don't read too much into it."

Aurora stood, moving toward the small kitchen to pour herself a glass of water. "You can't blame me for being curious," she said, glancing at him over her shoulder. "You're an enigma, Talon Hayes."

"An enigma," he echoed, his tone dry. "That's one way to put it."

Aurora turned to face him, leaning against the counter. "So, are you going to tell me why you're really tangled up in this smuggling mess? Because something tells me you're not just in it for the money."

Talon's expression hardened instantly. "You don't know what you're talking about."

"Then explain it to me," Aurora pressed, stepping closer. "Help me understand why someone who seems so controlled, so precise, would be involved in something so dangerous and messy." Talon's body tensed at her sudden advancement, but he didn't move away from her.

Talon stood, his full height and broad frame casting a shadow that made the small cabin feel even smaller. "I don't owe you an explanation," he said coldly.

Aurora held her ground, her hazel eyes locking onto his. "No, you don't. But if we're going to keep working together, I need to know who I'm trusting my life with."

Talon stared at her for a long moment, his jaw tight. Finally, he sighed, turning away and running a hand through his hair. "It's not that simple."

"Try me," Aurora said, her voice softer now.

Talon leaned against the table, his gaze distant. "I didn't choose this life. It chose me."

Aurora frowned, sensing the weight in his words. "That's a convenient excuse."

"It's the truth," Talon snapped, his voice sharp. He exhaled, forcing himself to calm down. "You think I like being hunted? Living in the shadows? Everything I've done has been about survival—mine and others."

"Others?" Aurora asked, curiosity piqued.

Talon hesitated, his eyes meeting hers for a fleeting moment before looking away. "People I cared about. People who needed protecting."

Aurora softened, her defenses lowering. "And the smuggling? How does that fit in?"

"It doesn't," Talon admitted, his voice heavy with regret. "I got involved with the wrong people, thinking I could control it. I thought I could make it work in my favor, but it's not that simple. It never is."

Aurora crossed her arms, her gaze unwavering. "You're trying to make up for something, aren't you?"

Talon flinched, his eyes narrowing slightly. "What do you know about it?"

"Enough to see the guilt written all over your face," Aurora said, her tone softer now. "You're not as cold as you pretend to be."

Talon's lips pressed into a thin line. He picked up the axe again, as if the simple act of sharpening it could shield him from the weight of her words. "I don't have the luxury of guilt," he said finally. "Not anymore."

Aurora didn't push further, sensing she'd already gotten more from him than he was used to giving. Instead, she shifted the conversation. "So what's the plan? You can't keep hiding forever."

Talon's focus returned to the blade in his hands. "We find out who's running the operation, and we take them down. It's the only way to end this."

"And what happens after that?" Aurora asked.

Talon didn't answer right away. He set the axe aside, his gaze fixed on the window. "That depends on whether we make it out alive."

Aurora frowned, her stomach twisting at the thought. "You make it sound like a suicide mission."

"It might be," Talon said bluntly. "But it's better than waiting for them to find us."

The weight of his words settled over her, and for the first time, Aurora truly understood the depth of the danger they were in. It wasn't just about survival—it was about fighting back, even when the odds were stacked against them.

"I'm in," she said firmly, her resolve hardening. "Whatever it takes."

Talon glanced at her, a flicker of surprise crossing his face before it disappeared. "You don't have to do this."

"Yes, I do," Aurora said, her voice steady. "Because if I don't, they'll come for my family. And because... I think you need someone to remind you that you're not as alone as you think."

Talon didn't respond, but the faintest hint of a smile tugged at the corner of his mouth. "You're stubborn," he muttered.

"Someone has to be," Aurora quipped.

The cabin fell into a comfortable silence, the tension between them easing slightly. Sensing the shift, Havoc trotted over to Aurora and nudged her leg with his nose. She knelt to scratch behind his ears, smiling faintly.

"You're lucky to have him," she said, glancing at Talon. "He's loyal."

"More than most people," Talon replied, his voice tinged with something unspoken.

Aurora studied him, seeing the cracks in his stoic facade. There was more to him than he let on—layers of pain, guilt, and something else she couldn't quite place. For the first time, she found herself wondering not just what had made him this way but whether he could ever find his way back.

As the day wore on, they worked in tandem to fortify the cabin, checking locks, securing windows, and setting up makeshift alarms using cans and fishing line. Talon's military precision was evident in every task, and Aurora followed his lead, her respect for him growing despite herself.

At one point, she caught him watching her, his gaze thoughtful. "You're not what I expected," he said.

Aurora raised an eyebrow. "And what did you expect?"

Talon shrugged, a faint smirk crossing his lips. "Someone less capable. More scared."

"I don't scare easily," Aurora said, meeting his gaze.

"I'm starting to see that," Talon replied, his tone almost approving.

As night fell, they sat by the wood-burning stove, the flickering flames casting warm light across the room. Havoc lay between them, his steady breathing filling the quiet. For the first time, the weight of their circumstances felt bearable, if only for a moment.

"You know," Aurora said softly, "you might not be as bad as you think you are."

Talon glanced at her, his expression unreadable. "Don't get used to it."

Aurora smiled faintly, leaning back against the couch. "We'll see."

Aurora leaned back against the couch, her eyes drifting toward the window. The forest outside was cloaked in darkness, its silence pressing against the cabin like an unseen force. She wondered how long they could stay hidden before the world outside came crashing in. "Do you ever think about walking away from all of this?" she asked suddenly, her voice cutting through the quiet.

Talon glanced at her, his expression thoughtful. "All the time."

Aurora tilted her head, surprised by his honesty. "So why don't you?"

Talon shrugged, poking at the fire with a metal poker. "Because running doesn't solve anything. Wherever you go, the ghosts follow."

Aurora considered his words, the weight of them settling heavily in her chest. "Sounds lonely."

"It is," Talon admitted. He set the poker aside and leaned against the mantle, his gaze distant. "But it's better than putting people in danger."

Aurora frowned, her curiosity about him deepening. "Is that why you keep everyone at arm's length? To protect them?"

Talon's jaw tightened, and for a moment, she thought he wouldn't answer. "Something like that," he said finally, his voice quieter. "It's easier that way."

"Easier for you, maybe," Aurora countered. "But what about the people who want to get close? Do you ever think about how it feels for them?"

Talon looked at her, his eyes sharp. "Why does it matter to you?"

Aurora hesitated, caught off guard by the directness of his question. "I don't know," she said honestly. "Maybe because I've been on the other side of it. Watching someone shut people out, thinking they're doing the right thing when all they're doing is pushing everyone away."

Talon didn't respond immediately. Instead, he crouched to add another log to the fire, the flickering flames casting shadows across his face. "You can't fix people like me," he said quietly. "We are what we are."

Aurora leaned forward, her hazel eyes steady. "Maybe. Or maybe you've just convinced yourself of that because it's easier than trying to change."

Talon's lips twitched into something that wasn't quite a smile. "You don't quit, do you?"

"Nope," Aurora said, a faint smirk playing on her lips. "Get used to it."

The tension between them softened again, replaced by something quieter and more introspective. Havoc let out a contented sigh, breaking the silence, and both of them glanced at the dog as if he'd spoken. "He's got the right idea," Aurora said, her voice lighter now.

Talon chuckled softly—a rare sound that caught Aurora off guard. It was like the first bird song after the chaos of a forest fire. "He usually does."

They sat in companionable silence for a while, the warmth of the fire and Havoc's steady breathing creating a rare sense of calm. But Aurora's thoughts kept circling back to Talon's words, the weight of his self-imposed isolation, and the pain he clearly carried. She couldn't shake the feeling that there was more to him than he let on—layers he kept buried under the surface.

After a while, Talon stood, his movements deliberate, retrieved a small box from the shelf, and opened it carefully. It contained a collection of old photographs and worn letters. Aurora watched as her curiosity piqued when he hesitated over one of the pictures.

"Who's that?" she asked, nodding toward the photo.

Talon glanced at her, his expression guarded. For a moment, it seemed like he might brush her off, but then he held up the photo, the edges frayed from years of handling. It showed a younger Talon in military fatigues, standing beside a man about his age. Both were smiling, their arms slung over each other's shoulders.

"An old friend," Talon said quietly, his voice tinged with something that sounded like regret.

Aurora didn't press further, sensing the heaviness in his words. "Looks like you were close," she said gently.

"We were," Talon said, setting the photo back in the box. "But life has a way of taking things from you when you least expect it."

Aurora's chest tightened at the rawness in his tone. "I'm sorry," she said softly, her earlier defiance replaced by genuine empathy.

Talon nodded, closing the box and placing it back on the shelf. "It's in the past," he said, though the way his shoulders slumped told her he didn't believe it.

The air between them felt heavier now, the unspoken emotions hanging like a storm cloud. Aurora wanted to say something—anything—to break the weight of the moment, but she also knew that some wounds couldn't be soothed with words.

Instead, she stood and walked over to the shelf, picking up a small, carved wooden figurine that caught her eye. "Did you make this?" she asked, holding it up.

Talon glanced at the figurine, a faint flicker of something like surprise crossing his face. "Yeah. It's been a while, though."

Aurora turned the figurine over in her hands, admiring the intricate details. "It's beautiful," she said, smiling faintly. "You've got talent."

Talon looked away, a faint hint of color rising to his cheeks. "It's just something I used to do. Keeps my hands busy."

Aurora set the figurine back on the shelf, her smile lingering. "You should keep doing it. You're good at it."

Talon didn't respond, but the faintest hint of a smile tugged at the corner of his mouth. For the first time, Aurora thought she saw a glimpse of the person he might have been before the weight of the world had settled on his shoulders.

As the fire crackled in the background, Aurora felt the first glimmer of something unexpected—a connection. It was fragile and unspoken, but it was there, lingering in the quiet moments they shared. And though neither of them would admit it, they both felt a little less alone for the first time in a long time.

Chapter 6

THE MORNING BROKE SLOWLY, light filtering through the cabin's curtained windows. Aurora stretched the stiffness in her side, a reminder of their chaotic escape days earlier. She swung her thick thighs over the side of the couch and stood, stretching with a sigh as she blinked the sleep from her eyes. The cabin was quiet, save for the occasional creak of the wooden floorboards under her feet. Talon and Havoc were nowhere in sight.

Exploring seemed harmless enough. She padded to the kitchen for water, noticing the neat arrangement of utensils and supplies—everything had its place, functional and deliberate, much like Talon himself. Her eyes wandered to a door she hadn't seen open before. It was slightly ajar, revealing what looked like a small bathroom.

Curiosity got the better of her. She stepped inside, scanning the space. It was spartan, like the rest of the cabin, but something on the counter caught her eye: a small, neatly arranged collection of medical supplies. There were syringes, vials, and a folded piece of paper that looked like a prescription. Aurora tilted her head, her brow furrowing as she leaned closer.

She didn't mean to pry, but one of the vials had rolled slightly, revealing the label. Testosterone. Aurora blinked, her heart skipping a beat as realization dawned on her. She glanced around the bathroom, noticing other subtle clues—razor blades and a binder hanging from a hook near the shower. It all clicked into place.

The floor creaked behind her, and Aurora turned sharply to find Talon standing in the doorway, his expression unreadable. Havoc stood at his side, tail wagging faintly, oblivious to the tension filling the room.

"What are you doing?" Talon's voice was low, his eyes burned with a mix of anger and vulnerability.

"I was just—" Aurora hesitated, holding up her hands. "I wasn't trying to snoop."

Talon's jaw tightened as he stepped inside, his presence suddenly overwhelming in the small space. "Then what were you doing?" he demanded, his tone sharper now. Talon stood like a force to be reckoned with. Daring Aurora to make one wrong move.

Aurora met his gaze, refusing to flinch. "I got curious. I didn't mean to... invade your privacy."

For a moment, neither of them moved. The weight of Talon's glare was almost unbearable, but Aurora held firm, her expression calm. "It's none of your business," he said finally, his voice quieter but no less tense.

"You're right," Aurora said softly. "It's not. But... I don't care."

Talon blinked, his brow furrowing. "What?"

"I don't care," Aurora repeated, her voice steady. "It doesn't change anything. You're still you."

Talon stared at her, his defenses wavering for a brief moment before he crossed his arms, his posture rigid. "You don't know anything about me."

"Then tell me," Aurora said, taking a tentative step closer. "Help me understand." The air around the two stood still, strangled by tension and waiting for any sudden movements.

Talon shook his head, turning away. "It's not that simple."

"Maybe not," Aurora admitted. "But you've been carrying this on your own for a long time, haven't you?"

Talon's shoulders stiffened, and Aurora realized she'd struck a nerve. "I don't need your pity," he said through gritted teeth.

"It's not pity," Aurora said gently. "It's respect. You've been through a lot—I can see that. And you've survived. That's not something that you have to hide."

Talon's breath hitched, and for a moment, Aurora thought he might snap at her again. Instead, he leaned against the sink, his hands gripping the edge tightly. "It's not about hiding," he said finally, his voice rough. "It's about keeping control. People like me don't get the luxury of trust."

Aurora felt a pang of sympathy but kept her expression neutral. "I get it," she said. "But you don't have to push everyone away."

Talon glanced at her, his eyes searching hers for something. Trust, maybe, or understanding. "Why are you so calm about this?"

Aurora smiled faintly. "Because it doesn't matter to me. What matters is that you've got my back—and I've got yours."

Talon didn't respond right away, his gaze dropping to the floor. Havoc nudged his leg with his nose as if sensing his unease. Slowly, Talon's shoulders relaxed, and he exhaled. "You're not what I expected," he muttered.

Aurora chuckled softly. "You've said that before."

"Well, it's true," Talon said, the faintest hint of a smirk tugging at his lips. The tension between them eased slightly, though the vulnerability lingered in the air.

Aurora leaned against the door frame, her arms crossed. "So, are you going to keep dodging my questions, or are you going to let me in?"

Talon glanced at her, the walls around him cracking just enough to let a sliver of emotion through. "What do you want to know?"

Aurora considered her words carefully. "Whatever you're willing to share. No pressure."

Talon hesitated, then straightened, his posture less defensive now. "I figured things out young," he said, his voice quieter. "But it didn't make it easier. The military... wasn't exactly welcoming."

Aurora nodded, her chest tightening. "You served anyway."

"Yeah," Talon said, his gaze distant. "I thought I could prove myself. That it would make me untouchable."

"And did it?" Aurora asked gently.

Talon's lips pressed into a thin line. "For a while. But eventually, someone always finds a reason to look closer. To judge."

Aurora's heart ached at the pain in his voice, but she kept her tone steady. "That's on them, not you."

Talon scoffed, shaking his head. "Doesn't change the outcome."

"No," Aurora agreed. "But it says a lot about your strength—that you kept going anyway."

Talon looked at her, his expression softening. For the first time, he seemed to believe her words. "I don't know why you care," he admitted. "But… thanks." Talon looked deep into Aurora's eyes, searching for deceit. Something to give him a reason not to trust her, just like he had learned to do with so many others and, eventually, everyone.

Aurora smiled. "You're welcome." Aurora stepped closer, nearly closing the distance between the two of them. Talon watched her like a predator, an unsure hawk. Even though Aurora could feel the man's gaze searing into her, she closed in. Aurora looked up at Talon, the two only a breath apart, "Talon…"

Before the moment could stretch further, a sharp, static-filled buzz broke the quiet. Both of them turned toward the sound, their tension reigniting. Talon strode into the main room, grabbing the radio from the table.

"Unknown vehicle spotted near the perimeter," a voice crackled through the speaker. "Repeat, unidentified vehicle near your location."

Talon cursed under his breath, grabbing his gun and motioning for Aurora to follow. "Stay close," he said, all traces of vulnerability replaced by sharp focus.

Aurora nodded, her heart pounding as she followed him out of the cabin. The woods around them felt alive with danger, every shadow a potential threat. Whatever connection they'd just formed would have to wait. Survival came first.

The radio crackled again as Talon adjusted the frequency, his brow furrowing. "Vehicle's about two clicks out, heading this way. No identifying marks. Could be random… or not."

"It's not random," Aurora said firmly, gripping the handgun she'd grown increasingly accustomed to holding. "They've found us."

Talon shot her a look, sharp and calculating. "You don't know that."

"And you don't believe it's a coincidence either," Aurora countered, her eyes narrowing.

Talon didn't argue. He crossed the room in quick, deliberate strides, grabbing a pair of binoculars from a shelf near the door. "Stay here," he ordered, his tone leaving no room for debate.

"Like hell, I will," Aurora said, moving to follow him.

Talon turned abruptly, his gaze locking onto hers. "If this goes sideways, I need you to cover the inside. That means staying put."

Aurora opened her mouth to protest, but the intensity in his eyes stopped her. He wasn't trying to control her; he was calculating risks, and her presence outside was one he couldn't afford. "Fine," she said reluctantly, gripping the gun tighter. "But don't do anything stupid."

Talon allowed himself a faint smirk. "That's my line."

He slipped out the door, Havoc close at his side, the two of them disappearing into the treeline-like shadows. Aurora stood frozen for a moment, her heart racing. She hated waiting—being sidelined—but she knew he was right. If this was a coordinated attack, they'd need someone inside to defend the cabin.

The minutes stretched into what felt like hours. Aurora paced the room, her mind replaying their earlier conversation. She couldn't shake the image of Talon, standing in the bathroom doorway, every muscle in his body tense as if bracing for a blow. The way his voice had softened when he spoke of his past—it was the most human she'd ever seen him.

Her thoughts were interrupted by the sound of movement outside. She froze, her hand tightening around the gun. A shadow flickered past the window, and her pulse quickened. "Talon?" she whispered, though she knew he wouldn't respond.

The cabin door creaked open, and Aurora raised the gun, her finger hovering over the trigger. Relief flooded her as Talon stepped inside, Havoc close behind. "It's clear," he said, though his tone suggested he wasn't convinced it would stay that way.

"What was it?" Aurora asked, lowering the gun.

"An old truck," Talon said, setting the binoculars on the table. "Could have been a drifter, but it stopped farther up the road. Too far to confirm."

Aurora frowned. "So what do we do? Wait for them to come back?"

Talon shook his head. "No. We prepare."

He moved with purpose, gathering supplies—extra ammunition, a pair of radios, and a map that he spread across the table. "If they're watching, they'll wait until dark to make a move. We need to be ready."

Aurora joined him at the table, her eyes scanning the map. "And if they don't come back?"

"Then we move," Talon said. "Staying here isn't an option anymore."

Aurora hesitated, her gaze flicking to him. "Talon… about earlier."

He stiffened slightly but didn't look up. "What about it?"

"I meant what I said," Aurora said softly. "It doesn't change how I see you. If anything, it makes me respect you more."

Talon's hand stilled over the map. He glanced at her, his expression unreadable. "Why?"

"Because you've been through hell," Aurora said simply. "And you're still standing. That takes strength."

For a moment, Talon didn't respond. Then, almost imperceptibly, he nodded. "Thanks," he said gruffly, his focus returning to the map. "But let's survive tonight before we get sentimental."

Aurora smirked faintly, recognizing his deflection but choosing not to push further. "Deal."

The two of them worked side by side, reviewing the layout of the cabin and its surroundings. Talon's military precision was evident in every plan he laid out, but he listened when Aurora offered suggestions. Their dynamic shifted into something closer to partnership, but Aurora wasn't sure that word was fitting either.

As dusk settled over the forest, the cabin was transformed into a fortress. Windows were barricaded, and makeshift alarms were rigged along the perimeter. Aurora took up a position near the front window, her gun within arm's reach.

"Talon," she said quietly, breaking the silence. "If this goes south, you should know… I'm not sorry I met you."

Talon looked at her from across the room, his gaze softening just slightly. "Let's make sure it doesn't go south," he said, his voice steady.

The shadows outside deepened, and the tension in the cabin became almost tangible. Whatever came next, Aurora knew they would face it together.

Chapter 7

THE CABIN WAS ALIVE with quiet activity, a tension hanging in the air like the calm before the storm. Aurora crouched near the front window, reinforcing the makeshift barricade Talon had set up earlier. Every creak of the wood or shift of the shadows outside kept her on edge, but her hands moved with practiced precision. The adrenaline of survival had become second nature.

Talon stood a few feet away, sorting through ammunition with methodical care. "You're pretty good at this," he said, his voice low but clear.

"Pretty good at what?" Aurora replied, glancing at him.

"Keeping your head," Talon said simply. "Most people would be panicking by now."

Aurora smirked faintly. "I don't have time to panic. Besides, you'd probably just tell me to suck it up."

Talon chuckled softly, the sound rare but not unwelcome. "You're not wrong." Talon watched Aurora's movements with precision.

They worked in companionable silence for a while; the occasional growl from Havoc was the only other sound in the room. Aurora grabbed a length of wire and began rigging a trip alarm near the door, her movements swift and confident. Talon watched her out of the corner of his eye, his respect for her growing with each task she tackled.

"Where'd you learn to do all this?" Talon asked, nodding toward the alarm she was setting up.

"Trial and error," Aurora said, tightening the wire. "When you're investigating dangerous people, you pick up a few tricks."

"Dangerous doesn't scare you, does it?" Talon said, his tone more curious than accusatory.

Aurora shrugged. "Not as much as it probably should."

Talon paused, studying her for a moment. "That's going to get you killed one day."

"Maybe," Aurora said, meeting his gaze. "But at least I'll go down fighting."

There was a flicker of something in Talon's expression—admiration, perhaps, or understanding. He nodded, acknowledging her resolve. "Let's make sure it doesn't come to that."

As the evening wore on, the preparations slowed, and the tension in the room shifted. Aurora found herself sitting near the wood-burning stove, her hands wrapped around a steaming mug of tea Talon had handed her without a word. He sat across from her, his shoulders slightly relaxed, though his eyes still carried the weight of their situation.

"You're different than I expected," Aurora said suddenly, breaking the silence.

Talon raised an eyebrow. "What did you expect?"

"Someone colder," Aurora admitted. "More detached."

Talon smirked faintly. "I can be when I need to."

"Yeah, but you're not just that," Aurora said, her voice softer. "You care. Even if you don't want to admit it."

Talon's gaze dropped to his mug, his fingers tracing the edge. "Caring gets you hurt," he said after a moment. "It makes you vulnerable."

"And shutting yourself off doesn't?" Aurora countered.

Talon didn't respond immediately. Instead, he leaned back in his chair, his eyes drifting to Havoc, who lay curled near the stove. "Sometimes it's easier," he said finally. "But you're right—it doesn't always work."

Aurora smiled faintly. "I'll take that as progress."

Talon rolled his eyes but didn't argue. The silence that followed was more comfortable this time, a quiet understanding settling between them. Aurora found herself studying him, noticing the way the firelight softened the sharp lines of his face. There was a warmth there, hidden beneath the layers of defenses he wore like armor.

Talon caught her staring and raised an eyebrow. "Something on your mind?"

Aurora hesitated, then shrugged. "Just trying to figure you out."

"Good luck with that," Talon said, his tone light but his gaze steady.

"I'm serious," Aurora said, leaning forward slightly. "You're not as hard to read as you think."

"Is that so?" Talon asked, his lips twitching into the faintest hint of a smile.

"Yeah," Aurora said. "You're stubborn, guarded, and maybe a little too serious, but you've got a good heart. Even if you don't want anyone to see it."

Talon's smile faded, replaced by something more introspective. "You see what you want to see."

"And you don't see yourself clearly," Aurora countered, her voice firm but not unkind.

Talon didn't respond, but the way his gaze softened told her she'd struck a chord. For a moment, the air between them felt charged, the unspoken connection growing stronger. Aurora wasn't sure when it had happened, but somewhere along the way, the tension between them had shifted into something... else.

Havoc stirred, breaking the moment as his ears perked toward the window. Talon tensed instantly, his focus snapping back to the present. He stood, crossing the room in a few quick strides to peer out into the darkness.

"What is it?" Aurora asked, setting her mug down and standing as well.

"Not sure," Talon said, his voice low. "But he heard something."

Aurora moved to the opposite side of the room, her hand instinctively reaching for the gun at her hip. The quiet of the forest outside felt oppressive now, every shadow a potential threat. Talon grabbed the binoculars and scanned the tree line, his posture rigid.

"There," he said, his tone sharp. "Movement, northeast."

Aurora followed his gaze, squinting into the darkness. She couldn't see anything, but she trusted his instincts. "Do you think it's them?"

"Could be," Talon said, lowering the binoculars. "We can't take chances."

He moved quickly, grabbing a second radio and handing it to Aurora. "If something happens, stay in contact. And don't engage unless you have to."

Aurora nodded, her pulse quickening as the reality of the situation sank in. "What's the plan?"

"We hold our ground for now," Talon said. "But if they're coming, we need to be ready to move."

The two of them worked in tense silence, double-checking their preparations and ensuring their weapons were loaded. The earlier ease between them had vanished, replaced by the sharp focus on survival.

As the minutes ticked by, the tension grew unbearable. Aurora found herself glancing at Talon, her chest tightening at the thought of what might happen if their luck ran out. "Talon," she said quietly.

He glanced at her, his expression softening just slightly. "What?"

"If this goes south..." Aurora hesitated, then forced herself to continue. "I'm glad I'm here with you."

Talon's gaze lingered on her, something unspoken passing between them. "We're not going down," he said firmly. "Not tonight."

Aurora nodded, the weight of his conviction bolstering her own resolve. Whatever came next, she knew they would face it together.

Suddenly, a sharp noise outside shattered the quiet—a snap of a twig, too deliberate to be natural. Talon raised a hand, motioning for Aurora to stay quiet. Havoc growled low, his body tense as he stared at the door.

The sound of footsteps followed, slow and measured. Aurora's heart pounded in her chest as she raised her gun, her hands steady despite the fear coursing through her veins. Talon positioned himself near the window, his own weapon at the ready.

The footsteps stopped just outside the cabin, and the world seemed to hold its breath. Talon glanced at Aurora, his expression grim but steady. "Stay close," he whispered.

Aurora nodded, her grip tightening on the gun. The quiet stretched on, each second feeling like an eternity. Then, without warning, the door burst open, and chaos erupted.

The door slammed against the wall, splinters flying as a shadowy figure stormed inside. Talon fired immediately, his shot striking the intruder in the shoulder and sending them staggering back with a pained grunt. Aurora instinctively dropped to a crouch behind the couch, her heart pounding as she trained her gun on the door.

"Stay low!" Talon barked, moving fluidly toward the window for a better angle.

Another figure appeared in the doorway, their silhouette framed by the faint glow of moonlight. Aurora squeezed the trigger, her shot grazing the edge of the doorframe and forcing the intruder to duck. Havoc growled, his body poised to strike as he waited for Talon's command.

"They're coming in from the side!" Aurora shouted, catching movement in her peripheral vision. Two more figures flanked the cabin, their footsteps crunching on the gravel outside.

Talon spun toward the window, firing off two precise shots that sent one of the attackers diving for cover. "They're testing us," he muttered, his tone grim. "Seeing how well we're defended."

"Well, they're about to find out," Aurora snapped, shifting her position to cover the back door.

She heard the faint click of a radio coming to life and realized one of the attackers was calling for reinforcements. The pit in her stomach deepened. "They're not stopping, are they?" she asked, glancing at Talon.

"No," Talon said, his jaw tightening. "And if we don't end this fast, it'll only get worse."

Aurora's mind raced, searching for options. The cabin was secure for now, but it wasn't a fortress. If the attackers had heavier firepower—or worse, explosives—they wouldn't last long. "We need to draw them away from the cabin," she said, her voice firm.

Talon hesitated, his eyes narrowing as he processed her words. "That's a gamble."

"Everything we do is a gamble," Aurora said sharply. "But if we stay here, we're sitting ducks."

Talon exhaled sharply, nodding. "Fine. But we do it on my terms."

He moved quickly, grabbing a flare gun from a shelf near the door. "I'll fire this to lead them toward the clearing," he said. "You follow Havoc and circle around. Use the tree line for cover."

Aurora frowned. "What about you?"

"I'll catch up," Talon said, his tone brooking no argument. "Just stick to the plan."

Aurora's chest tightened, but she nodded. "Be careful."

Talon glanced at her, his expression softening just slightly. "You too."

He opened the back door a crack and slipped outside, Havoc at his side. Aurora followed, her movements quiet as she crouched low and kept to the shadows. The forest was alive with tension, every rustle of leaves or snap of a twig, setting her nerves on edge.

Talon fired the flare, the bright red light arcing into the night sky and landing in the clearing beyond the cabin. The attackers reacted instantly, their attention drawn to the glow as they moved cautiously toward it.

"Come on," Aurora whispered to herself, her heart racing as she crept through the underbrush.

Havoc stayed close, his ears twitching as he scanned their surroundings. Aurora reached out to pat his side, grounding herself in his steady presence. "Good boy," she murmured, her voice barely audible.

Suddenly, a figure broke from the group and started toward the tree line—directly toward her. Aurora froze, her breath catching in her throat as the attacker drew closer. She raised her gun, her hands steady despite the adrenaline coursing through her veins.

The intruder stepped into a patch of moonlight, their face partially obscured by a mask. Aurora aimed for their leg and fired. The shot hit its mark, and the figure crumpled to the ground with a muffled cry.

Havoc growled low, but Aurora placed a hand on his back, keeping him from charging. "Stay," she whispered, her eyes locked on the downed attacker.

The noise drew another figure toward her position, and Aurora cursed under her breath. She glanced around, spotting a cluster of dense bushes nearby. "Come on, boy," she said softly, retreating into the foliage.

The second figure passed by, their focus on their injured comrade. Aurora stayed perfectly still, her breathing shallow as she waited for the right moment. Talon's voice crackled over the radio in her pocket, barely audible. "Status?"

"All good for now," Aurora whispered back, her heart still pounding. "What about you?"

"Almost clear," Talon replied. "Just keep moving."

Aurora nodded, even though he couldn't see her. She tightened her grip on her gun and signaled for Havoc to follow as she continued through the forest. The flare's glow was fading now, and the attackers' movements grew more frantic as they searched for their targets.

When she finally reached the edge of the clearing, she spotted Talon crouched behind a fallen log, his rifle trained on the remaining intruders. His movements were precise, and every shot was deliberate as he picked off their attackers one by one.

Aurora's chest tightened with a mix of admiration and relief. Despite the danger, Talon was calm, composed, and entirely in control. She couldn't help but feel a surge of respect—and something deeper—watching him work.

"Talon," she whispered, moving to his side. "What's the plan now?"

He glanced at her, his eyes sharp but steady. "We finish this."

Chapter 8

THE CABIN WAS QUIET, save for the soft crackle of the fire in the wood-burning stove. Shadows danced across the walls, flickering like restless spirits. Aurora sat cross-legged on the couch, a blanket draped over her lap. Havoc lay sprawled at her feet, his rhythmic breathing a comforting presence in the stillness. Across the room, Talon sat in his usual chair, his sharp profile illuminated by the firelight.

"You're quiet tonight," Aurora said, her voice low, not wanting to break the fragile calm.

Talon glanced at her, his lips twitching into a faint smirk. "I'm always quiet."

Aurora chuckled softly, pulling the blanket tighter around her. "Fair point. But this feels… different."

Talon leaned back in his chair, his gaze fixed on the fire. "Just thinking."

Aurora tilted her head, watching him carefully. There was a heaviness about him tonight, a weight she couldn't quite name. "About what?"

He didn't answer right away, his fingers idly tapping the armrest. "About everything," he said finally. "How it all went to hell so fast."

Aurora waited, sensing there was more he wasn't saying. "You've been through worse, haven't you?"

Talon's eyes flicked to her, sharp and assessing. "Why do you ask?"

"Because I see it in you," Aurora said honestly. "The way you handle yourself, the way you talk—it's like you've been carrying the world on your shoulders for a long time."

Talon exhaled, his shoulders tensing. "The military taught me how to carry weight like that. It also taught me that it doesn't matter how strong you are—eventually, something will break you."

Aurora leaned forward slightly, her curiosity piqued. "What broke you?"

For a moment, Talon didn't respond. Then, slowly, he reached into his pocket and pulled out a small, worn coin. He turned it over in his fingers, his expression unreadable. "Silas," he said quietly.

"Who's Silas?" Aurora asked, her brow furrowing.

Talon's jaw tightened. "Someone I trusted. Someone who decided I wasn't worth protecting when things got tough."

Aurora's chest tightened at the rawness in his voice. "What happened?"

"He sold me out," Talon said, his tone sharp with bitterness. "Turned me over to the people who wanted me gone. All for his own gain."

Aurora's heart ached for him, but she kept her tone steady. "I'm sorry," she said softly. "That must have been... devastating."

Talon laughed bitterly, the sound hollow. "It taught me a valuable lesson: trust is a liability."

"You don't really believe that," Aurora said, her voice firm. "You trust Havoc."

Talon's gaze softened as it drifted to the dog at her feet. "Havoc's different. He doesn't lie."

Aurora smiled faintly. "No, he doesn't. But maybe not everyone does, either."

Talon didn't respond, his eyes returning to the fire. The silence stretched between them, heavy but not uncomfortable. Aurora hesitated, then decided to take a risk. "You're not the only one who's been let down by people they trusted," she said.

Talon glanced at her, his expression cautious. "What do you mean?"

Aurora shifted, tucking her legs beneath her. "My family… they've always had high expectations. Everything I did had to be perfect—perfect grades, perfect behavior, perfect future. I tried to live up to it, but no matter how hard I worked, it was never enough."

Talon's brow furrowed. "That sounds exhausting."

"It was," Aurora admitted. "But it also made me who I am. It taught me how to fight for what I want—even if it means going against what people expect of me."

Talon studied her, a flicker of respect in his gaze. "That's why you're here, isn't it? Why you're chasing this smuggling ring?"

Aurora nodded. "I wanted to prove that I could do something meaningful. Something that mattered."

"And has it?" Talon asked.

Aurora hesitated, her gaze dropping to her hands. "I don't know. Sometimes, it feels like I'm just… running in circles. Trying to fix things that are too broken to fix."

Talon's voice softened. "That's not on you."

Aurora looked up, meeting his gaze. "Maybe not. But it feels like it is."

The quiet between them grew heavier, their shared vulnerabilities creating a fragile bond. Talon leaned forward, resting his elbows on his knees. "You're stronger than you give yourself credit for."

Aurora smiled faintly. "You're not so bad yourself."

Talon huffed a soft laugh, the sound lighter than she'd ever heard from him. "Don't let that get out."

"I won't," Aurora teased. "Your reputation is safe with me."

Their conversation drifted into more casual territory, the intensity of the earlier moments easing. They talked about small things—Havoc's quirks, the cabin's history, and the places they'd both been. Aurora found herself relaxing in a way she hadn't expected, the walls between them crumbling bit by bit.

At one point, Talon reached for a battered deck of cards on the table. "Do you play?"

Aurora raised an eyebrow. "Depends. Are you any good?"

"Good enough," Talon said with a smirk. "But I'll go easy on you."

"We'll see about that," Aurora said, her competitive streak flaring.

They played a few rounds, the game providing a distraction from the weight of their situation. Aurora surprised herself by winning more often than not, and Talon's feigned frustration earned a genuine laugh from her.

"You're cheating," he accused, though his tone was light.

"Just admit I'm better," Aurora shot back, grinning.

Talon shook his head, a rare smile tugging at his lips. "Fine. But only because I let you win."

"Sure you did," Aurora said, her laughter fading into a comfortable silence.

As the night wore on, the fire dwindled, casting the cabin in dim, flickering light. Havoc stretched out beside Talon's chair, his contented sigh filling the quiet. Aurora leaned back against the couch, her gaze drifting to the shadows on the ceiling.

"Do you think it's possible to start over?" she asked softly, the question slipping out before she could stop it.

Talon glanced at her, his expression thoughtful. "I don't know," he admitted. "But maybe it's worth trying."

Aurora smiled faintly, his words offering a small glimmer of hope. "Yeah. Maybe it is."

For the first time in what felt like forever, the weight on her chest lightened just a little. And as she glanced at Talon, she realized she wasn't the only one feeling it. Whatever walls he'd built around himself were starting to crack, and she hoped that, just maybe, they could find a way to rebuild—together.

Aurora shifted her position on the couch, watching the firelight dance across Talon's face. She hadn't seen this side of him before—the quiet, contemplative version of the man who had, until now, been all sharp edges and stoic resolve. She wondered how many people had ever gotten close enough to witness this part of him.

"Talon," she began hesitantly, "what made you join the military in the first place?"

He glanced at her, his brow furrowing slightly. "I guess I thought it would give me purpose," he said after a moment. "Structure. A way to prove something to myself."

"Did it?" Aurora asked softly.

Talon's lips pressed into a thin line. "At first. It gave me focus and taught me discipline. But... it came with a cost."

"What kind of cost?" Aurora probed gently.

He looked down, his fingers tracing the edge of the worn coin in his hand. "The kind that leaves scars," he said simply, his voice heavy. "Some visible, some not."

Aurora's heart ached at the weight in his tone, but she didn't press further. Instead, she leaned back against the couch, her own thoughts swirling. "You know," she said quietly, "I get why you're so guarded. But you don't have to carry all of this alone."

Talon huffed a quiet laugh, though there was no humor in it. "You say that like it's a choice."

"It is," Aurora said, her voice firm. "It might not feel like it, but it is."

Talon's gaze shifted to her, his expression unreadable. "And what about you? What's your excuse for trying to take on the world by yourself?"

Aurora smiled faintly, the question hitting closer to home than she'd expected. "Stubbornness, mostly," she admitted. "And maybe a little bit of stupidity."

Talon smirked, shaking his head. "I'll give you stubborn. Stupid? Not so much."

Aurora raised an eyebrow. "Is that a compliment?"

"Don't get used to it," Talon said, though the faint smile tugging at his lips softened the words.

The comfortable silence stretched between them again, broken only by the occasional pop of the fire. Aurora found herself studying Talon, noticing the way the lines of his face softened in the low light. He looked younger, less weighed down, as though the walls he usually kept so tightly in place finally gave him a moment of reprieve.

"You're strange, you know," she said suddenly.

Talon glanced at her, his brow arching. "Is that a good thing?"

"I think so," Aurora said, her voice thoughtful. "You're more... human than I thought you'd be."

Talon chuckled softly, shaking his head. "I'll take that as a compliment."

"It is," Aurora said, her tone sincere.

For a moment, the vulnerability in his gaze matched her own, and the air between them felt charged with unspoken possibilities. Aurora's heart quickened, though she wasn't sure if it was from fear or something else entirely.

"You're different, too," Talon said, his voice quieter now. "Most people would've bailed by now. You didn't."

Aurora shrugged, trying to mask the warmth that crept into her cheeks. "Guess I'm stubborn, remember?"

Talon smirked, but the weight in his gaze lingered. "You've got guts. I'll give you that."

"Thanks," Aurora said, her tone light. "I think."

Their conversation shifted again, this time into lighter territory. Aurora told him stories about her younger sister, whose rebellious streak rivaled her own, and Talon shared a rare, fleeting smile when Aurora described the disastrous camping trips her family had attempted during her childhood.

"You'd think we'd learn after the first one," Aurora said, laughing. "But no, we kept going back for more."

"Sounds like a nightmare," Talon said, though his lips twitched into a faint grin.

"It was," Aurora agreed, wiping a tear of laughter from her eye. "But looking back, it's… nice to remember. Even the bad parts."

Talon's expression grew thoughtful, and Aurora wondered if he was replaying his own memories—ones he likely hadn't shared with anyone else. She decided not to ask, sensing he needed the quiet.

After a while, the fire began to burn low, casting the cabin in deeper shadows. Havoc stirred at Talon's feet, his ears twitching as he let out a contented sigh. Aurora felt the weight of the day settle over her, her body aching but her mind oddly at ease.

"I should get some rest," she said, though she made no move to stand.

Talon suddenly grabbed her wrist and pulled her close without thinking. Aurora gasped at the sudden movement and caught herself on the arm of the chair where Talon sat.

Aurora looked deep into Talon's eyes. They held words that he didn't know how to say. Words that screamed to be spoken to someone — and be true finally.

"I just wanted to say thank you," Talon released Aurora's wrist and cleared his throat. "For this morning, I mean."

Aurora was stunned at the sudden personality switch. What once was a calculated and remorseful killer and ex-soldier was now a human just like her. For the first time, Aurora didn't see him as cold; she saw him the same way she saw herself. She was tired of being alone and fighting the same battle.

"Of course," Aurora's voice was calm, barely audible. Aurora found herself looking at Talon's lips, plump and then his nose. Then, something she realized was her favorite part: his eyes. Eyes roaming her the same way she was him.

"Aurora, we-" Talon's words cut off as he lifted his hand to her cheek. He grazed his fingertips over her cheekbone and savored the feeling. The tips of his fingers felt electric as they were connected.

Aurora didn't fight it. She didn't want to fight it.

Aurora found herself yearning for his touch. Aurora shut her eyes and leaned into him.

Talon's thumb traced over the soft skin of her cheek, and when Aurora opened her eyes, her breath caught in her throat.

Talon's eyes were heavy with something she couldn't quite place.

His fingers snaked around to the back of Aurora's neck, and he pulled her close, closing the distance between the two and connecting their foreheads.

"Talon-"

"Shhh"

Talon's eyes were shut, and his breathing was strong and staggered. He was gentle with her, and Aurora leaned in and pressed a gentle kiss on his forehead.

"I shouldn't want this, I shouldn't want you." Talon looked up at Aurora, and his eyes were filled with an internal war.

"It's okay," Aurora's heart ached. How could she admit to him that she wanted this just as badly as he did? How could she tell him that he wasn't crazy?

The snapping branch sounded like a whisper in the air, and within seconds, Talon was standing at the door.

As suddenly as it began, the moment was cut off. After a moment of standing guard, Talon cleared his throat.

"It's getting late."

There it was again. His mask that he had so tightly tied around his face that it hid his demons. Aurora stood up, dizzy by the whirlwind of emotions she had been caught up in. "You're right. I'm gonna head to bed." Aurora's chest ached from how his touch — their connection had been ripped away so suddenly.

Talon nodded, his gaze flicking to her before returning to the fire. "Good idea."

Aurora hesitated, then smiled faintly. "Goodnight, Talon."

"Goodnight, Aurora," he replied, his voice softer than she'd ever heard it.

As she lay down on the couch, pulling the blanket over herself, Aurora couldn't help but feel that something had shifted between them. The walls they'd both built so carefully were beginning to crumble, piece by piece, revealing parts of themselves neither had shared in years.

As she drifted off to sleep, she realized that, for the first time in a long while, she felt safe—not just because of Talon's presence but because of the fragile trust they were beginning to build together.

Chapter 9

Morning sunlight streamed through the cabin windows, casting a warm glow across the wooden floor. Aurora sat at the small table, her hands wrapped around a steaming mug of coffee, watching Talon move around the kitchen. He wasn't exactly graceful, but there was something comforting about his steady movements, the quiet purpose he brought to even the simplest tasks.

"So," Aurora said, breaking the silence, "we've decided this is home. What now?"

Talon glanced over his shoulder, his brow furrowing slightly. "What do you mean?"

"I mean, how do we make this work?" she asked, gesturing to the cabin around them. "This place feels like a fresh start, but we can't just sit here forever, hoping the world forgets about us."

He leaned against the counter, crossing his arms as he considered her words. "We make it work one step at a time. Start with the basics—food, security, keeping a low profile."

"And after that?" she pressed. "What happens when we need more than the basics? When we need supplies or—God forbid—medical help?"

Talon's jaw tightened, but his gaze didn't waver. "Then we figure it out. We've always figured it out."

Aurora sighed, her fingers drumming lightly against her mug. "I want this to work. I want us to have something real here. But it feels like we're balancing on the edge of something that could collapse at any moment."

Talon moved closer, resting a hand on her shoulder. "We've survived worse. This is the easy part."

She looked up at him, her gaze searching his. "You really believe that?"

"I do," he said simply. "Because we're not doing this alone."

The day unfolded quietly. Talon spent hours outside chopping firewood and reinforcing the cabin's perimeter while Aurora worked inside, organizing their supplies and jotting down a list of what they still needed. Havoc alternated between following Talon and lounging near the fireplace, his presence a steady reminder of their new reality. By mid-afternoon, Aurora stepped outside, list in hand, and found Talon near the edge of the clearing, hammering nails into a makeshift fence. He looked up as she approached, wiping sweat from his brow.

"Busy?" she asked, her tone teasing.

"Always," he replied, his lips quirking into a faint smile. "What's on your mind?"

She held up the list. "We need a few things—more food, tools, maybe some seeds if we're serious about staying here long-term."

Talon took the list, scanning it before handing it back. "There's a town about an hour from here. Quiet, small. We can check it out."

Aurora raised an eyebrow. "I thought we were in the middle of nowhere."

"We are," he replied. "But nowhere still has edges."

The next morning, they packed light, taking only what they needed for the trip. Aurora felt a pang of hesitation as they left the cabin, the sense of safety it provided lingering in her mind. Havoc trotted ahead, his tail wagging as though he had no such reservations. The drive was quiet, the narrow dirt road winding through dense forest before giving way to open fields. Aurora glanced out the window, her thoughts drifting to the life they were trying to build. It felt fragile like it could shatter with the slightest misstep, but she was determined to hold onto it.

When they reached the town, it was exactly as Talon had described—small, quiet, and unassuming. The main street was lined with a handful of shops, their faded signs and weathered exteriors speaking to a simpler way of life. Aurora followed Talon into a general store, the bell above the door jingling softly as they entered. The woman behind the counter greeted them with a polite smile, her gaze lingering briefly on Talon before shifting to Aurora.

"Let me know if you need any help," she said, her tone warm but cautious.

Talon nodded, his expression neutral as he began scanning the shelves. Aurora moved toward a display of seeds, her fingers brushing against the packets as she considered their options. She felt a twinge of unease, the sense that she was being watched, but when she glanced over her shoulder, the store was empty save for the clerk and Havoc, who waited patiently by the door.

"Find anything good?" Talon asked, appearing at her side.

"Maybe," she replied, holding up a packet of tomato seeds. "What do you think?"

"I think you're getting ahead of yourself," he said, though his tone was more amused than critical.

"Call it optimism," she said with a shrug. "You should try it sometime."

Talon chuckled softly, his hand brushing against hers as he reached for the seeds. "I'll leave that to you."

By the time they returned to the cabin, the sun was dipping below the horizon, casting the sky in hues of orange and gold. Aurora carried the supplies inside while Talon tended to Havoc, who seemed content to flop down by the fire after their long day. The cabin felt warm and welcoming, a stark contrast to the tension that had followed them for so long. As they unpacked, Aurora placed the seeds on the windowsill, a small but meaningful symbol of the life they were trying to build.

Talon watched her, his expression softening as he crossed the room to stand beside her. "You did good today," he said, his voice low but steady.

"Thanks," she replied, her smile faint but genuine. "So did you."

They stood there for a moment, the weight of the day easing as the quiet enveloped them. Havoc let out a contented sigh from his spot near the fire, his tail thumping softly against the floor. Aurora glanced at Talon, her heart swelling at the way he looked at her—not with the guarded intensity she was used to, but with something warmer, something that felt like hope.

Aurora placed her forehead against Talon's shoulder. A move she swore would be too far. But Talon didn't move.

Talon's heart raced with hope for the first time in a long time. He had been operating on pure survival for as long as he can remember. And for the first time, he had another reason to fight. Hope for a life he could for once imagine. And for the person he had begun to trust even against the odds of their situation.

"This is going to work," she said, her voice barely above a whisper.

Talon reached for her hand, his fingers curling around hers. "Yeah," he said softly. "It is."

Chapter 10

Aurora stood frozen, her breath shallow and uneven as she watched Talon through the dim haze of the abandoned industrial building. The faint glow of a flickering overhead light painted the scene in harsh shadows. He was relentless, his fists connecting with his target with calculated brutality. The man beneath him coughed and wheezed, blood streaking his face as he begged for mercy.

Talon's voice was low, chillingly calm. "Tell them," he said, his words cutting through the air like a blade. "Tell them if they so much as look at her again, I'll make them wish they were dead."

The man stammered through his pain. "I—I didn't mean—"

Talon silenced him with another blow, sending him sprawling. The cold finality in his movements wasn't just a warning; it was a statement. This wasn't just about protecting her—it was about sending a message to anyone foolish enough to think they could touch her.

"Talon," Aurora's voice cut through the heavy air, trembling but firm.

He stilled, his shoulders tightening as if her presence had caught him off guard. Slowly, he turned his head, his piercing gaze locking onto hers. For a moment, neither of them spoke. The silence stretched, filled with unspoken tension and the weight of everything she'd just seen.

"Go home, Aurora," he said, his voice rough and detached.

"No," she replied, taking a hesitant step closer. "Not until you stop this."

The man on the ground groaned, trying to crawl away, but Talon reached out and grabbed his collar, dragging him back effortlessly. "We're not finished," he muttered coldly, his grip tightening.

Aurora's heart pounded. "Yes, you are," she said, her voice firmer now. "Let him go."

Talon didn't move, his jaw clenching as he stared down at his bloodied prey. "If I let him go, he'll go back to them. He'll tell them I'm weak."

"Then let him," she countered. "Because this? This isn't strength, Talon. This is cruelty."

Her words hung in the air, sharp and unrelenting. Talon's hand loosened slightly, but he didn't release the man. Instead, he glanced at her, his expression hard and unreadable. "You don't understand. If they fear me, they'll leave you alone."

"I don't want them to fear you," she said, her voice breaking. "I want you to stop losing yourself to this."

Talon stood slowly, his hand finally letting go of the man's shirt. The figure on the ground scrambled away, gasping and coughing, but neither of them paid him any mind. Talon turned to Aurora, his presence towering and suffocating.

"You think this is about me?" he asked, his voice low and cutting. "This is about keeping you alive."

Aurora shook her head, tears stinging her eyes. "You're scaring me, Talon. Don't you see that? You're doing all of this for me, but you're turning into someone I can't recognize. Someone I can't trust."

Her admission seemed to hit him like a physical blow. For a fleeting moment, something raw and vulnerable flickered across his face, but it was gone as quickly as it came. He stepped closer, the space between them charged with tension.

"I'm doing what needs to be done," he said, his voice softer but no less resolute.

"No," she said, her voice trembling but unyielding. "You're doing what you think will protect me because you don't know how to let me in."

His expression darkened, his jaw tightening as if her words had struck a nerve. "You don't get it, Aurora. I don't know how to be anything else. This—" he gestured to the scene around them, his bloodied knuckles, the crumpled man. "This is all I know."

Aurora's throat tightened, frustration boiling over. "Then learn. If you care about me, if I mean anything to you, you'll try."

Talon exhaled sharply, turning away from her. His shoulders slumped slightly, the weight of her words pressing down on him. But when he spoke, his voice was distant, hollow. "Go home, Aurora."

Her heart sank, the finality in his tone slicing through her resolve. She stepped back, shaking her head. "No. Not until you meet me halfway. Not until you prove that you can be more than this."

Talon's hands curled into fists at his sides, and for a moment, she thought he might say something. But he didn't. He stood there, silent and immovable, his gaze fixed on the ground.

Tears blurred her vision as she turned to leave. "You said I was your weakness," she said over her shoulder, her voice breaking. "Then stop using me as an excuse to destroy yourself."

She didn't wait for his response. Her footsteps echoed in the empty space as she walked away, her chest tight with anger, fear, and heartbreak.

Talon watched her go, his chest tightening with every step she took. When the sound of her footsteps faded, he sank to his knees, his hands trembling as they buried themselves in his hair. He sat there in silence, the blood on his knuckles a stark reminder of the line he'd crossed.

"What have I done?" he whispered, his voice cracking under the weight of his regret.

The man he'd beaten lay groaning a few feet away, but Talon didn't hear him. All he could see was the look in Aurora's eyes—the fear, the pain, the disappointment. She had asked him to step back from the edge, to choose her instead of the darkness that had consumed him.

And he'd failed.

"What have I done?" he whispered, his voice cracking under the weight of his regret. The words felt hollow, barely audible against the oppressive silence of the abandoned building. Talon stared at his bloodied hands, the crimson stains smearing his knuckles and the tremor in his fingers that he could no longer suppress. For years, he had operated on instinct, living in a world where violence was survival, but now, for the first time, his actions felt like a cage closing in around him.

Aurora's footsteps had long faded, but her voice echoed in his mind, cutting deeper than any blade ever could. "You're scaring me," she had said, the raw pain in her words twisting something inside him. He had seen her fear, her heartbreak, and still, he had let her walk away. He had told himself it was for the best, that she was better off without him, but the lie tasted bitter now. She had asked him to choose her, to step away from the darkness that consumed him, and he hadn't. Instead, he had chosen the only thing he knew—violence, control, destruction.

His knees buckled, and he sank to the floor, the cold concrete biting against his skin. His breathing was ragged as the reality of what he'd done settled in. He had tried to protect her, to shield her from the world he lived in, but in doing so, he had become the very thing she feared. His hands dragged through his hair, smearing blood across his face as he sat there, the weight of his failure pressing down on him.

The knife on the table caught his eye, its edge glinting faintly in the dim light. It was a symbol of everything he hated about himself—the precision, the cold efficiency, the damage he caused without hesitation. He reached for it, his fingers curling around the hilt, but the weight of it felt unbearable. He thought of her again, of the way she had looked at him with a mixture of defiance and desperation, begging him to come back from the edge.

With a growl of frustration, Talon hurled the knife across the room, the clang of metal against concrete echoing in the empty space. The sound broke the suffocating silence but did nothing to ease the turmoil inside him. He stood abruptly, his movements jerky and uncoordinated, and paced the room like a caged animal. Every step felt heavier than the last as he replayed the events of the night over and over in his mind.

Hours passed in a haze, the faint light of dawn creeping through the cracks in the building's walls. Talon had barely moved, his body and mind locked in a battle he didn't know how to win. He thought of Aurora again, of her unwavering determination, her strength in standing up to him even when she was afraid. She had been his tether to something better, something he had long believed he couldn't have. And now, he might have destroyed it.

The drive back to the safehouse was a blur, the roar of the engine drowned out by the storm raging in his head. He didn't know what he was going to say to her or if she would even listen, but he had to try. The thought of leaving things as they were, of letting her walk away without fighting for her, was unbearable.

When he arrived, the house was silent. He hesitated at the door, his hand resting on the handle as doubt clawed at him. What if she didn't want to see him? What if he had pushed her too far? He pushed the thoughts aside and stepped inside, the door creaking softly as it swung open.

Aurora was sitting at the small table, her arms crossed tightly over her chest as she stared out the window. Her posture was tense, her shoulders rigid, and she didn't look up as he entered. The sight of her, so closed off, sent a pang of guilt through him. He had done this to her—made her retreat into herself, her defenses rising against him.

"Aurora," he said, his voice low and unsteady.

She didn't respond at first, her gaze fixed on some distant point outside. When she finally turned to face him, her eyes were red-rimmed, but her expression was sharp and guarded. "What do you want, Talon?"

Her words hit him like a blow, but he forced himself to step closer. "I came to apologize," he said, his voice hoarse.

"For what?" she asked sharply. "For scaring me? For hurting me? Or for proving me right?"

Talon flinched, the weight of her words cutting deep. "For all of it," he admitted. "I never wanted to hurt you, Aurora."

"But you did," she said, her voice trembling with anger and pain. "You keep saying you're doing this for me, but all you're doing is pushing me away."

"I know," he said, his tone raw and unfiltered. "I'm a coward, Aurora. I was too afraid to believe that I could be something more, that I could be the man you deserve."

Aurora's expression softened slightly, but the pain in her eyes remained. "I never asked you to be perfect, Talon. I just needed you to try. But instead, you pushed me away and proved that this—" she gestured to him, to the blood on his clothes, the exhaustion etched into his face—"is all you want to be."

"It's not," he said desperately, taking a step closer. "I want to be better for you, Aurora. I don't know how, but I'm willing to try. Just… don't give up on me."

Her gaze softened for a moment, but the fear and doubt lingered. "What happens the next time, Talon?" she asked quietly. "What happens when you lose control again, and I can't pull you back?"

"I don't know," he admitted, his voice barely above a whisper. "But I'll fight it. For you. Because losing you is worse than losing myself."

Aurora looked at him for a long moment, her expression unreadable. She wanted to believe him, wanted to hold onto the hope that he could be the man she saw glimpses of beneath the darkness. But the hurt he had caused was fresh, the wounds still raw.

"I can't keep saving you, Talon," she said finally, her voice trembling. "You have to save yourself."

Her words hung in the air, heavy and final. Talon felt the weight of them settle over him, but he nodded slowly, his gaze steady on hers. "Then I'll save myself. For you."

Aurora turned away, her arms wrapping tightly around herself as she faced the window again. Talon didn't move, his chest tight with the realization that this was his last chance. He had to prove to her—and to himself—that he could be better.

As the silence stretched between them, he took a step back, his hand lingering on the doorframe. "I'll fix this, Aurora," he said softly. "I swear it."

She didn't reply, but he saw the way her shoulders tensed, the faint tremble in her hands. It wasn't forgiveness, not yet, but it was enough to give him hope.

Talon stepped outside, the cool morning air biting against his skin. He clenched his fists, determination settling in his chest. He would fight the darkness within him, not just for her, but because she deserved more than the man he had been.

And for the first time, he believed he could try.

Chapter 11

THE STORM OUTSIDE MATCHED the tension brewing inside the cabin. Rain lashed against the windows, wind howling through the trees, as if nature itself had decided to reflect the storm raging between Talon and Aurora. The cabin, which had felt like a refuge just days ago, now seemed suffocatingly small.

Aurora stood near the couch, her arms crossed and her jaw tight. "You can't just make decisions for me, Talon," she snapped, her voice sharp.

Talon, pacing near the table, stopped abruptly and turned to face her. "I'm trying to keep you alive," he growled, his tone ice-cold. "Is that such a terrible thing?"

"I didn't ask for your protection," Aurora shot back, stepping closer. "I can handle myself."

"You've got a funny way of showing it," Talon said, his voice dripping with sarcasm. "Running into danger every chance you get? That's not handling yourself—that's reckless."

Aurora's eyes narrowed. "Reckless? Coming from the guy who takes every threat as a personal challenge?"

Talon's jaw clenched, his hands curling into fists at his sides. "This isn't a game, Aurora."

"I know that," she said, her voice rising. "But you treat me like I'm some liability, like I can't think for myself."

Talon stepped closer, his eyes blazing. "Because if something happens to you—"

"What?" Aurora challenged, her heart pounding. "What happens then, Talon? You lose someone else? You feel guilty? Or maybe—just maybe—you actually care about someone for once?"

The words hit like a blow, and for a moment, Talon just stared at her, his chest heaving. The air between them was electric, charged with the kind of tension that could ignite at any second. Aurora refused to back down, her gaze locked on his, defiant and unyielding.

Talon's eyes blazed with fury. Aurora knew that the words struck home, but they needed to be said. It broke each and every time that Talon held back his emotions. He deserved to feel loved and needed. He deserved to be able to rely on someone.

"Talon, you can't always distance yourself the moment you begin to get close to someone."

"Like Hell, I fucking can't," Talon stomped up to Aurora.

Aurora stepped back, hitting her back on the nearby wall. Havoc sat nearby, watching and licking the tension in the air.

Talon's hands slammed into the wall on either side of Aurora's head, sending dust and small wood splinters to the floor around her. But she didn't flinch. She refused to hide from his demons the way that he did.

Talon's breath was like an angry bull. His eyes blazed in a way that Aurora had never seen before. It was at this moment that she realized she felt fear.

With shaking hands, Aurora grabbed Talon's face gently. Talon flinched, shutting his eyes, and his breath staggered for a moment. Aurora internally celebrated the small win when Talon didn't pull away.

"I'm not going anywhere," she whispered.

Talon opened his eyes but didn't say anything.

"My place is at your side. Just like Havoc." Aurora brought his face down and pressed a gentle kiss on Talon's forehead. "You're home to me."

Talon shut his eyes and leaned into her touch now, his walls slowly falling.

"You will be home to me no matter how far you travel or try to run. No corner of this earth would be far enough for you to hide. Because I would spend the rest of my life searching for you."

"You don't get it," Talon said finally, his voice low and rough. "You don't understand what it's like to lose everything."

Aurora stepped closer, her eyes softening but her tone firm. "Then help me understand. Stop shutting me out."

Talon's walls cracked, just enough for her to see the pain lurking behind his sharp exterior. "I can't," he muttered, his voice barely audible.

"Why not?" Aurora asked, her voice softening further. "What are you so afraid of?"

Talon's breath hitched, and before he could stop himself, he reached out, grabbing her by the arms and backing her against the wall. The movement was sudden, almost rough, but controlled. Aurora gasped, her heart pounding as her back pressed against the wood.

"Because you're making me care," Talon said, his voice strained. "And that terrifies me."

Aurora's lips parted, her breath shallow as she stared up at him. His face was inches from hers, his hands braced on either side of her. The heat between them was undeniable, their emotions raw and exposed. "Talon—"

Her words were cut off as his mouth crashed against hers. The kiss was rough, almost punishing, as if he was trying to silence every thought and emotion swirling in his head. Aurora gasped against his lips, her hands instinctively gripping his shirt as she kissed him back with matching intensity.

The world around them seemed to fade, the storm outside a distant roar compared to the fire burning between them. Talon's hands moved to her waist, pulling her closer as the kiss deepened. It was consuming, needy, and raw, every ounce of frustration and longing pouring out in the way their mouths moved against each other.

Aurora felt her knees weaken, her body pressing against his as if trying to close the gap between them entirely. She'd never felt anything like this—this combination of fury and desire that left her breathless and wanting more. Their bodies moved in sync, music that faded into something neither of them had truly known.

Just as quickly as it started, Talon pulled back, his breathing ragged. His hands dropped to his sides, his gaze a mixture of shock and regret. "This shouldn't have happened," he muttered, stepping back.

Aurora stared at him, her lips tingling from the kiss and her heart racing. "Why not?" she asked, her voice trembling. "What are you so afraid of?"

Talon ran a hand through his hair, turning away. "Because I can't afford to care about you like this."

Aurora stepped forward, her voice steady despite the whirlwind of emotions inside her. "But you do care."

Talon froze, his back to her. "That's the problem," he said quietly.

Aurora's chest ached at the vulnerability in his voice. She wanted to reach out, to pull him back and tell him it was okay to let his guard down. But she knew better than to push too hard, too fast.

"Talon," she said softly, her tone careful. "You don't have to do this alone. Whatever this is—whatever we are—we'll figure it out. Together."

He turned slowly, his eyes locking onto hers. For a moment, the weight of his walls seemed to lift, his gaze softer than she'd ever seen it. But then he shook his head, stepping back further. "I can't," he said again, his voice rough. "I can't let this happen."

Aurora crossed her arms, her jaw tightening. "You keep saying you can't, but you already have. That kiss—whatever it meant—you can't take it back."

Talon's gaze dropped to the floor, his shoulders slumping. "That's what scares me."

Aurora sighed, the tension in her shoulders easing as she stepped closer. "You're not the only one who's scared, you know."

Talon looked up at her, his expression conflicted. "Then why aren't you running?"

"Because I trust you," Aurora said simply. "And I think, deep down, you trust me too."

Talon's breath hitched, and for a moment, he looked like he might say something. But then he shook his head, turning toward the door. "I need some air," he muttered, stepping outside into the storm.

Aurora stood there, her chest tightening as she watched him go. She touched her lips, still tingling from the kiss, and exhaled shakily. Whatever had just happened between them, it was far from over.

The rain lashed against Talon's face as he stood on the porch, his hands gripping the railing tightly. His mind raced, every thought a chaotic swirl of anger, fear, and something he didn't want to name. The kiss had been a mistake—a moment of weakness he couldn't afford.

But it had also been real, and that terrified him more than anything.

Inside, Aurora leaned against the wall, her fingers tracing the grain of the wood as she replayed the moment in her mind. Her heart was still pounding, a mix of confusion and longing swirling in her chest. She didn't regret the kiss, but she couldn't ignore the way it had shaken them both.

When Talon finally stepped back inside, his expression was guarded, his eyes avoiding hers. Aurora stood her ground, her arms crossed as she waited for him to speak. But he said nothing, instead moving toward the fire and stoking it with unnecessary force.

"We need to talk about this," Aurora said finally, breaking the silence.

"There's nothing to talk about," Talon said, his voice flat.

Aurora frowned, stepping closer. "You don't get to kiss me like that and pretend it didn't happen."

Talon glanced at her, his jaw tightening. "I'm trying to protect you."

"From what?" Aurora challenged. "From you? Or from how you feel?"

Talon didn't answer, his silence speaks volumes. Aurora sighed, her frustration giving way to understanding. "I'm not asking you to change overnight," she said softly. "But you can't keep running from this."

Talon met her gaze, his expression torn. "I don't know how to stop."

Aurora smiled faintly, stepping closer. "Then let me help."

Aurora didn't back down, standing firm as Talon's conflicted gaze darted between her and the floor. The firelight flickered across his face, casting shadows that mirrored the storm raging inside him. His fists clenched at his sides, his breathing uneven as he struggled to find the words.

"You think this is easy for me?" Talon finally said, his voice low and strained. "You think I don't want to just—" He stopped himself, exhaling sharply. "It's not that simple."

"Nothing about this is simple," Aurora replied, her voice steady but gentle. "But running away from it isn't going to make it any less complicated."

Talon shook his head, taking a step back as if putting distance between them would ease the tension. "You don't understand. This... us—it's dangerous."

Aurora frowned, crossing her arms. "You keep saying that, but what's the real danger here, Talon? Is it them—our enemies—or is it you?"

Talon flinched as though her words had struck him physically. "It's me," he admitted after a long pause, his voice barely above a whisper. "You don't know the things I've done, Aurora. The people I've hurt. If you get too close... I don't know if I can protect you from that."

Aurora softened, her heart aching at the vulnerability etched into his features. "I'm not asking you to protect me from yourself," she said. "I'm asking you to let me in."

Talon's jaw tightened, his eyes glistening with emotions he rarely let surface. "Why?" he asked, his voice breaking. "Why would you want this? Why would you want me?"

Aurora stepped closer, her voice unwavering. "Because I see you, Talon. The real you—the one you try so hard to hide. And I think you're worth fighting for."

Her words seemed to unravel something inside him. Talon's walls, the ones he'd spent years building, cracked further. He reached for her, his hand trembling slightly as it brushed against her cheek. Aurora didn't pull away; instead, she leaned into his touch, her breath catching at the warmth of his skin.

"I don't deserve this," Talon murmured, his voice raw.

"That's not for you to decide," Aurora replied softly. "Let me choose."

The storm outside raged on, the wind howling as the cabin seemed to shrink around them. Talon's thumb brushed her cheekbone, and for a moment, the weight of the world melted away. His lips parted as though he wanted to say something, but instead, he closed the gap between them.

The kiss was slower this time, less frantic but just as consuming. Talon's hand slid to the back of Aurora's neck, holding her gently as their lips moved together in perfect sync. Aurora felt her knees weaken, but she held onto him, grounding herself in the moment.

When they finally pulled apart, both of them were breathing heavily. Talon rested his forehead against hers, his eyes closed, savoring the closeness. "This scares the hell out of me," he admitted.

Aurora smiled faintly, her fingers brushing against his chest. "Good. That means it matters."

Talon chuckled softly, the sound both foreign and welcome. "You really don't give up, do you?"

"Not on the things that matter," Aurora said firmly.

They stood there for a while, the storm outside their only witness. Talon's arms encircled her waist, pulling her closer as if to shield her from everything he feared. Aurora rested her head against his chest, listening to the steady rhythm of his heartbeat.

For the first time in a long while, Talon allowed himself to feel safe—not from the threats outside, but from the ones he carried within. Aurora had broken through his defenses, and though it terrified him, it also brought a sense of peace he hadn't known he needed.

Eventually, Talon sighed, pulling back slightly. "This doesn't mean it'll be easy," he said, his tone cautious.

"Nothing worth having ever is," Aurora replied, her eyes locking onto his. "But I think we're worth it."

Talon nodded, a faint smile tugging at his lips. "You're something else, you know that?"

Aurora smirked, stepping back and crossing her arms. "You're just figuring that out now?"

Talon chuckled, shaking his head. "I've known for a while. Guess I just didn't want to admit it."

The lightness of their exchange eased the tension, but the reality of their situation loomed over them. Talon's gaze drifted toward the window, his expression darkening. "We need to focus. They're still out there."

Aurora followed his gaze, her smirk fading. "Then let's make sure we're ready for whatever comes next."

The next few hours were spent reinforcing their defenses, double-checking weapons, and mapping out escape routes. The storm began to subside, leaving the air heavy with the promise of a coming reckoning. Talon worked silently, his movements efficient and purposeful, but Aurora noticed the subtle shifts in his demeanor—small moments of hesitation, the way his eyes lingered on her when he thought she wasn't looking.

As the fire dwindled to embers, they found themselves back in the living area. Aurora sat on the couch, her legs tucked beneath her, while Talon leaned against the mantle, his arms crossed. Havoc lay between them, his tail thumping softly against the floor.

"You ever think about what you'll do after this is over?" Aurora asked, breaking the silence.

Talon's brow furrowed as he considered her question. "Not really. Haven't had the luxury."

Aurora tilted her head, studying him. "What if you did? What would you want?"

Talon hesitated, his gaze dropping to the floor. "I don't know," he admitted. "I've spent so long just trying to survive. Thinking beyond that… it feels impossible."

"It's not," Aurora said softly. "Maybe it's time you started thinking about more than just surviving."

Talon looked at her, his expression unreadable. "And what about you? What do you want?"

Aurora smiled faintly. "To make a difference. To know that all of this meant something."

Talon nodded slowly, his eyes reflecting a depth of understanding that words couldn't capture. "You already have."

Aurora's chest tightened at the quiet sincerity in his voice. She leaned forward slightly, her eyes searching his. "So have you."

Talon's lips parted as if to respond, but instead, he pushed off the mantle and crossed the room. He sat beside her on the couch, the space between them shrinking to nothing. "Whatever happens next," he said quietly, "we face it together."

Aurora nodded, her voice steady despite the storm of emotions inside her. "Together."

Chapter 12

THE MORNING SUN SEEPED through the cabin's windows, casting a warm, golden glow that contrasted starkly with the storm of thoughts swirling in Aurora's mind. She sat at the small table, absently stirring her cup of tea, her gaze fixed on the horizon outside. The kiss they'd shared the night before lingered in her mind, every detail replaying in vivid clarity. It was unlike anything she'd ever felt before—raw, unfiltered, and intense.

Yet, it also came with complications. Talon wasn't an open book, and she'd only begun to scratch the surface of his guarded nature. There was a lifetime of pain behind his eyes, layers of defenses built to keep the world at bay. She wanted to understand him, to know the man beneath the armor. But she knew that breaking through would require patience.

"Lost in thought?" Talon's voice broke the silence, drawing her attention.

Aurora glanced up to find him leaning against the doorway, his arms crossed. He looked more relaxed than usual, but his sharp gaze betrayed his ever-present vigilance. "Something like that," she replied, offering a faint smile.

Talon stepped inside, his boots making soft thuds against the wooden floor. "You've been quiet all morning."

"Just... thinking," Aurora said, her tone thoughtful. "About you. About us."

Talon's brow furrowed, and he hesitated before sitting across from her. "Regretting last night?" he asked his voice low.

Aurora shook her head firmly. "No. But I'd be lying if I said I wasn't trying to figure out what it means."

Talon's gaze softened, his shoulders relaxing slightly. "You're not the only one," he admitted. "I'm not used to this… letting someone in."

Aurora tilted her head, studying him. "I get that. But if we're going to make this work, we need to be honest with each other."

Talon exhaled, running a hand through his hair. "That's not easy for me."

"I'm not asking for easy," Aurora said gently. "Just real."

For a moment, Talon didn't respond. Then, as if steeling himself, he leaned forward and rested his forearms on the table. "There are things about me—things you need to know if you're going to stay in this."

Aurora's heart quickened, but she nodded. "I'm listening."

Talon hesitated, his jaw tightening as he gathered his thoughts. "You know I'm trans," he began, his voice steady but guarded. "But there's more to it than just that."

Aurora stayed silent, sensing he needed space to continue.

"I've made choices—some of them weren't really choices at all," Talon said, his tone heavy. "When I started transitioning, I thought it would fix everything. But life doesn't work that way."

Aurora's brow furrowed. "Fix everything?"

Talon nodded, his gaze dropping to the table. "For a long time, I thought that if I looked the way I felt, it would make the rest of the world fall into place. But… it didn't. There's always something more to deal with."

Aurora reached out, placing her hand on his. "Like what?"

Talon hesitated before meeting her gaze. "Like medical issues. I can't pursue bottom surgery—not because I don't want to, but because it's not safe for me. And even if it were... it doesn't define who I am."

Aurora's chest tightened at the vulnerability in his voice. "I don't care about that," she said softly. "I care about you."

Talon's lips twitched into a faint smile. "I've spent so long worrying about how people see me. Hearing that... it's not something I'm used to."

"Well, get used to it," Aurora said with a smirk, squeezing his hand. "Because I'm not going anywhere."

Talon chuckled softly, shaking his head. "You're something else."

Later that day, Aurora found herself standing in the middle of the cabin's living room, her arms crossed as Talon circled her like a predator assessing his prey. "I don't see why this is necessary," she said, eyeing him warily.

"You froze during the last fight," Talon said bluntly. "If you want to stay alive, you need to know how to defend yourself."

"I know how to defend myself," Aurora shot back. "I've handled plenty of tough situations before."

Talon smirked, his gaze sharp. "Handling isn't enough. You need to dominate."

The word sent a shiver down Aurora's spine, though she refused to show it. "Fine," she said, her chin lifting defiantly. "Show me."

Talon stepped closer, his presence overwhelming as he towered over her. "First rule: control the situation. Don't let your opponent dictate the fight."

Aurora nodded, her eyes locked on his. "Got it."

"Good," Talon said, his voice dropping. "Now try to get out of this."

Before she could react, his hand shot out, gripping her wrist and twisting it gently but firmly behind her back. He stepped closer, his chest brushing against her shoulder as he leaned in. "What's your move?"

Aurora's breath hitched, the closeness making it hard to think. She shifted her weight, attempting to pivot out of his grip, but Talon anticipated the move, his free arm wrapping around her waist to keep her in place.

"Not bad," he murmured, his breath warm against her ear. "But not good enough."

Aurora twisted again, managing to free her wrist, but Talon countered immediately, spinning her around and pinning her against the wall. His hands braced on either side of her head, their faces inches apart. "You're hesitating," he said, his voice low and rough. "That'll get you killed."

Aurora glared up at him, her chest heaving. "You're not giving me much room to work with."

"You think your enemies will?" Talon shot back, his tone challenging.

The tension between them crackled like a live wire, the line between training and something far more dangerous blurring with every passing second. Aurora refused to back down, her defiance blazing in her eyes. "You're enjoying this, aren't you?"

Talon's lips curled into a faint smirk. "Maybe."

Aurora's pulse quickened, but she kept her voice steady. "You think you can intimidate me?"

"I don't need to intimidate you," Talon said, his voice dropping to a near whisper. "I just need to remind you who's in control."

Aurora's breath caught, the heat between them almost unbearable. "And who's that?" she challenged, her voice daring.

Talon leaned in, his lips brushing her ear as he spoke. "Me."

The single word sent a shiver down her spine, but Aurora refused to let him win. She lifted her knee, aiming for his side, but Talon blocked the move effortlessly, his hand catching her thigh and holding it firmly. "Better," he said, his voice tinged with approval. "But you'll have to do better than that."

Aurora's frustration and attraction burned in equal measure, her chest heaving as she stared up at him. "You're impossible."

"And you're stubborn," Talon said, his smirk widening. "It's why we work."

Aurora couldn't help the smile that tugged at her lips, even as her heart raced. "This isn't over."

Talon chuckled, finally stepping back and releasing her. "It never is."

That night, as Aurora sat by the fire, nursing the faint soreness from their training session, she couldn't help but reflect on how far they'd come. Talon was still an enigma, his walls far from completely down, but she'd seen more of him than anyone else likely had.

And despite the chaos around them, she found herself drawn to him—not just to his strength, but to the man he was underneath. It terrified and thrilled her in equal measure.

Across the room, Talon caught her gaze, his expression softening. "You're staring," he said, a hint of teasing in his voice.

Aurora shrugged, a faint smile playing on her lips. "Maybe I like what I see."

Talon chuckled, shaking his head. "Careful, Aurora. You're playing a dangerous game."

Aurora's smile widened, her eyes gleaming with mischief. "I think I can handle it."

Talon's gaze lingered on her, his lips twitching into a rare smile. "We'll see."

Aurora leaned back against the couch, her body still buzzing from their self-defense lesson. Her muscles ached in places she hadn't known existed, but it wasn't just the physical exertion that left her breathless. Talon's proximity, his commanding presence, and the quiet power in his every move lingered in her mind like an intoxicating echo.

Across the room, Talon stood at the sink, washing his hands. The sleeves of his shirt were rolled up, revealing the strong lines of his forearms. He moved with the same fluidity that had disarmed her so effortlessly earlier, but his expression was distant as if he were lost in thought.

"You're quiet," Aurora said, breaking the silence.

Talon glanced over his shoulder, his brow furrowing. "So are you."

Aurora smirked faintly. "Touché. But I think I earned a little quiet after getting tossed around like that."

Talon dried his hands on a towel, turning to face her. "You held your own," he said, his tone thoughtful. "Most people would've panicked."

"I almost did," Aurora admitted, shifting to sit cross-legged on the couch. "But then I remembered who I was dealing with."

Talon tilted his head, a faint smirk tugging at his lips. "And who's that?"

"Someone who doesn't take it easy on anyone," Aurora replied, raising an eyebrow. "Not even someone they kissed last night."

Talon froze for a fraction of a second before recovering, his smirk fading into something softer. "I thought we weren't talking about that."

Aurora shrugged, her eyes gleaming with mischief. "You didn't say it was off-limits."

Talon sighed, crossing the room and leaning against the mantle. "You're impossible, you know that?"

"Maybe," Aurora said, her smirk widening. "But you like it."

Talon didn't respond immediately. Instead, he studied her, his gaze lingering a moment longer than necessary. "You don't make it easy to stay guarded."

Aurora tilted her head, her expression softening. "Maybe that's a good thing."

Talon exhaled, his shoulders relaxing slightly. "Or maybe it's dangerous."

"You're always worried about danger," Aurora said, leaning forward. "But what about what's worth the risk?"

Talon's gaze darkened, but not with anger—something else entirely. "You're pushing your luck."

Aurora stood, crossing the room until she was standing just a foot away from him. "Maybe I am," she said, her voice low. "But I think it's worth it."

For a moment, the air between them crackled with tension. Talon's jaw tightened, his hands gripping the edge of the mantle. Aurora could see the conflict in his eyes—the war between his instincts to protect and his desire to let go.

"You don't understand what you're asking for," Talon said finally, his voice strained.

"Then explain it to me," Aurora countered. "Show me."

Talon's breath hitched, and for a moment, she thought he might close the distance between them. But instead, he stepped back, shaking his head. "Not yet."

Aurora's chest tightened, but she nodded, sensing the fragility of the moment. "Okay," she said softly. "I'll wait."

Talon's expression softened, gratitude flickering in his eyes. "Thank you."

The next morning, Aurora woke early, the cabin still shrouded in the soft light of dawn. She found Talon outside, chopping firewood with precise, practiced movements. His shirt clung to his back, damp with sweat, and his jaw was set in quiet concentration.

"You're up early," Aurora said, stepping onto the porch.

Talon glanced at her, wiping his brow with the back of his hand. "Couldn't sleep."

"Me neither," Aurora admitted, leaning against the railing. "Too much on my mind."

"Same," Talon said, splitting another log with a single, fluid strike.

Aurora watched him for a moment before speaking again. "You don't talk about your past much."

Talon paused, resting the axe against the stump. "What's there to talk about?"

"A lot, I think," Aurora said, her tone careful. "But I get why you don't. Sometimes, it's easier to keep it locked up."

Talon leaned on the axe handle, his expression unreadable. "What about you? What keeps you up at night?"

Aurora hesitated, then sighed. "My sister," she said finally. "I promised her I'd keep her safe. That I'd make things better for both of us."

Talon's gaze softened. "And do you think you've kept that promise?"

Aurora smiled faintly, though it didn't reach her eyes. "I'm trying. But sometimes it feels like I'm fighting a losing battle."

"You're still fighting," Talon said quietly. "That's what matters."

Aurora met his gaze, the sincerity in his voice making her chest ache. "You're not as tough as you pretend to be," she said softly.

Talon chuckled, shaking his head. "Don't tell anyone. It can be our little secret."

Later that afternoon, Talon led Aurora through another round of self-defense training. This time, the moves were more complex, and the contact was more intimate. Aurora found herself pressed against him more often than not, her body hyper-aware of every brush of his hands.

"You're hesitating again," Talon said, his breath warm against her ear. Shivers shot down her spine and she hoped he didn't notice.

"I'm trying not to break something," Aurora shot back, her voice laced with frustration.

"You're not going to break me," Talon said, his tone teasing but firm. "But if you don't commit, someone else might break you."

Aurora glared at him, her pulse quickening. "You're awfully confident."

"Because I know what I'm doing," Talon replied, his smirk infuriatingly charming.

Aurora shoved against his chest, managing to push him back a step. "Maybe I do too."

"Prove it," Talon challenged, his eyes glinting with amusement.

Aurora lunged, catching him off guard and locking his arm behind his back. For a moment, she thought she'd won—until Talon spun out of her grip, pinning her against the wall with maddening ease.

"You were saying?" he asked, his voice low and rough.

Aurora's breath hitched, her full chest rising with each breath as she glared up at him. "You're impossible."

"And you're stubborn," Talon countered, his smirk softening into something warmer. "It's why we work."

Aurora couldn't help the laugh that escaped her, the tension between them easing as she shook her head. "You're ridiculous."

"Maybe," Talon said, stepping back. "But you're getting better."

Aurora smiled, the praise warming her more than she wanted to admit. "Thanks."

"Don't mention it," Talon said, his gaze lingering on her for a moment before turning away. "Same time tomorrow?"

"Wouldn't miss it," Aurora said, her voice light.

That night, as they sat by the fire, Aurora couldn't help but feel a sense of peace she hadn't known in years. The connection she and Talon were building was fragile, but it was real. And for the first time, she allowed herself to believe that maybe—just maybe—they had a chance at something more.

Across the room, Talon caught her gaze, his expression softer than she'd ever seen it. "You're staring again," he said, his voice teasing.

Aurora shrugged, a playful smile tugging at her lips. "Maybe I like what I see."

Talon chuckled, shaking his head. "You're going to be the death of me."

"Worth it," Aurora said, her tone light but her words heavy with meaning.

Talon's smile faded, replaced by something deeper. "You're worth a lot more than you know."

Aurora's chest tightened at the quiet sincerity in his voice, and she realized, at that moment, that she felt the same.

Chapter 13

The first thing Aurora noticed was the cold. The alley felt impossibly dark, the air thick with the stench of damp garbage and metallic blood. Her shoulder throbbed where one of the attackers had struck her with a blunt object, and her legs trembled as she tried to steady herself against the wall.

Her mind raced as she replayed the ambush. She had been following a lead, her guard up but not enough, when two men had jumped her. They were after information, their questions rapid and cruel, their threats laced with malice. She'd fought back, landing a few solid hits, but they'd overwhelmed her.

A low growl broke through her haze. Aurora looked up to see Havoc standing at the mouth of the alley, his hackles raised, and his teeth bared. Relief flooded her chest, though it did little to quell the adrenaline coursing through her veins.

Then she heard him.

Talon's voice was low and guttural, filled with a cold fury that sent a shiver down her spine. "You've got about five seconds to explain why you're still breathing."

Aurora turned her head just in time to see him emerge from the shadows, his broad frame moving like a predator stalking its prey. He didn't look at her—his focus was entirely on the two men who now cowered before him.

One of the attackers scrambled backward, his hands raised in a feeble attempt to placate Talon. "We didn't mean anything by it—"

"Shut up," Talon growled, his voice sharp enough to cut through steel. He grabbed the man by the collar, hauling him to his feet with terrifying ease. "Who sent you?"

The man stammered, his eyes darting to his accomplice, who was already trying to make a run for it. Havoc intercepted, leaping forward with a vicious snarl and pinning the man to the ground. The alley echoed with the sound of his cries.

"Talon," Aurora croaked, her voice strained. "I'm fine."

He froze for a fraction of a second, his head snapping toward her. His eyes, dark and blazing with fury, softened just slightly when they met hers. "You're hurt," he said, his tone a mix of anger and concern.

"It's not bad," Aurora insisted, though the way her hand clutched her side told a different story.

Talon turned back to the man in his grip, his lips curling into a snarl. "You think you can touch her and walk away?" His voice was venomous, the words low and deliberate. "You don't get to lay a finger on her."

The man whimpered, his protests devolving into incoherent pleas. Talon didn't release him, his grip tightening. "Start talking. Now."

"W-We were just following orders!" the man sputtered. "We didn't know she was with you!"

Talon's jaw clenched, his teeth grinding audibly. "Who sent you?" he demanded again, his voice rising.

"The name's Silas!" the man cried. "We were just supposed to scare her!"

Talon's eyes narrowed, his voice a dangerous whisper. "You've done a lot more than that."

Once the attackers were incapacitated—one unconscious, the other too terrified to move—Talon finally turned his attention back to Aurora. He strode toward her, his expression still dark but his movements gentler as he crouched in front of her.

"Aurora," he said softly, his hand brushing her arm. "Let me see."

Aurora winced as she shifted, the adrenaline wearing off enough for the pain to take center stage. "It's nothing serious," she muttered.

Talon's brow furrowed, his gaze flicking to the small gash on her temple and the way she held her side. "You're bleeding," he said, his voice tight.

"It's not the first time," Aurora quipped, though her attempt at humor fell flat under the weight of his intense gaze.

"Stop," Talon said, his voice calm but firm. "Let me take care of you."

Aurora sighed, leaning back against the wall as Talon inspected her injuries. His touch was surprisingly gentle, his fingers brushing against her skin with a tenderness that belied the fury he'd just unleashed on her attackers.

"You shouldn't have been out here alone," he said quietly, his tone laced with frustration.

"I can handle myself," Aurora replied, though her voice lacked conviction.

"You shouldn't have to," Talon countered, his gaze locking onto hers. "Not when you're with me."

The words sent a shiver down Aurora's spine, her breath catching in her throat. She stared at him, her heart pounding as the weight of his protectiveness settled over her. "Talon—"

"No," he interrupted, his voice low and firm. "No one touches you but me. Do you understand?"

Aurora's chest tightened, her pulse quickening at the raw intensity in his voice. She nodded, unable to find her words.

Talon exhaled, his hand resting on her shoulder as he looked her over one more time. "Let's get you out of here."

Back at the cabin, the atmosphere was heavy with unspoken emotions. Talon guided Aurora to the couch, his hand lingering on her arm as she sat down. Havoc lay at her feet, his watchful eyes a comforting presence.

Talon moved with precision, gathering medical supplies from the small cabinet near the kitchen. When he returned, he knelt in front of her, his movements deliberate, and began cleaning the cut on her temple.

Aurora winced, hissing softly as the antiseptic stung. "You're enjoying this, aren't you?" she muttered.

Talon's lips twitched into a faint smirk. "Not as much as you think."

Aurora chuckled, though the sound was weak. "Could've fooled me."

"Stay still," Talon said, his voice soft but commanding. "This won't take long."

Aurora complied, her gaze fixed on him as he worked. She couldn't help but notice the way his jaw tightened, the furrow in his brow as if tending to her injuries was a personal affront. "You're blaming yourself," she said quietly.

"I should've been there," Talon replied, not looking up.

"You can't protect me from everything," Aurora said gently. "And I wouldn't want you to." Aurora placed a gentle hand on Talon's arm, and he froze underneath her touch.

Talon finally met her gaze, his eyes filled with a vulnerability that caught her off guard. "But I'll try," he said simply.

Aurora's chest ached at the sincerity in his voice. She reached out, her fingers brushing against his cheek. "I know."

"Aurora, you don't understand." Talon averted his gaze, and Aurora watched as the familiar storm returned to him. "My life was chaos, then in the middle of it came you. And for the first time in a long time, you silenced the noise. Aurora, being at your side is like breathing to me now. How can you expect me to stop?" Talon shut his eyes as if thinking about his next words carefully. "Please don't ask me to stop."

For a moment, the world seemed to stop. The fire crackled softly in the background, and the tension between them shifted into something warmer, deeper. Talon's hand covered hers, his grip firm yet gentle.

"You're stronger than you think," Talon said, his voice barely above a whisper. "But that doesn't mean I'll stop fighting for you."

Aurora's breath caught, her heart pounding in her chest. "And I'll fight for you," she said, her voice trembling with emotion.

Talon leaned closer, his forehead resting against hers. "You're mine, Aurora," he murmured, his voice raw. "No one touches you. No one hurts you. Not while I'm here."

Aurora closed her eyes, her body leaning into his. "I'm not going anywhere," she whispered.

The rest of the night passed in a haze of quiet intimacy. Talon stayed close, his presence a steady reassurance as Aurora rested on the couch. His protectiveness, once overwhelming, now felt like a shield she hadn't known she needed.

As dawn broke, Aurora stirred, finding Talon still seated beside her, his head resting against the back of the couch. Havoc lay at his feet, his tail wagging softly as Aurora shifted.

"You didn't sleep," she said, her voice hoarse.

Talon opened his eyes, his lips curling into a faint smile. "Didn't need to."

Aurora rolled her eyes, though her heart swelled at the sight of him. "You're impossible."

"And you're stubborn," Talon replied, his voice teasing. "But we make it work."

Aurora laughed softly, her hand brushing against his. "Yeah, we do."

As the sunlight filled the cabin, it felt like a new beginning—one forged in trust, vulnerability, and a connection neither of them could deny.

The first rays of dawn filtered through the cabin's windows, casting a soft light over Aurora's still form. Talon sat in the chair beside the couch, his elbows resting on his knees and his hands clasped tightly. His gaze never left her, as though by sheer will, he could ensure her safety.

Havoc stirred at his feet, letting out a soft huff as he looked up at his master. Talon glanced down, scratching behind the dog's ears absently. "I know," he murmured. "She's tougher than she looks. But still…"

The weight of the previous night clung to him like a second skin. He replayed the ambush over and over, every detail seared into his mind—the fear in Aurora's eyes, the blood staining her temple, the way her breath hitched as she'd tried to downplay the severity of her injuries. And the men—Silas's lackeys—thinking they could touch her, harm her, and walk away unscathed.

Talon's fists clenched at the memory. They hadn't walked away.

Aurora stirred, her face scrunching slightly as she woke. Talon straightened immediately, his body on high alert despite the exhaustion tugging at his limbs. "Morning," he said softly, his voice a low rumble.

Aurora blinked up at him, her eyes hazy with sleep. "You're still here?" she asked, her voice hoarse.

"Where else would I be?" Talon replied, a faint smirk tugging at his lips. "You think I'd leave you after last night?"

Aurora pushed herself up, wincing as her muscles protested. "You didn't need to stay up all night watching me."

"Didn't I?" Talon asked, his tone pointed. "After what happened, you think I'd take any chances?"

Aurora sighed, her gaze softening. "I'm fine, Talon. Really."

"You keep saying that," Talon said, his voice sharp with frustration. "But you don't get to decide how I feel about this."

Aurora raised an eyebrow. "And how do you feel?"

"Like I failed," Talon admitted, his jaw tightening. "I should've been there."

Aurora leaned forward, her hand brushing against his knee. "You didn't fail me," she said firmly. "You showed up when it mattered. That's what counts."

Talon's gaze softened, his hand covering hers. "I'll make sure it doesn't happen again."

Aurora smiled faintly, though her chest ached at the vulnerability in his voice. "You can't control everything, Talon. And you can't protect me from the world."

Talon leaned closer, his voice dropping to a near whisper. "Maybe not. But I'll die trying."

The intensity of his words left Aurora breathless, her heart pounding as she stared at him. There was no denying the raw, unfiltered emotion in his gaze, the depth of his protectiveness wrapping around her like a shield.

"Talon," she began, her voice trembling, "I don't want you to carry that kind of weight. Not for me."

"Too late," Talon said simply, his lips twitching into a faint smirk. "You don't get to decide how I feel, either."

Aurora laughed softly, her laughter easing the tension between them, "Fair enough."

The moment lingered, their eyes locked as an unspoken connection passed between them. Talon's hand lingered on hers, his touch warm and grounding. Aurora felt the urge to lean closer, to close the gap between them and lose herself in the quiet intensity of his presence.

But the memory of the ambush lingered, a cold reminder of the danger that loomed over them. "What happens now?" Aurora asked, breaking the silence.

Talon's expression hardened, his gaze shifting to the fire. "We make them pay."

Aurora's stomach tightened at the steel in his voice. "You're talking about Silas."

"Who else?" Talon replied, his tone sharp. "He's behind this. He sent them after you."

Aurora nodded slowly, her mind racing. "And what's the plan?"

Talon leaned back, his arms crossing over his chest. "We take the fight to him. No more waiting, no more running. We end this."

Aurora's chest ached at the determination in his voice, but she couldn't shake the unease that settled over her. "It's not just about us, Talon. If we go after him, we're putting a target on ourselves."

"There's already a target on us," Talon said darkly. "The difference is, now we aim back."

Later that afternoon, as the storm clouds cleared and sunlight bathed the cabin, Talon insisted on continuing their training. Aurora protested at first, her body still sore, but she knew better than to argue for long.

"You need to be ready," Talon said as they stood outside in the clearing. "No excuses."

"I thought I did okay last night," Aurora said, smirking as she adjusted her stance.

"Okay, doesn't cut it," Talon replied, stepping closer. "You hesitate. You second-guess yourself. That'll get you killed."

Aurora rolled her eyes. "You really know how to inspire confidence, you know that?"

Talon smirked, his hands on his hips. "I'm not here to make you feel good. I'm here to make sure you survive."

Aurora's heart skipped a beat at the conviction in his voice. "Fine," she said, raising her fists. "Show me."

Talon moved in quickly, his hands darting out to grab her wrists and twist her arms behind her back. Aurora gasped, struggling against his hold, but he was unyielding. "You're still holding back," he said, his voice low and rough.

"I'm not," Aurora shot back, twisting her body to break free. She managed to slip out of his grip, spinning around to face him. "See?"

Talon's smirk widened, his eyes gleaming with approval. "Better. But not good enough."

Before she could respond, he lunged, his hands gripping her waist and spinning her around until her back hit the tree behind her. Aurora's breath caught, her heart hammering as he pressed closer, his hands braced on either side of her head.

"You have to commit," Talon murmured, his voice a dark whisper. "No hesitation. No second-guessing."

Aurora's chest heaved, her gaze locked on his. "I'm trying."

"Not hard enough," Talon said, his lips twitching into a faint smirk. "But we'll get there."

The tension between them was electric, their proximity sending a rush of heat through Aurora's body. She swallowed hard, her voice shaky as she said, "You're enjoying this."

"Maybe," Talon admitted, his smirk softening. "But only because I know you can handle it."

Aurora glared up at him, though her lips twitched into a smile. "You're insufferable."

"And you're stubborn," Talon countered, his voice teasing. "It's why we work."

Aurora laughed, the sound breaking the tension. "You keep saying that."

"Because it's true," Talon said, stepping back and releasing her. "Now, let's try again."

As the sun dipped below the horizon, casting the clearing in shades of gold and amber, Aurora found herself standing beside Talon, both of them breathing heavily from the day's training. Havoc lay nearby, his tail wagging lazily as he watched them.

"You're getting better," Talon said, his voice softer now. "Not there yet, but better."

"High praise," Aurora teased, brushing a strand of hair from her face.

Talon chuckled, shaking his head. "Don't let it go to your head."

Aurora smiled, her chest warming at the rare lightness in his tone. "Thanks, Talon. For everything."

Talon glanced at her, his expression softening. "Always." Aurora lay still, the warmth of Talon's body barely a breath away. His steady breathing should have reassured her. It didn't.

Because he wasn't asleep.

She could feel it—the tension in his frame, the way his fingers flexed and stilled, flexed and stilled. The way his mind was miles away, retreating.

By morning, he'd be gone again. Not physically, but in every way that mattered.

She just had to decide if she was willing to chase him.

Chapter 14

The night was unnervingly quiet. The forest surrounding the cabin seemed to hold its breath, as if it knew danger was just beyond the trees. Talon paced near the window, his sharp gaze scanning the darkness for any signs of movement. Havoc lay nearby, and his ears perked, attuned to every sound.

Aurora sat on the couch, her arms wrapped around her knees. She was exhausted from the day's events, her body sore and her mind racing. They'd barely escaped an ambush, and though they'd managed to fight their way out, the close call left her shaken.

"You should get some rest," Talon said, his voice low but commanding. He didn't turn from the window, his focus still on the shadows outside.

Aurora let out a soft laugh, though there was little humor in it. "Like I'd be able to sleep after that."

Talon finally turned, his piercing gaze landing on her. "You need to. You won't be any good to me if you're running on fumes."

Aurora raised an eyebrow, her lips curving into a faint smirk. "You really know how to comfort a girl, don't you?"

Talon's lips twitched into a brief smile before his expression hardened again. "You're safe here. For now."

"For now," Aurora echoed, her voice soft. She stood, crossing the room to stand beside him. "You don't have to carry all of this alone, you know."

Talon glanced at her, his jaw tightening. "I know."

"Do you?" Aurora pressed, her hand brushing against his arm. "Because it feels like you're always trying to keep me at arm's length."

Talon's breath hitched, his gaze softening just slightly. "I'm trying to protect you."

Aurora tilted her head, a faint smile playing on her lips. "Maybe I don't need protecting. Maybe I just need you."

Talon's chest rose and fell with a deep breath, his eyes locked on hers. The tension between them crackled like electricity, the air growing heavier with unspoken words. "Aurora..."

"You don't have to say anything," she whispered, stepping closer. "Just... let me in."

Talon reached an unsteady hand up and gripped Aurora's cheek. His fingers grazed over her skin with a yearning he had never felt before — one he had never allowed himself to feel before.

"Talon," Aurora couldn't bring her gaze away from his lips.

"Don't talk," Talon's voice was commanding as his hand slipped to the back of her neck, where he pulled her body flush with his own. Aurora gasped at the sudden proximity.

Talon's lips crashed into Aurora's and she couldn't bring herself to fight back with her usual attitude. Talon guided her to the chair and pulled Aurora onto his lap, straddling her on his hips.

Aurora felt her heart hammering against the cage inside her. She wanted him, all of him. Aurora traced Talon's body, memorizing each and every inch of him.

"Aurora, I don't know if I can hold back anymore," Talon's teeth grazed over the soft skin of her neck like a whisper before Talon bit down, claiming her. The nearby candles flickered with anticipation, silent witnesses to the shattered restraints that once bound Talon's wrists like cuffs.

"I don't want you to hold back," Aurora pushed her hips further into Talons, molding her body against his like warm, golden clay and honey. Talon's arm wrapped around her waist, trapping her. "I need you not to hold back. I want you. All of you." Aurora whispered the words like a silent plea. She needed to know him. She wanted to know his flaws, his fears, and what he loved. If he was nervous around bugs- something simple. Something human.

Talon claimed her mouth once more, spearing his tongue and immediately winning the battle. He ravaged her, taking careful time to savor each and every moan that escaped her lips. He needed her. Talon slipped a hand between them, earning a groan in protest from Aurora.

"Patience," Talon popped the button off her pants and slipped in a finger, pushing in soft circles against Aurora's core.

"Talon," Aurora's voice snaked through the air, pleasure heavy on her tongue. Talon took the opportunity to slip his tongue inside once more. He savored the moment as their breath became an intricate tango of heat and passion that both of them had tried so hard to push down.

Aurora's back arched as Talon dipped a gentle finger inside of her.

"Just from touch alone, I can tell your pussy is pretty," Talon nipped Aurora's ear, and another moan escaped her. Her eyes were shut in pleasure, and Talon could feel his finger slipping further inside from just the mess alone that now soaked her pants. Without hesitation, he slipped another finger inside and curled them. Talon couldn't take his eyes off of the goddess above him as her eyebrows gathered in pleasure.

Aurora began to grind on Talon's fingers, earning a smile from the man beneath her. She felt her core begin to grow tight as Talon curled and pumped his fingers in a rhythmic pattern that dripped with sin.

"You want me, huh?" Talon kissed down Aurora's neck, landing gentle bites along her now bruised skin.

"Yes," Aurora's voice was barely above a whisper as she pushed her core further against Talon. She opened her eyes for a moment — she needed to see him. His eyes were dark with lust, with desire. And all at once, she felt herself lose control and as her body rippled with pleasure. Talon held her tightly, pumping his fingers gently to help her ride out her climax.

Talon didn't allow her to finish her orgasm before his hand shot up and around the front of Aurora's throat. His fingers wrapped so tightly he was sure it would bruise. But he didn't care- he wanted the world to see where her loyalties were. Where her heart came home to each and every second.

Aurora's body flowed like warm silk above him, sending Talon's nerves over the edge. He pulled the siren close, planting soft kisses along her exposed skin and savoring the bruise he knew he was leaving.

Would she try and hide them?

Talon grinned and left a bite right underneath her jaw, earning him a moan from Aurora. His name slipped from her tongue. Talon stole her lips in a kiss to taste the pleasure he was sure his name tasted like.

"Talon, please, I-"

"Please, what, my dear?" Talon tightened his fingers only a fraction more around her pretty throat, cutting her air, and his hand slipped out from between her thighs. "Open those pretty lips for me, dear."

Aurora did as she was told, all spark and attitude now a servant to the man beneath her. Talon's fingers slipped past her lips, and they danced over her tongue, coating her own passion over her taste buds. She tasted sweet, like a pomegranate. Talon grabbed her tongue and pulled it out of her mouth before sliding his own over it. Talon slipped his hand from her throat and to her breast, where he rolled the soft mound in his hand.

"You taste heavenly," Talon whispered to her. His eyes were heavy with lust and need, and Aurora feared she could no longer fully hide her own. He slipped his fingers in his mouth and shut his eyes with a moan. "Absolutely heavenly."

Aurora couldn't answer. She didn't know what to say. She wanted to give everything to this man. She needed to give him all of her. And as he rolled and plucked her rosy nipple, she feared she would never be able to deny him.

Talon slipped his fingers back between her thighs and, this time, added a third. Aurora arched her back at the pleasure that racked her body, and Talon took the opportunity to take her perked nipple into his mouth. He rolled the bud with his tongue, and as his fingers curled inside of her, his teeth clamped down gently, claiming her.

Aurora felt another wave beginning to build beneath the surface. She molded her body against Talon's chest, gripping the back of his shirt and grinding her hips against his hungry fingers.

Talon ripped his shirt off completely, buttons flying everywhere. He tossed the shirt onto the floor, not caring where it landed. He stood there, bare-chested, his chiseled abs and broad shoulders on display, but his expression was thunderous.

In a sudden burst of dominance, Talon spun Aurora onto her hands and knees. His breath was ragged as he pressed himself against her back, one hand firmly gripping her waist to keep her steady. The other hand dove between her legs, two fingers pushing deep inside her pussy. "Shit…"

Aurora's eyes rolled back in ecstasy as Talon's fingers plunged into her, still wet from her previous orgasm. She cried out, tears of pure pleasure streaming down her face as she pressed back against him, desperate for more. "Ahhhhhh! Talon! Fuck! Fuck me!"

Talon's mind screamed at him to stop, to pull away before it was too late. But his body refused to listen, his mouth still pressed against Aurora's ass, his fingers still buried in her pussy. He gripped her hair tighter, his breath hot against her skin as he fought against his own will.

With a growl, Talon buried his face between Aurora's ass cheeks, his tongue immediately finding her pussy. He ate her out fiercely, his tongue lapping at her folds, pushing inside her. His fingers continued to pump in and out of her, matching the rhythm of his tongue.

Aurora's back arched, pushing her round breasts up and out as she wiggled her hips back against Talon's face. He could feel her shaking, her entire body trembling as he held her waist down, not letting her collapse under the intense pleasure. "Oh god! Oh god!"

Talon's hesitation returned, his mind screaming at him to stop, to get control back. But Aurora wasn't having it. She reached back and grabbed a handful of his hair, forcing his face harder against her pussy. "Eat it! Eat my fucking pussy!" she demanded.

Talon gave up control completely. He spread Aurora's cheeks wider and buried his face again, his tongue going wild. He added another finger inside her pussy, pumping them hard and fast. Her breasts bounced uncontrollably with each thrust. He growled against her pussy, making her scream.

The room filled with the obscene wet sounds of Talon's face buried between Aurora's thighs. His fingers squelched inside her, his tongue lapping loudly against her swollen folds. Her juices dripped down his chin and onto the bed beneath her.

As Aurora's knees nearly gave out, Talon reluctantly released her hip, fighting against every instinct screaming at him to hold her, protect her. He straightened up, wiping his mouth with the back of his hand. He stood up, his hand still dripping with Aurora's juices, and walked to the bathroom to clean it off. He stared at himself in the mirror, his reflection showing a man struggling with his own demons. He returned to the room, his expression hard once more.

The room was deafeningly quiet after their intense encounter. Aurora sat on the bed, waiting for Talon to say something, anything. But he stood by the window, his back turned to her, his face unreadable. Minutes ticked by, and still, no words were spoken.

Finally, Aurora broke the silence. "Talon..." She trailed off, not sure what to say. She wanted to ask him if he was okay, if she was okay, if they were okay. But before she could, he spoke, his voice cold and distant. "I'm leaving."

Talon stepped out of the room, closing the door softly behind him. He leaned against the wall, breathing heavily. His heart hammered in his chest - not from exertion, but from something else entirely. Something far more dangerous. "Fuck," he whispered to himself, running a hand through his hair.

Aurora sat on the rumpled bed, her body still humming from their intense sex. She brought her knees up to her chest, wrapping her arms around them. Her eyes scanned the room - the messed-up sheets, the discarded condom wrapper, Talon's shirt thrown on the floor.

Later, the cabin was bathed in the soft glow of firelight, the tension between them simmering just beneath the surface. Talon sat in his usual chair, his elbows resting on his knees as he stared into the flames. Aurora sat across from him, her hands fidgeting in her lap.

The silence was thick, charged with the weight of everything unsaid. Aurora finally broke it, her voice quiet but steady. "What if we stopped running? Just for one night?"

Talon looked up, his brow furrowing. "What do you mean?"

"I mean... what if we let ourselves feel something other than fear?" Aurora said, her gaze steady. "What if we just... existed, without the weight of everything hanging over us?"

Talon leaned back, his eyes narrowing as he studied her. "And how do you propose we do that?"

Aurora smiled faintly, standing and crossing the room to him. "Trust me."

Talon's idea of letting go wasn't what Aurora had expected. He led her to the small bedroom tucked away in the back of the cabin, the space sparse but comfortable. The bed was neatly made, the only decoration a small, framed photograph on the nightstand.

"Are you sure about this?" Talon asked, his voice low as he turned to face her.

Aurora nodded, her heart pounding. "Yes."

Talon's gaze softened, and he reached out, his fingers brushing against her cheek. "This is about trust," he said, his tone firm but gentle. "If you're not comfortable, we stop. No questions asked."

Aurora swallowed hard, her chest tightening at the sincerity in his voice. "I trust you."

Talon nodded, his hand sliding down to take hers. "Good."

The air between them grew heavy with anticipation as Talon reached into the nightstand, pulling out a length of soft rope. Aurora's breath caught, her pulse quickening as she watched him test the strength of the knots.

"Give me your hands," he said, his voice a low command.

Aurora hesitated for only a moment before holding out her wrists. Talon's fingers brushed against her skin as he looped the rope around her wrists, his movements slow and deliberate. The sensation sent a shiver down her spine, the vulnerability both thrilling and terrifying.

"Too tight?" Talon asked, his eyes locking onto hers.

"No," Aurora whispered, her voice trembling. "It's perfect."

Talon's lips curved into a faint smirk. "Good."

He stepped back, his gaze raking over her as if committing every detail to memory. "You look beautiful like this," he said, his voice rough. "So trusting. So ready."

Aurora's cheeks flushed, her body responding to the heat in his words. "Talon…"

"Not yet," he interrupted, holding up a finger. "We're doing this my way."

Talon reached for a black bandana, folding it neatly before stepping behind her. "Close your eyes," he murmured.

Aurora obeyed, her breath hitching as the soft fabric slid over her eyes. The world went dark, and her other senses heightened as she felt the warmth of Talon's body close to hers.

"Do you know what I love about this?" Talon whispered, his breath brushing against her ear. "You have to trust me completely. Every touch, every sound... it's all up to me."

Aurora's pulse raced, her lips parting as she tried to form a response. "I do trust you."

"Good girl," Talon murmured, his voice dripping with approval.

The next moments blurred together in a haze of sensation. Talon's hands were everywhere—light, teasing touches that sent shivers down her spine, firm, commanding grips that left her breathless. His words, low and rough, guided her through every moment, building anticipation until she thought she might come undone.

"You're so responsive," he murmured, his lips brushing against her neck. "Every sound you make drives me insane."

"Talon," Aurora gasped, her body arching toward him. "Please..."

"Patience," Talon said, his voice teasing. "You'll get what you need. But only when I decide."

Aurora whimpered, the sound earning a low growl of approval from him. "That's it," he said, his hand sliding down her arm. "Let me take care of you."

The night stretched on, their connection deepening with every moment. Talon's dominance was unyielding but never harsh, his every action laced with care and attention. Aurora gave herself over completely, her trust in him unwavering.

When he finally removed the blindfold and untied her wrists, Aurora blinked up at him, her eyes shimmering with emotion. "Talon... thank you."

He cupped her face, his thumb brushing against her cheek. "You don't have to thank me," he said softly. "You're mine, Aurora. Always."

Aurora's heart swelled at the raw sincerity in his voice. "And you're mine," she whispered.

Talon's lips curved into a rare, genuine smile. "Damn right, I am."

As they lay together, tangled in the sheets, Aurora rested her head on Talon's chest, listening to the steady rhythm of his heartbeat. The weight of the world still loomed over them, but for the first time, it felt manageable—because they had each other.

"You're incredible," Talon murmured, his fingers tracing patterns on her back. "Do you know that?"

Aurora smiled, her eyes drifting closed. "Only because I have you."

Talon pressed a kiss to her forehead, his hold on her tightening. "And you always will."

As sleep claimed them, the shadows outside seemed to retreat, giving way to the warmth and light they'd found in each other. But deep down, they both knew this moment of peace wouldn't last forever.

The warmth of the fire and the safety of Talon's arms lingered long after Aurora drifted into sleep. She had never felt so vulnerable yet so secure, and as her breathing evened out, Talon remained awake, his hand idly brushing through her hair. His mind raced, not with fear but with a sense of clarity he hadn't felt in years.

He looked down at her, her features soft and peaceful in the dim light. The tension she carried throughout the day was gone, replaced by a trust that both humbled and terrified him. He wasn't used to this—to being someone's anchor.

Havoc let out a soft huff from the corner of the room, drawing Talon's gaze. "She's something else, isn't she?" Talon muttered under his breath, his lips curving into a faint smile. Havoc wagged his tail once, agreeing.

The weight of their situation still pressed on him. Every decision felt like a delicate balance between keeping Aurora safe and not pushing her away. But tonight had been different. She'd handed him her trust so completely that it made him question every defense he'd built around himself.

Talon sighed softly, his fingers tracing the faint rope marks on her wrists. They weren't harsh—he'd been careful—but they were there, a reminder of how much she'd given him. "You don't even realize how much you've changed me," he murmured, his voice barely audible.

The next morning, Aurora stirred before the sun fully rose. She blinked awake to find Talon already up, standing by the window with his arms crossed. His silhouette was stark against the faint glow of dawn, his posture tense but steady.

"You're staring again," Aurora said, her voice still thick with sleep.

Talon glanced over his shoulder, a faint smirk tugging at his lips. "You're awake."

"You sound surprised," Aurora teased, sitting up and wrapping the blanket around her shoulders. "After last night, I thought you'd be the one needing rest."

Talon chuckled, shaking his head. "I don't rest, remember?"

Aurora rolled her eyes but couldn't help the smile that spread across her lips. "You should try it sometime. You might like it."

"Maybe," Talon said, turning back to the window. "But not today."

As the day began, the ease of the morning slowly gave way to the reality of their situation. The lingering warmth of their intimacy was overshadowed by the knowledge that Silas was still out there, and the ambush the previous day had proven just how close the threat was.

Aurora leaned against the kitchen counter, sipping her coffee, as Talon laid out a map on the table. His focus was razor-sharp, and his jaw was tight as he traced their potential routes and escape plans.

"This is where we ran into trouble yesterday," Talon said, tapping the map with his finger. "If Silas has people watching that area, he knows we're close."

Aurora frowned, setting her mug down. "Then why haven't they come for us yet?"

"Because he's waiting for us to slip up," Talon replied, his tone grim. "He wants us desperate, off-balance. That's when he'll strike."

Aurora crossed her arms, her gaze hardening. "Then let's not give him the satisfaction."

Talon looked up, his expression softening slightly. "You're tougher than you look, you know that?"

Aurora smirked. "You're just figuring that out now?"

Talon chuckled, shaking his head. "I've known for a while."

The day passed in a haze of preparation. Talon insisted on another round of self-defense training, though this time the atmosphere was lighter, the tension between them replaced with an easy camaraderie.

"You're getting better," Talon said as Aurora managed to break free from one of his holds.

"Better than you?" Aurora teased, stepping back and catching her breath.

Talon smirked, advancing on her with deliberate slowness. "Not even close."

Aurora laughed, raising her fists. "You're impossible."

"And you're stubborn," Talon countered, his voice teasing. "It's why we work."

Aurora lunged, her movements sharper and more confident than before. Talon caught her wrist, twisting it gently but firmly as he stepped behind her. His arm wrapped around her waist, pinning her against him. "Still predictable," he murmured, his breath warm against her ear.

Aurora's pulse quickened, her chest heaving as she twisted in his grip. "You're infuriating."

"And yet, here you are," Talon said, releasing her with a smirk.

Aurora glared at him, though her lips twitched into a smile. "Next time, I'm winning."

"I'll hold you to that," Talon said, his tone light.

As the sun dipped below the horizon, casting the forest in shades of gold and crimson, Aurora found herself sitting beside Talon on the porch. The air was cool, carrying the faint scent of pine and earth, and the silence between them was comfortable.

"You ever think about what comes next?" Aurora asked, breaking the quiet.

Talon glanced at her, his brow furrowing. "What do you mean?"

"I mean, after all of this," Aurora said, gesturing vaguely to the forest around them. "When Silas is gone. When the danger's over. What happens then?"

Talon leaned back, his gaze drifting to the treetops. "I've never thought that far ahead."

Aurora tilted her head, studying him. "Why not?"

"Because thinking ahead means hoping for something better," Talon said quietly. "And hope... hasn't always been kind to me."

Aurora's chest tightened at the vulnerability in his voice. She reached out, her hand brushing against his. "Maybe it's time you tried again."

Talon looked at her, his expression softening. "Maybe."

The evening was quiet, the kind that settled deep into the bones. Aurora leaned against the couch, her head resting on the armrest, as she watched the fire flicker and dance. Talon sat in the chair across from her, his legs stretched out and his hands resting on his thighs.

"You're staring again," Talon said, his voice teasing.

Aurora smiled faintly. "Maybe I like what I see."

Talon chuckled, shaking his head. "You're going to be the death of me."

"Worth it," Aurora said, her tone light but her words heavy with meaning.

Talon's expression softened, and he leaned forward, his elbows resting on his knees. "You know you don't have to do this, right?"

"Do what?" Aurora asked, tilting her head.

"Stay," Talon said quietly. "Be part of this fight. You could walk away."

Aurora sat up, her gaze steady. "I'm not walking away, Talon. Not from you."

Talon's breath hitched, his eyes locking onto hers. "You're too good for this."

"Maybe," Aurora said with a faint smile. "But you're worth it."

The night stretched on, the shadows deepening as the fire burned low. Talon and Aurora sat together, their hands brushing occasionally as the distance between them slowly disappeared. For the first time in a long while, the weight of the world felt just a little bit lighter.

And though the shadows outside still loomed, they didn't feel quite so overwhelming—not when they had each other.

Chapter 15

The room was dim, the only light coming from a flickering lantern on a table in the corner. The air was heavy, thick with unspoken emotions and the tension that had been building between them for weeks. Talon paced near the edge of the room, his movements restless, his jaw clenched. Aurora sat quietly on the edge of the bed, her eyes tracking his every move. She could feel the storm brewing within him, the way he was fighting himself, resisting the pull between them.

"Are you going to keep pacing, or are you going to talk to me?" Aurora finally asked, her voice calm but laced with challenge.

Talon stopped abruptly, his hand gripping the edge of the table. His back was to her, his broad shoulders rising and falling with each uneven breath. For a long moment, he didn't answer, and Aurora thought he might shut her out again. But then his voice cut through the silence, low and rough. "I can't keep pretending."

Aurora's heart skipped a beat. "Pretending what?" she pressed, though she already knew.

"That I don't need you," he said, turning to face her. His steel-gray eyes were darker than usual, shadowed by frustration and something deeper. "That I don't want you."

She stood slowly, her pulse quickening as she crossed the small space between them. "Then stop pretending."

Talon's hand clenched against the table as if he were holding himself back. "You don't understand," he said, his voice tight. "This isn't something I can do halfway. If I start... I won't be able to stop."

"Then don't stop," Aurora said simply, her gaze steady.

The space between them disappeared in an instant. Talon closed the distance with a single stride; his hands braced on either side of her head as he pressed her back against the wall. His face was close, his breath warm against her skin. "You have no idea what you're asking for," he murmured, his voice a dangerous mix of warning and want.

"Then show me," she replied, her voice unwavering.

His control snapped. Talon's lips crashed against hers in a bruising kiss, his hands gripping her hips as he pulled her closer. The kiss was raw, demanding, filled with all the tension and need they had both been holding back. Aurora responded eagerly, her fingers tangling in his hair as she surrendered to the intensity of the moment.

Talon growled low in his throat, breaking the kiss to trail his lips along her jawline and down her neck. His teeth grazed her skin, and she gasped as he bit down gently, leaving a mark. "Mine," he muttered against her skin, his voice rough with possession.

"Yes," Aurora whispered, her head tipping back to give him better access. "I'm yours."

Each bite, each scratch, was deliberate, a visible claim that left no room for doubt. Aurora's skin burned with each touch, but the fire was one she welcomed. She felt his need in every movement, his desperation to make her his in every way.

When her hands moved to explore his body, Talon's grip on her wrists stopped her. "Not there," he said, his voice steady but firm. His gaze softened for a moment, searching hers. "Not yet."

Aurora nodded, her respect for his boundaries only deepening her love for him. "Okay," she said softly. "Tell me what you need."

Talon's grip loosened, and he brought her hands back to his shoulders. "Just stay here," he said. "Let me take care of you."

He guided her to the bed, his movements deliberate as he laid her down. His hands skimmed over her body, every touch a mix of dominance and reverence. When his fingers brushed her neck, she stilled, her pulse racing beneath his touch.

"Trust me," he murmured, his fingers applying just enough pressure to make her aware of him. "Just feel this."

Aurora's breathing hitched, but she didn't pull away. "I trust you," she whispered, her voice trembling with anticipation.

Talon's fingers tightened slightly, his eyes never leaving hers. "Good," he said, his voice a low rumble. "Now breathe."

She obeyed, her breaths coming shallow and uneven as she surrendered completely to him. The sensation heightened everything—the weight of his hands, the heat of his body against hers, the raw intensity of his gaze.

"You're perfect," Talon muttered, his voice rough with emotion. "Do you know that?"

Aurora smiled faintly, her hands moving to cup his face. "I'm just me," she said. "And I'm yours."

Her words seemed to break something in him. Talon's usually guarded nature shattered as he let out a quiet groan, his head dropping to rest against her shoulder. "You're mine, Aurora," he said, his voice thick with feeling. "Every inch of you."

"Always," she whispered, wrapping her arms around him.

The vulnerability in his voice brought tears to her eyes, and she kissed him again, slow and tender. The rawness between them gave way to something softer, deeper, as they moved together in perfect harmony. Every touch, every breath, was a promise—a vow that neither of them spoke aloud, but both understood.

When the passion finally subsided, Talon collapsed beside her, his chest rising and falling with each heavy breath. Aurora turned to face him, her fingers brushing over the marks he had left on her skin.

"Does it hurt?" he asked, his voice quieter now.

"Not enough to regret it," she replied, her smile teasing.

Talon chuckled softly, his hand moving to trace the same marks. "I wasn't too rough?"

"You were exactly what I needed," Aurora said, her voice sincere.

For the first time, Talon looked at her without hesitation, his expression open and unguarded. "You're the only one who's ever made me feel like this," he admitted. "Like I'm not broken."

Aurora cupped his face, her thumb brushing against his cheek. "You're not broken, Talon. You're just human."

He closed his eyes, leaning into her touch. "No one's ever looked at me like you do."

"Then maybe you've been looking in the wrong places," she said, her lips curving into a soft smile.

Talon pulled her closer, his forehead resting against hers. "I don't deserve you," he murmured.

"You don't have to," Aurora said. "You just have to let me love you."

Talon's eyes glinted with a wild, unrecognizable light as he picked Aurora up from the bed and slammed her against the wall, his large hands pinning her wrists above her head. He growled, the sound rumbling through his chest like an animal about to snap its jaws shut. "Look at me."

"Look. At. Me." Talon snarled, his grip on her wrists tightening. He was losing control, the beast inside him clawing at the surface. Love? Her loving him? That simple word triggered the sleeping beast and brought him forward. His breathing came in ragged pants, chest heaving, as he tried and failed to rein himself in.

Aurora's breath caught in her throat, her eyes going wide at the dangerous tone. Instead of fear, something primal ignited within her - desire mixed with a healthy dose of excitement. Even though they had finished not long ago she wanted, no needed, him again. She challenged him with a whisper, "And what if I don't?" Her hips pressed slightly against his, testing his control.

Talon's breathing hitched again, deeper this time. Their lips were inches apart, breaths mingling. He could taste her breath - sweet like honey and dangerous like whiskey. He growled softly; his body tensed as he felt her hips move against him again. His hands tightened around her wrists possessively.

Aurora leaned in, her lips pressing against Talon's in an aggressive kiss. She bit his bottom lip, tugging on it gently before sinking her teeth into his full lip. Talon groaned, his hands finally releasing her wrists to wrap around her head and pull her deeper into the kiss.

With his hands now free, Talon took full advantage. He pressed her against the wall, his touch heavy and hungry. He gripped her hips possessively, pulling her against his growing arousal. His other hand cupped her full bust hungrily through the fabric of her dress, squeezing it roughly.

Talon tried desperately to regain control, but Aurora's bold move shattered any semblance of restraint. She jumped onto his lap, wrapping her long legs tightly around his waist. The new position pinned him harder against the wall, his arousal pressing insistently against her core. He groaned, hands gripping her thighs.

Talon, try to regain control - there. Talon's heavy breathing, Aurora's aggressive touches as she grinds, forcing herself to press closer against him, grinding despite his protests, her lips near his ear whispering teasingly, "Come on, Talon, I can feel how much you want this..."

His control finally snapped, and Talon's hands moved from her thighs to her waist, gripping harshly - almost bruising. With one hand, he held her firmly in place while the other moved to her neck, tilting her head back with more force than usual, exposing her neck completely.

Talon's body betrayed him. His muscles tightened as if ready for a fight, his breath coming out raggedly like he'd been running. He was hard-pressed not to yank those sexy curves closer. His body reacted to her aggression - his blood ran hotter, his touch rougher.

As Talon's body continued to react uncontrollably, a loud gunshot echoed in the distance. It was like a cold bucket of water being poured over him, instantly snapping him back to reality. He released Aurora abruptly, pushing her away from him. They separated, both standing heavily and breathing.

Their eyes locked again, his gaze lingering on her heaving chest before sighing heavily, "I'll go check it out." With one last intense look, he turned and strode away, leaving Aurora breathless and flushed against the wall. As soon as he was out of sight, she slumped down, trembling slightly.

As the night stretched on, they stayed tangled together, their breaths mingling in the quiet of the room. Talon's walls had come down, and for the first time, he let himself believe in the possibility of a future with her.

When dawn broke, the light spilling into the room felt like a promise—a new beginning. Talon kissed Aurora's forehead, his voice steady as he said, "We'll figure this out. Together."

Aurora smiled, her fingers lacing with his. "Together," she echoed, her heart full.

And for the first time, Talon didn't feel afraid.

Chapter 16

THE WORLD SEEMED TO tilt as Aurora watched him, her breath caught somewhere between awe and fear. Talon stood in the dim light, his chest heaving, his fists clenched at his sides. The faint glow of the streetlamp outside sliced through the darkness, illuminating the blood splattered across his knuckles and the cold, detached fury etched into his face.

This wasn't the man who had guarded her with silent determination or made her laugh with a rare, fleeting smirk. This was something else entirely—a predator, coiled and ready to strike, even in the aftermath of his violence.

He hadn't seen her yet.

Aurora pressed herself against the wall, her heart hammering. Her mind raced, screaming for her to leave, to run, to do anything but stand there and watch. But her legs wouldn't move.

And then he looked up.

His eyes locked on hers, and the world seemed to stop.

For a moment, Talon didn't move. His expression didn't change, but she could see something flicker behind his gaze—recognition, then something darker. His shoulders sagged slightly, and the hand that had been clenched so tightly at his side relaxed, though his fingers still twitched; they didn't know how to let go of the violence.

"Aurora..." His voice was a hoarse whisper, raw and unsteady.

She didn't respond. Couldn't.

Talon took a step toward her, his movements slow and deliberate as though he were approaching a wounded animal. His gaze dropped to his hands, and for the first time, she saw it: the faint tremor and the way his jaw clenched as if he were trying to keep himself together.

"What did you see?" he asked, his voice quieter now, almost fragile.

"Enough," she said, her voice trembling.

Talon winced, his eyes narrowing slightly. He turned away, scrubbing a hand down his face as if trying to erase what had just happened.

Aurora's mind spun. The scene she'd just witnessed played on a loop, vivid and unforgiving. The way he'd moved—precise, calculated, almost inhuman in his efficiency. The way his opponent had crumpled, the life draining from his eyes as Talon's hands stayed steady, unforgiving.

And yet, there had been no hesitation. No second-guessing.

Her heart ached in a way that felt unbearable. This was the man she'd trusted with her life, the man she'd begun to see as something more. But now? Now, she wasn't sure she recognized him at all.

"Talon," she said, her voice cutting through the thick silence.

He froze but didn't turn around.

"What are you?" she asked, the words slipping out before she could stop them.

His shoulders tensed, and for a moment, she thought he wouldn't answer. When he finally spoke, his voice was low, almost resigned.

"Exactly what you saw," he said.

Aurora's chest tightened. "That's not an answer."

He turned to face her then, his expression hard, though his eyes betrayed something softer—something broken. "It's the only one I have."

The room felt too small, the air too thick. Aurora's gaze darted to the door, her body screaming at her to leave, to put as much distance between herself and this man as possible.

But she didn't move.

"Do you even regret it?" she asked, her voice shaking but insistent.

Talon flinched as if the question had struck him physically. He looked down at his hands again, his brows furrowing. "I don't know," he admitted. "I don't... know how to feel about it."

Aurora stepped closer, her fear warring with something deeper, something she couldn't name. "How can you say that? You—" She stopped herself, the words catching in her throat.

"I did what I had to," he said, cutting her off. His voice was firmer now, though his gaze remained fixed on the ground. "I always do what I have to."

The weight of his words hung between them, heavy and suffocating. Aurora felt a sharp pang of anger rise within her—anger at him, at herself, at this entire situation.

"Do you even care?" she demanded, her voice rising.

At that, Talon's head snapped up, his eyes blazing with something fierce and unrelenting. "Of course I care," he said, his voice rough and raw. "That's the problem. I care too damn much, and that's why I keep breaking everything I touch."

Aurora recoiled slightly at the force of his words, but she didn't back down. "Then why—"

"Because I don't know how to be anything else!" he shouted, his voice echoing off the walls.

The silence that followed was deafening. Talon's chest heaved, his fists clenching and unclenching at his sides. He looked like a man teetering on the edge of something he couldn't control, something that terrified him.

Aurora took a deep, shaky breath. She had to decide.

Her mind screamed at her to leave, to run, and never look back. But her heart... Her heart wouldn't let her.

Because beneath the predator, beneath the violence, she saw the man. The one who had protected her, fought for her, cared for her in ways no one else ever had.

"I'm still here," she said softly, breaking the silence.

Talon's head snapped up, his eyes wide with disbelief. "What?"

"I'm still here," she repeated, her voice steadier this time.

For the first time, Talon looked truly shaken. He stared at her as if he couldn't quite believe what he was hearing, as if he didn't deserve it.

"Why?" he asked, his voice barely above a whisper.

Aurora stepped closer, her gaze never leaving his. "Because I see you. All of you. And I'm not running."

Talon's breath hitched, and for a moment, she thought he might break entirely. Instead, he reached for her, his movements hesitant, almost afraid. When their fingers brushed, Aurora felt a jolt of something electric, something undeniable.

"You shouldn't," he said, his voice trembling. "You deserve better."

"Maybe," she said, a faint smile tugging at her lips. "But I want you."

They stood there for what felt like an eternity, the weight of their words sinking in. Talon's hand tightened around hers, and for the first time, she saw something close to hope flicker in his eyes.

"Don't let me break you," he whispered.

Aurora squeezed his hand, her gaze steady. "I'm stronger than you think."

Chapter 17

Aurora's breath came in slow, measured draws, but her heart raced beneath her calm exterior. The steel of Talon's knife hovered near her collarbone, cold against her skin. Her pulse pounded in her ears, not from fear but from something deeper—an awareness of the danger he embodied and the power she was giving him in this moment.

Talon's eyes held hers, intense and searching. His hand, steady and sure, betrayed none of the conflict she knew simmered beneath his surface. Yet she saw it—the way his jaw tightened, the way his fingers flexed against the hilt of the blade.

"Why aren't you afraid?" he asked, his voice low and rough.

Aurora swallowed hard but didn't break his gaze. "Because you won't hurt me."

The words hung between them, charged and fragile. Talon's expression didn't change, but something in his eyes softened and flickered with an emotion she couldn't name. He lowered the blade slowly, deliberately, and set it on the table between them.

"You shouldn't trust me like that," he said, his voice quieter now.

"But I do," Aurora replied. "Even after everything I've seen."

Talon ran a hand through his hair, his frustration evident. "You don't know what you're doing."

"Don't I?" she challenged.

He froze, his gaze snapping back to her. The room felt impossibly small, the weight of their shared silence pressing down on them.

The drive here had been suffocating. Talon hadn't said a word, his focus fixed on the road, his hands gripping the wheel with a force that turned his knuckles white. Aurora had wanted to speak, to break the silence, but the whirlwind of emotions inside her had made it impossible. She'd spent every moment replaying what she'd seen—the brutality, the precision, the part of him that scared her even as it drew her closer.

They'd arrived at the safe house just before dawn. The air had been crisp, the horizon painted in muted golds and grays. Talon had moved with practiced efficiency, securing the place before finally sitting across from her at the small table. And now here they were, the blade between them, the distance they kept from the truth closing inch by inch.

"You said I was your weakness," Aurora said, her voice breaking the tension.

Talon stiffened, his gaze narrowing. "I shouldn't have said that."

"But you meant it."

He didn't respond, his jaw tightening as he leaned back in his chair.

Aurora leaned forward, refusing to let him retreat. "You can't keep shutting me out, Talon. Not after what we've been through."

He laughed bitterly, shaking his head. "You think this is me shutting you out? You don't get it, Aurora. Letting you in—that's the problem."

"Why?"

"Because it makes me weak. It makes you a target. And I don't know how to protect you from me."

The confession hit her like a punch to the chest, but she didn't back down. "I don't need you to protect me from you," she said firmly. "I need you to trust me."

Talon's eyes blazed with anger, but beneath it was something else—desperation. "You don't understand what you're asking."

"Then explain it to me," Aurora countered. "Help me understand."

For a long moment, he didn't move, didn't speak. When he finally did, his voice was low, heavy with something she couldn't place.

"You saw what I did back there," he said. "You saw what I'm capable of. That wasn't an exception, Aurora. That's who I am. It's who I've always been."

Aurora's throat tightened, but she forced herself to stay calm. "That's not all you are," she said.

Talon's laugh was hollow. "You think you know me?"

"I think I see you," she said, her voice softer now.

His gaze snapped to hers, sharp and piercing. "Then you see a man who destroys everything he touches."

Aurora stood, closing the space between them. She reached out, her fingers brushing against his, and for a moment, he didn't pull away.

"You didn't destroy me," she said quietly.

Talon looked at her, his expression unreadable. "Not yet," he murmured.

The blade on the table gleamed faintly in the dim light. Aurora glanced at it, then back at him. "Pick it up."

Talon frowned. "What?"

"Pick it up," she repeated, her voice steady.

He hesitated, but her unwavering gaze pushed him to obey. He lifted the knife, his hand steady despite the uncertainty in his eyes.

Aurora stepped closer, her breath shallow but even. "I trust you," she said, her voice soft but firm.

Talon's grip tightened on the hilt, and for a moment, she thought he might refuse. But then he raised the blade, the edge glinting as it caught the light.

His hand trembled.

Aurora placed her fingers over his, steadying him. "You're not going to hurt me," she said.

He exhaled shakily, the tension in his body palpable. "You don't know that."

"Yes, I do."

The knife clattered to the table, the sound sharp and jarring in the quiet room. Talon turned away, his hands curling into fists at his sides. "Why are you doing this?"

Aurora moved closer, her voice gentle. "Because I see the man you're trying to hide. And I believe in him."

Talon's shoulders sagged, the weight of her words breaking something inside him. He turned to face her, his expression raw, his walls crumbling.

"I don't deserve this," he said, his voice trembling.

"Maybe not," Aurora said. "But I'm giving it to you anyway."

They stood there, the space between them charged with something unspoken. Talon reached for her, his touch hesitant, almost reverent. Aurora stepped into his arms, her head resting against his chest, and for the first time, she felt him relax.

In that moment, they weren't predator and prey, danger and trust. They were just two broken people, holding on to each other in the dark.

Chapter 18

THE CABIN HAD FELT like a safe haven at first. The quiet was almost surreal, a stark contrast to the chaos they'd left behind. Aurora sat on the edge of the couch, her knees drawn to her chest, and watched Talon as he moved methodically around the room. He checked the locks, his hand brushing his holstered weapon every so often, and Havoc followed him like a shadow.

But something shifted. The silence grew heavier, less like peace and more like the calm before a storm. Aurora's unease bubbled to the surface, and Talon's tension was palpable—though he'd never admit it outright.

"You're pacing," she said softly.

Talon stilled for a moment, his sharp gaze cutting toward her. "I'm keeping us alive."

Aurora hugged her knees tighter. "It felt safer a minute ago."

He didn't reply, but the ghost of an emotion flickered across his face—regret, maybe. He sank into the chair opposite her, running a hand through his hair. Havoc settled at his feet, ears perked.

"I'm not going to let anything happen to you," Talon said finally, his voice low but firm.

It was the first time he'd spoken so plainly about her safety, and it made her heart stumble. There was no bravado in his tone, just a promise that felt heavier than the air between them.

"Why do you care?" she asked, the words slipping out before she could stop them.

He leaned back in the chair, his expression guarded. "I don't know," he admitted. "Maybe because you're different."

Aurora frowned. "Different, how?"

"You just... are," he said, his words clipped, like he wasn't ready to dig deeper.

Aurora didn't push. She watched him instead, noticing how his hands curled into fists, the tension in his jaw. He wasn't just guarded—he was afraid. Not for himself, though. For her.

The knock came suddenly, shattering the fragile stillness. Talon's head snapped toward the door, and Havoc growled low in his throat. Aurora froze, her breath catching.

"Stay here," Talon ordered, his voice a harsh whisper.

Before she could argue, he was already moving, his gun drawn and his body poised like a coiled spring. Havoc followed, silent and alert.

Aurora's instincts screamed at her to do something—anything—but she stayed rooted to the couch, her heart hammering.

Talon eased the door open just enough to peer outside. The figure on the other side didn't get a chance to speak before Talon yanked them inside, shoving them against the wall with one hand while his gun pressed to their ribs.

"Talon, wait—" Aurora started, but he cut her off with a sharp glance.

"Talk," he demanded, his voice cold as steel.

The man stammered, his eyes wide. "I—I'm just the messenger. They sent me to deliver a warning."

Talon's expression didn't soften. "Who sent you?"

"Does it matter?" the man wheezed. "They're coming for her. They know she's here."

Aurora's stomach dropped. She shot to her feet, ignoring the sharp protest of her ribs. "Who's coming?"

The man's gaze darted to her, then back to Talon. "They didn't say. But they're serious. You've got maybe an hour before they show up."

Talon's jaw tightened, and he shoved the man toward the door. "Get out."

The man didn't need to be told twice. He stumbled outside, disappearing into the shadows.

Talon turned to Aurora, his expression unreadable. "We're leaving. Now."

The drive was tense and silent, the hum of the engine the only sound between them. Talon's grip on the steering wheel was tight, his knuckles white. Aurora wanted to say something—anything—but the weight of what had just happened pressed down on her chest.

"They're not going to stop," Talon said finally, his voice breaking the silence.

Aurora glanced at him. "What do you mean?"

"They know about you. About your family. They'll use whatever leverage they can find to get to you."

A cold knot of fear twisted in her stomach. "Then what's the plan?"

Talon's jaw tightened. "We stop them before they can get close."

She let out a shaky breath. "You make it sound so simple."

"It's not," he admitted. "But we don't have a choice."

For a moment, the vulnerability in his voice caught her off guard. He wasn't invincible, no matter how much he pretended to be.

"You've been hurt before," she said softly, not as a question but a statement.

Talon's lips pressed into a thin line. "Haven't we all?"

It wasn't an answer, not really, but it was enough. Aurora leaned back in her seat, the weight of everything sinking in.

By the time they reached the safehouse, the air between them was thick with unspoken words. Talon parked the car and stepped out without a word, Havoc close behind. Aurora followed, her gaze sweeping over the run-down building.

"This is safe?" she asked skeptically.

"It's secure," Talon said.

They stepped inside, and Talon immediately began checking the windows and doors. Aurora watched him, her mind racing. This man, so guarded and distant, had layers she couldn't begin to unravel.

"You're different than I thought you'd be," she said quietly.

Talon paused, glancing at her. "You keep saying that."

"Because it's true." She crossed her arms. "You act like you don't care, but you do. You act like you don't feel, but I see it."

Talon's expression hardened. "Don't psychoanalyze me."

Aurora shrugged, her gaze steady. "I'm just saying what I see."

For a long moment, he didn't respond. Then he sighed, the tension in his shoulders easing just slightly. "If you're done, get some rest. Tomorrow's going to be hell."

She wanted to argue, but the exhaustion weighing her down won out. As she settled onto the couch, she couldn't help but steal one last glance at Talon.

Beneath the walls and thorns, there was something raw and human—a man who cared more than he wanted to admit.

Chapter 19

THE ROOM WAS TOO quiet, the kind of silence that made Aurora's skin prickle with unease. She stood beside Talon, arms crossed tightly over her chest as her gaze flickered to Havoc, who lay alert at her feet. The dog's ears twitched at every faint creak or shift in the old building, his sharp eyes scanning the shadows. At least Havoc was here. His presence, steady and watchful, was one thing that felt normal in the swirl of everything else.

Aurora hadn't expected to find herself back at Talon's side so soon, not after the way she had walked away from him. Yet here she was, drawn back into his world by circumstances too dire to ignore. The mission had come together in a blur of phone calls and whispered warnings, Talon's clipped tone leaving no room for argument. "They've escalated," he had said. "I need you on this."

At first, she had been angry. After everything that had happened, he thought he could just call her and expect her to come running? But as the details unraveled, it became clear that this wasn't about him or even her—it was about something bigger, something neither of them could afford to let slip through their fingers. Reluctantly, she had agreed.

Now, standing in the stale air of the safe house, she wondered if she had made a mistake. The tension between them was palpable; a fragile thread stretched taut by unresolved emotions and lingering doubts. Talon, however, seemed unfazed—or at least, he was good at pretending.

"You don't have to be here," Talon said finally, breaking the silence. His voice was low, almost hesitant.

"I know," Aurora replied. "But I am."

She could see the flicker of relief in his eyes before he turned away, his expression hardening again. Havoc let out a low growl, his body tensing as he turned toward the door. Talon crouched beside the dog, resting a hand on his head and murmuring something too quiet for Aurora to hear. Havoc stilled, but his gaze remained locked on the door.

"Someone's coming," Talon muttered, rising to his feet.

Aurora's heart quickened, but she forced herself to stay calm. This was her first time back in the field with Talon since their fallout, and she wasn't about to let him see her falter.

The door swung open, revealing a man who seemed to command the room without effort. His suit was sharp, his eyes sharper, and the air around him seemed to hum with quiet menace. Aurora didn't need Talon's barely audible curse to know who this was. The big bad.

The man's voice was smooth, his words laced with veiled threats and icy confidence. Talon stepped forward, placing himself firmly between Aurora and the man. Havoc moved closer to her side, his growl low and continuous. The exchange that followed was tense, a battle of wills fought with words rather than weapons. Talon's responses were measured but pointed, his tone carrying an edge that promised retribution.

Aurora watched, her mind racing as she tried to piece together the implications of what the man was saying. This wasn't just a threat—it was a challenge, a warning of what was to come. But as the man finally retreated, leaving them in silence once more, Aurora couldn't shake the feeling that they had just been outmaneuvered.

Talon closed the door with a sharp exhale, leaning against it for a moment as though the weight of the confrontation had finally hit him. Aurora remained still, her thoughts swirling. "What now?" she asked, her voice quieter than she intended.

"We regroup," Talon said, straightening. "And we make sure he doesn't get the upper hand."

His words carried conviction, but there was something in his tone that made her pause. He wasn't just thinking about the mission—he was thinking about her, about them, and about the fragile thread they were trying to hold onto. Havoc pressed his nose against Aurora's hand, grounding her for a moment as she absently scratched behind his ears.

Later, when the adrenaline had begun to fade, they found themselves alone in the quiet of the safe house. Havoc lay curled up near the corner, his breathing steady and rhythmic. The tension in the room had eased slightly, but the unspoken weight of everything still lingered.

They stayed like that for a moment longer, the world outside forgotten. In that quiet, intimate space, they were just Talon and Aurora—two people who had faced the darkness and found their way back to each other.

Aurora shifted, leaning her head against his shoulder. "You don't have to do this alone," she said softly.

"I know," Talon replied, his voice equally quiet. "But I don't know how to do it with you, either."

She tilted her head to look at him, a faint smile tugging at her lips. "You'll figure it out. You always do."

He met her gaze, his expression softer than she had seen in a long time. "You make it sound so simple."

"It's not," she admitted, her voice steady but warm. "But nothing worth it ever is."

Havoc let out a contented sigh, his ears twitching slightly as he shifted in his sleep. For the first time in what felt like forever, Aurora felt a flicker of peace. The battle wasn't over—not by a long shot—but for now, they had this. They had each other, and for now, that was enough.

Aurora let herself relax against Talon's shoulder for a moment longer, the quiet warmth of his presence grounding her in a way she hadn't expected. Havoc stirred nearby, lifting his head to watch them with an expression that was almost knowing. She reached down to ruffle his fur, earning a soft huff in response, and for a brief moment, the world outside seemed far away.

But the reprieve was short-lived. Talon straightened slightly, his body tense again as if he couldn't allow himself to stay in this fragile peace for too long. "We can't stay like this forever," he said softly, his voice tinged with regret.

"I know," Aurora replied, pulling back just enough to meet his eyes. "But for now, it's okay to rest."

Talon hesitated, his gaze flickering to Havoc, who had resumed his vigilant watch of the room. "Resting isn't exactly in my skill set," he said, his lips quirking in the faintest ghost of a smile.

Aurora couldn't help but smile back, though it didn't quite reach her eyes. "Maybe it's time you learned."

Talon didn't respond immediately, his gaze shifting to the window. The faint light of dawn was starting to creep through the cracks in the curtains, painting the room in muted golds and grays. "I don't know how to stop, Aurora," he admitted finally, his voice barely above a whisper. "Not when every instinct I have tells me to keep moving, to keep fighting."

"You don't have to stop completely," she said gently. "But you can't fight everything all the time, Talon. You'll burn out. And then what?"

He leaned forward, his elbows resting on his knees as he stared at the floor. "Then they win."

Aurora placed a hand on his arm, her touch firm but comforting. "Not if you've already built something stronger than what they're trying to take from you."

He turned to look at her, something unreadable flickering in his eyes. "You make it sound so simple."

"It's not," she said, echoing her earlier words. "But you're not doing this alone anymore."

Havoc let out a low, rumbling growl, his ears pinning back as he rose to his feet. Both Talon and Aurora tensed, their focus snapping to the dog as he moved toward the door. Talon's hand instinctively went to his weapon, his movements controlled and precise.

"Stay here," he said, his voice low but commanding.

Aurora frowned but didn't argue. She watched as he approached the door, Havoc by his side, the dog's muscles taut with tension. Talon opened the door slowly, his gaze sweeping the area outside. After a moment, he relaxed slightly, but his hand didn't leave his weapon.

"It's clear," he said, stepping back inside. "But we need to move soon. I don't trust that we're not being watched."

Aurora nodded, standing as she adjusted the strap of her bag over her shoulder. Havoc returned to her side, his tail brushing against her leg as if to reassure her. "What's the plan?" she asked, her tone steady despite the unease curling in her stomach.

Talon's expression hardened, his focus sharpening as he outlined their next steps. They would meet with an informant who claimed to have critical information about the man they had encountered earlier. It was risky, but the potential payoff was too great to ignore.

As they prepared to leave, Aurora couldn't shake the feeling that they were walking into something far more dangerous than either of them had anticipated. The weight of the earlier confrontation still lingered, and the man's calculated demeanor and cryptic words left her uneasy. She glanced at Talon, wondering if he felt the same.

"You're quiet," she said as they walked to the car, Havoc trotting ahead of them.

"I'm always quiet," Talon replied, though there was a faint edge to his voice that suggested he was deep in thought.

"More than usual," Aurora pressed. "What's on your mind?"

He hesitated, his jaw tightening. "That man we met earlier. He wasn't just sending a message—he was testing us. He wanted to see how far we'd go."

"And?" she prompted, her heart sinking at the implication.

Talon stopped, turning to face her. "And we didn't give him enough to stop him. Whatever he's planning, he's already three steps ahead."

Aurora swallowed hard, her pulse quickening. "Then we'll catch up. We always do."

Talon's lips curved into a faint, humorless smile. "Always?"

She met his gaze, her determination unwavering. "Always."

They climbed into the car, Havoc settling in the backseat with a quiet huff. The drive was tense, the air between them heavy with unspoken fears and unresolved emotions. Talon's grip on the steering wheel was tight, his knuckles white as he navigated the winding roads. Aurora stole a glance at him, noting the hard set of his jaw and the flicker of vulnerability in his eyes.

"Do you trust me?" she asked suddenly, breaking the silence.

Talon's gaze flicked to her briefly before returning to the road. "With my life."

"That's not what I meant," she said softly. "Do you trust me to see all of you—the good, the bad, the parts you try to hide—and still stand by you?"

He didn't answer immediately, his fingers tightening around the wheel. When he finally spoke, his voice was low, almost hesitant. "I'm trying to."

"That's enough for now," she said, offering him a small, reassuring smile.

The rest of the drive passed in silence, but it wasn't the uncomfortable kind. It was the kind that spoke of unspoken understanding, of two people finding their way back to each other even as the world threatened to tear them apart. Havoc's soft breathing filled the space, a steady reminder of the bond they all shared.

When they arrived at their destination, the air was thick with tension. Talon parked the car and turned to Aurora, his expression unreadable. "Stay close," he said simply.

"I always do," she replied, her voice steady.

They stepped out, Havoc falling into step beside them as they approached the meeting point. The shadows seemed to stretch longer here, the air colder, heavier. Aurora's heart raced, but she pushed the fear aside, focusing instead on the warmth of Havoc's fur against her leg and the solid presence of Talon at her side.

No matter what waited for them in the darkness, she knew one thing for certain: they would face it together.

Chapter 20

The safe house was eerily quiet. Too quiet. The night's unease still clung to the air like a warning.

The safe house was eerily quiet, and a fragile peace replaced the tension between Talon and Aurora. Havoc lay near the door, his ears twitching at every creak or whisper of wind. Aurora leaned against the edge of the table, her gaze flicking toward Talon as he sifted through a map spread out across the surface. His focus was intense, his brow furrowed as he traced a route with his finger.

"We'll need to move soon," Talon said, breaking the silence. "Staying here much longer isn't safe."

Aurora nodded, though her mind was elsewhere. She couldn't shake the feeling that something was coming, a shift in the air that made her uneasy. Before she could voice her thoughts, Havoc's ears perked, his head snapping toward the door. A low growl rumbled in his throat.

"Talon," Aurora said, her voice sharp.

He straightened immediately, his hand moving to the weapon at his side. Havoc rose to his feet, his body tense as he positioned himself between Aurora and the door. The knock that followed was deliberate, measured, and far too calm for Aurora's liking.

"Stay behind me," Talon ordered, his tone leaving no room for argument.

Aurora grabbed her knife from the table and followed him to the door, her heart pounding. Talon opened it cautiously, his stance defensive, but the figures on the other side didn't move.

A man and a woman stood there, both dressed in tactical gear that had clearly seen better days. The man was tall and broad-shouldered, his dark hair cropped short and his expression unreadable. The woman, slightly shorter but no less imposing, had sharp features and piercing green eyes that seemed to take in everything at once.

"Talon," the man said, his voice calm but firm. "It's been a while."

Talon stiffened, his hand tightening on the door frame. "Logan."

Aurora's eyes darted between them, confusion swirling in her chest. "You know them?" she asked.

"Unfortunately," Talon muttered, stepping aside to let them in.

Logan smirked as he entered, his gaze sweeping over the room before landing on Aurora. "And you must be the reason he's not dead yet. Nice to meet you."

The woman rolled her eyes, giving Logan a light shove as she passed him. "Ignore him. He thinks he's funny," she said, her tone dry. She extended a hand toward Aurora. "I'm Elise."

Aurora hesitated for a moment before shaking her hand. "Aurora."

"Elise and Logan are... old acquaintances," Talon explained, his tone clipped. "We worked together. Once."

"More than once," Logan corrected, his smirk widening. "And don't act like you didn't miss us."

"I didn't," Talon said flatly.

Aurora raised an eyebrow. "What are you doing here?"

Elise folded her arms, her expression turning serious. "We're here because we heard about the ambush. Word travels fast in our circles, and it sounds like someone wants you dead, Talon. Again."

"Nothing new," Talon replied, his tone dismissive.

Logan leaned against the wall, crossing his arms. "This isn't like before. Whoever is after you isn't playing around. We're here to help."

Talon scoffed. "I don't need your help."

Aurora stepped forward, her frustration bubbling to the surface. "Actually, we do. If they know enough to set up an ambush, we're not as invisible as we thought. And two extra pairs of eyes wouldn't hurt."

Logan grinned at her. "I like her."

Elise shot him a warning look before turning back to Aurora. "We're not here to cause trouble. We're here because we owe Talon a debt. And because we know what's coming."

"What's coming?" Aurora asked, her unease growing.

Elise's expression darkened. "The man you ran into—the one behind the ambush—he's not just a threat to you. He's connected to something much bigger. And if he gets what he wants, none of us will be safe."

Talon's jaw tightened. "What do you know?"

"Enough to know you can't do this alone," Logan said. "And whether you like it or not, we're not going anywhere."

Aurora glanced at Talon, watching the tension in his posture as he weighed their words. She could see the conflict in his eyes—his instinct to handle everything on his own, warring with the realization that they were outmatched.

"We need information," Talon said finally, his voice reluctant. "If you have it, start talking."

Elise nodded, her expression grim. "It's not just you they're targeting. They're after anyone connected to you. That includes Aurora."

Aurora's blood ran cold, and she felt Talon's hand brush against hers in a silent gesture of reassurance. "Why me?" she asked.

"Because you're his weakness," Logan said bluntly. "And they think they can use you to get to him."

The room fell into a tense silence, the weight of Logan's words sinking in. Aurora's mind raced, but she forced herself to stay calm. "Then we make sure they can't."

Talon glanced at her, his expression unreadable, before turning back to Logan and Elise. "If you're staying, you follow my lead. No freelancing."

"Wouldn't dream of it," Logan said with a smirk.

Elise sighed. "We'll follow your lead, but don't forget—we're on your side."

"We'll see," Talon muttered, moving back toward the map on the table.

As they began to strategize, Aurora watched the dynamic between Talon and his old allies. There was history there, tension mixed with a begrudging respect that hinted at shared experiences she couldn't begin to imagine. She didn't trust them yet, but if they could help, she was willing to give them a chance.

Havoc padded over to her, pressing his nose against her hand. She smiled faintly, scratching behind his ears as she watched Talon and Logan argue over their next move. Whatever came next, Aurora knew one thing for certain—they couldn't afford to fail.

The tension in the room was palpable as Logan leaned over the map, gesturing animatedly while Talon stood rigid, his arms crossed and his expression unreadable. Elise paced near the window, her sharp eyes darting between the outside world and the conversation unfolding in the safe house.

"Look, I get it," Logan said, pointing to a circled area on the map. "You're used to doing things your way, but if you think you can go into their stronghold alone and come out alive, you're an idiot."

"I've done it before," Talon replied flatly, his tone cold.

"And it nearly got you killed," Elise cut in, her voice razor-sharp. "This time, they're expecting you. You don't have the element of surprise anymore."

Aurora stepped closer, her gaze flicking between the three of them. "What's the plan, then? Because sitting here arguing isn't getting us anywhere."

Logan straightened, his smirk fading as he turned to face her. "We don't rush in, for starters. We gather intel, find their weak points, and make a plan that doesn't end with all of us in body bags."

"And while we're gathering intel, they're gathering strength," Talon said, his voice rising slightly. "We don't have time to sit around playing it safe."

"You think rushing in blind is going to help anyone?" Elise countered. "Because if you do, you're more reckless than I remember."

Havoc let out a low growl from his spot by the door, breaking the escalating tension. Aurora placed a calming hand on the dog's head, then turned back to the others. "Enough. We're all on the same side here, right? So let's act like it."

The room fell into an uneasy silence, the weight of Aurora's words hanging over them. Logan sighed, running a hand through his hair before leaning back against the wall. "She's right. We need to focus."

Talon's jaw tightened, but he gave a reluctant nod. "Fine. Where do we start?"

Logan exchanged a glance with Elise before pulling a folded piece of paper from his jacket. "We intercepted this a few days ago," he said, handing it to Talon. "It's a list of known associates. Your name's on it. So is hers."

Aurora's stomach twisted as Talon unfolded the paper. His expression darkened as his eyes scanned the list. When he handed it to her, she felt her chest tighten. Her name was scrawled near the bottom, a stark reminder of just how much danger they were in.

"They're targeting anyone connected to you," Elise said, her tone grim. "Friends, allies, even people you've worked with in the past. They want to isolate you."

"And use Aurora to get to me," Talon muttered, his hands curling into fists.

Aurora swallowed hard, the weight of the situation pressing down on her. "Then we don't let them."

Logan's smirk returned, though it lacked its usual humor. "Easier said than done. These guys don't play fair."

"They don't have to," Aurora said firmly. "We just have to be smarter."

Talon's gaze flicked to hers, a faint glimmer of admiration in his eyes. "You're right," he said, his voice steady. "But that means working together."

Logan grinned. "Did he just say we should work together? Mark this day on the calendar."

"Don't push your luck," Talon snapped, though the edge in his voice was softer now.

Elise stepped forward, her expression serious. "If we're going to do this, we need to move quickly. The longer we wait, the more vulnerable we become."

"Agreed," Talon said. "Logan, you focus on tracking their movements. Elise, see if you can find out where they're keeping their resources. Aurora and I will figure out how to secure our location and keep them off our trail."

"And Havoc?" Logan asked, glancing at the dog. "What's his job?"

"Being smarter than you," Talon replied without missing a beat.

Logan laughed, shaking his head. "Touché."

As the group began to strategize, Aurora couldn't help but feel a flicker of hope amidst the tension. For all their differences, they were united by a common goal, and that was more than she had dared to hope for.

Hours passed in a blur of planning and preparation. Elise worked tirelessly at the window, her sharp eyes scanning for any signs of movement outside. Logan sat at the table, piecing together fragmented bits of intel while occasionally throwing out sarcastic remarks that earned him glares from Talon. Aurora focused on securing their supplies, her mind racing with a thousand possibilities of what could go wrong.

By the time the sun dipped below the horizon, the plan was starting to take shape. It wasn't perfect, but it was better than nothing. Aurora sat beside Havoc, her hand idly stroking his fur as she tried to quiet the unease bubbling in her chest.

"You okay?" Talon asked, his voice low as he sat down beside her.

She nodded, though the tension in her shoulders didn't ease. "I'm just trying to wrap my head around all of this. A week ago, my biggest worry was figuring out how to keep you from shutting me out. Now we're planning a takedown of people who want us dead."

Talon's lips curved into a faint smile. "Life comes at you fast."

Aurora laughed quietly, the sound tinged with exhaustion. "That's one way to put it."

He reached out, his hand brushing against hers in a gesture that was both reassuring and grounding. "We'll get through this," he said, his voice steady. "Together."

She met his gaze, her heart swelling at the quiet determination in his eyes. "Yeah," she said softly. "Together."

Logan's voice interrupted the moment, his tone laced with amusement. "Am I interrupting something, or can we get back to saving the world?"

Aurora rolled her eyes, though a small smile tugged at her lips. "You're impossible."

"And you're welcome," Logan shot back, earning another glare from Talon.

As the group gathered around the table to finalize their plans, Aurora felt a renewed sense of purpose. The road ahead was dangerous, and the stakes were higher than ever, but she wasn't alone. For the first time in a long time, she felt like they had a fighting chance.

Chapter 21

Aurora gritted her teeth as she helped Talon through the door of the safe house, his arm slung heavily over her shoulders. His weight was almost too much for her, but she refused to falter. Blood seeped through his shirt, dripping onto the floor with every step. Havoc darted ahead of them, his sharp eyes scanning the room as if sensing the tension. Talon let out a low groan, the sound barely audible but enough to twist something in her chest.

"What were you thinking?" she muttered, half to herself, as she lowered him onto the couch. His body stiffened as he sank into the cushions, his face pale and drawn.

"It wasn't supposed to go that way," he said through clenched teeth, his voice weak but defiant.

"Clearly," Aurora snapped, grabbing the first aid kit from the cabinet. She dropped it onto the table beside him and knelt in front of him, her fingers already pulling at the blood-soaked fabric of his shirt. He tried to push her hands away, but she slapped his wrist lightly. "Stop being stubborn. Let me see."

"I'm fine," Talon muttered, though the tremor in his voice betrayed him.

"You're bleeding all over the place, and you call this fine?" she shot back. "Just shut up and let me help you." She peeled back his shirt, her breath catching at the sight of the gash running along his ribs. It wasn't deep enough to be fatal, but it was bad enough to make her stomach churn. "You're lucky it didn't hit anything vital."

Talon leaned his head back against the couch, his eyes closing as he exhaled sharply. "Lucky," he echoed, the word laced with sarcasm.

Aurora worked quickly, cleaning the wound with steady hands despite the anxiety clawing at her insides. The mission had been a disaster from the start. What they thought was a straightforward exchange had turned into an ambush. Talon had thrown himself into the fray without hesitation, shielding her from the worst of it. She hadn't even realized he'd been hurt until they were already on the run, his movements slowing as the blood loss took its toll.

"You could have died," she said quietly, her voice tight with restrained emotion.

"But I didn't," Talon replied, his tone as dismissive as ever.

"You always do this," she snapped, her frustration boiling over. "You act like your life doesn't matter, like you're expendable."

Talon's eyes opened, meeting hers with an intensity that made her breath catch. "It matters," he said softly. "More than you think."

"Then start acting like it," she countered, her voice cracking slightly. "Because I can't keep doing this if you don't."

The silence that followed was heavy, punctuated only by the soft clink of metal as she stitched his wound. Havoc, who had been pacing the room, settled at Aurora's side, resting his head on her leg as if to offer comfort. She scratched his ears absently, her focus never leaving Talon.

"You're good at this," Talon said after a moment, his voice quieter now.

"Stitching people up?" she asked, arching a brow. "Not exactly a skill I wanted to perfect."

"No," he said, a faint smirk tugging at his lips despite the pain. "Keeping me alive."

Aurora rolled her eyes, but a small smile tugged at the corner of her mouth. "Someone has to."

Talon's gaze softened, and for a moment, he looked at her like she was the only thing tethering him to the world. "I trust you," he said simply, the weight of the words hanging between them.

Aurora froze, her hands stilling as she processed his admission. "Then stop making it so hard," she whispered, her voice barely audible.

Talon didn't reply, but the way he held her gaze said everything he couldn't put into words. She finished the stitches in silence, her hands lingering briefly on his skin before she pulled away. Talon reached out, his fingers brushing against hers, stopping her retreat.

"I don't deserve this," he said, his voice raw.

"Maybe not," Aurora replied, meeting his eyes. "But you have it anyway."

She leaned forward slightly, her forehead resting against his. His breath was warm against her skin, steady despite the pain he was clearly in. For the first time in what felt like forever, she saw him without the walls he usually kept between them. This was Talon—vulnerable, human, and heartbreakingly real.

They stayed like that for a moment, the world outside forgotten. Havoc let out a soft huff, shifting slightly as if to remind them he was still there. Aurora smiled faintly, her fingers brushing against Talon's jaw. "You're stubborn," she said softly.

"So are you," he replied, his voice laced with warmth.

She chuckled the sound light despite the tension still lingering in the air. "Maybe that's why we work."

Talon's lips curved into a faint smile, his hand moving to rest against her cheek. "Do we?" he asked, his voice tinged with uncertainty.

Aurora's smile faded slightly, but her resolve didn't waver. "We do," she said firmly. "But only if you stop trying to shoulder everything alone."

"I'm trying," he admitted, his voice barely above a whisper.

"Try harder," she said, her tone soft but insistent. "For both of us."

Talon nodded slowly, his gaze never leaving hers. Havoc shifted again, letting out a low groan as he stretched out at their feet. Aurora laughed quietly, her hand brushing through the dog's fur. "At least Havoc's on my side," she said.

"He always liked you better," Talon muttered, though there was no bitterness in his tone.

"Because he knows I won't let you get away with your bullshit," she replied, grinning.

Talon's laugh was quiet, almost reluctant, but it was real. "Guess I don't stand a chance then."

Aurora leaned in, her forehead brushing against his again. "Not even a little."

They stayed like that, wrapped in a fragile peace that felt too rare to last. The danger wasn't gone, and the wounds—both physical and emotional—were far from healed. But in that moment, with Havoc lying at their feet and the world temporarily held at bay, it was enough.

For now, it was enough.

For now, it was enough. But Aurora knew "enough" was fleeting. The silence between them stretched, not uncomfortable but heavy with things unsaid. She could feel the tension in Talon's body, the way he held himself so tightly; letting go even for a moment, would shatter the fragile peace they had found. Havoc's steady breathing filled the room, a soft reminder that not everything in their world was broken.

"You don't have to fight this alone anymore," Aurora said quietly, her hand still resting lightly on Talon's arm.

He didn't respond at first, his gaze fixed on some distant point beyond her shoulder. When he finally spoke, his voice was low, almost hesitant. "I don't know how not to."

"Then start with me," she said. "Start small. Trust me to carry some of it."

His eyes flicked to hers, and for a moment, she thought he might argue. But instead, he gave a faint nod, his lips pressing into a thin line. "I'm not good at this."

Aurora smiled softly, her thumb brushing against his arm. "Good at what?"

"Letting people in," he admitted. "Every time I have, it's gone wrong. People get hurt. Or worse."

She tilted her head, her expression gentle but unwavering. "I'm still here."

Talon let out a shaky breath, his fingers flexing slightly as if testing the weight of her words. "I don't want to lose you, Aurora."

"Then stop pushing me away," she said simply. "Stop treating me like I'm something fragile. I've been through hell with you, and I'm still standing."

"That's what scares me," he murmured, his voice barely above a whisper.

Aurora leaned closer, her forehead brushing against his. "It shouldn't."

For a long moment, neither of them moved. The quiet stretched, but it wasn't heavy this time. It was filled with something else, something lighter, more hopeful. Havoc stirred at their feet, his tail thumping softly against the floor as if he could sense the shift in the room.

"You're really good at this whole pep talk thing," Talon said, his voice tinged with dry humor.

Aurora grinned, leaning back slightly. "Someone has to keep you in check."

"Lucky me," he replied, a faint smile tugging at his lips.

She gave his arm a playful nudge before rising to her feet. "I'll take that as a thank you."

"Don't push it," he muttered, though there was no bite in his tone. He watched as she moved around the room, gathering supplies to clean up the remnants of her work. Havoc followed her movements with his gaze, his tail wagging lazily.

As Aurora worked, Talon's thoughts drifted. He couldn't remember the last time he'd felt this... steady. Not safe, exactly—he didn't think he'd ever truly feel safe—but anchored. Aurora had a way of pulling him out of the chaos in his head, of reminding him there was still something worth fighting for. Worth protecting.

"Thank you," he said suddenly, the words surprising even himself.

Aurora paused, glancing over her shoulder at him. "For what?"

"For not giving up on me," he said, his voice quieter now. "I don't make it easy."

She set the supplies down and walked back over to him, her expression soft. "You don't have to thank me for that."

"I do," he insisted. "Because I know I don't deserve it."

Aurora crouched in front of him again, her hands resting lightly on his knees. "You don't get to decide what you deserve, Talon. That's not how this works."

He held her gaze, something unspoken passing between them. The weight of her words settled over him, and for the first time in a long time, he didn't feel the urge to push back.

Havoc let out a low huff, drawing their attention. Aurora laughed quietly, reaching out to ruffle the dog's fur. "Looks like he agrees with me."

Talon chuckled softly, wincing slightly at the movement. "Of course he does. He's always on your side."

"Maybe because he knows I'm right," she teased, her smile widening.

Talon shook his head, but his expression softened. "You're impossible."

"And you're stubborn," she shot back, standing and crossing her arms. "Guess that makes us even."

The warmth in the room lingered as they settled back into a comfortable rhythm. Aurora busied herself tidying up while Talon watched her with a quiet intensity that made her heartache. She could see the wheels turning in his mind, the way he was processing everything they'd said, everything they hadn't.

"You know," she said after a while, breaking the silence, "you don't have to have all the answers right now."

Talon raised an eyebrow. "That's not how my brain works."

"Well, maybe it's time to rewire it," she replied lightly. "Start with baby steps."

"Like trusting you to take care of me?" he asked, his tone teasing but his eyes serious.

"Exactly," she said with a grin. "See? You're already halfway there."

"Halfway is generous," he muttered, though the corner of his mouth twitched upward.

Aurora rolled her eyes, but she couldn't hide the amusement in her expression. "You're impossible."

"You already said that," he pointed out.

"And I stand by it," she retorted, leaning against the edge of the table. "But at least you're my kind of impossible."

Talon didn't reply immediately, his gaze dropping to Havoc, who had stretched out at their feet. "I don't know what I did to deserve you two," he said quietly.

Aurora's heart softened at the vulnerability in his voice. "Maybe it's not about what you've done, Talon. Maybe it's about what you're willing to do from here on out."

His eyes met hers, and for the first time, she saw a flicker of something she hadn't dared hope for—acceptance. Not just of her but of the possibility that he could be more than what his past had made him.

"I'm trying," he said simply.

"And that's enough," Aurora replied, her voice steady. "For now."

They fell into a companionable silence, the weight of the world pressing a little less heavily on their shoulders. Havoc stretched with a satisfied groan, his tail thumping against the floor, and Aurora couldn't help but laugh.

"Looks like someone's finally relaxed," she said, gesturing to the dog.

"Wish I could say the same," Talon muttered, though there was no real edge to his words.

"You will," Aurora said confidently. "One step at a time."

Talon watched her for a moment longer, then nodded. "One step at a time."

And for the first time in a long time, he believed it.

Talon pulled Aurora closer, his arms wrapping around her as he picked her up and settled her onto his stomach. She let out a surprised laugh as he wrapped his arms around her, holding her securely in place.

As Aurora's thighs rested on either side of his stomach, Talon's large hands began to caress them soothingly. He felt the heat through the thin fabric of her pants, and his own stomach tensed under her as she unconsciously shifted her position, grinding slightly.

Aurora leaned in closer, her breath mingling with Talon's as she traced a hesitant finger along his chest. Talon, unable to resist, giving in to the urge, pulled her against him, capturing her lips with hers in a searing, passionate kiss.

Their kisses deepened as fumbling hands worked at each other's clothing - Aurora meticulously careful around Talon's still tender wound, while Talon's urgency outweighed his usual restraint. Shirts were discarded, and pants slipped down until bare skin met bare skin, igniting sparks wherever they touched.

Aurora continued her sensual assault, kissing and nipping at Talon's neck, marking him as hers. A deep, possessive groan escaped Talon's lips as she claimed him openly. "I am all yours," he declared fiercely, hands gripping her hips tightly, pulling her flush against him.

Talon, his control snapping, flipped Aurora onto her back, looming over her. He leaned down, licking his finger, then brought it to her core, rubbing slow circles around her sensitive nub. Aurora's eyes rolled back in pure pleasure, her back arching off the floor.

Talon's finger slid inside her, curling upwards, hitting that perfect spot that made Aurora see stars behind her closed eyelids. He added another finger, stretching her slowly as he leaned down to nuzzle her neck, inhaling her scent deeply.

Talon kissed his way down her jawline, capturing her mouth again as his fingers moved faster, deeper. Aurora's legs spread wider, heels digging into the mattress as she gripped his arms tightly. "Talon," she moaned, "Faster." Her body arched, breasts pressing against his chest.

Talon's mouth moved to her breasts, suckling hard as his fingers continued their rhythm inside her. "Every inch," he growled against her skin, "Mine." His thumb found her sensitive bundle of nerves, rubbing in circular motions, making her whimper and writhe beneath him.

In the heat of the moment, Talon suddenly paused, his hand moving away from Aurora's core. He reached into his bedside drawer and pulled out a strap-on, holding it up for her to see. "I'm going to claim you from behind," he said, his voice low and dominant.

Talon didn't say a word, his dominant grip on her wrist immobilizing her as he positioned the strap-on. The 8-inch long, 2.5-inch thick device rubbed against her clit, making her breathe heavily. He squeezed her ass cheeks together, spreading them apart to gain entry.

Talon thrust his hips forward slowly, pushing the thick strap-on inside Aurora an inch at a time. She whimpered, her body tensing as it stretched around the invasion. He squeezed her ass again, spreading her cheeks wider, and slid in another inch. "Talon," she breathed heavily,

"Shh…" Talon whispered, continuing his slow, deep thrusts. His hand still firmly gripping her wrist, preventing her from moving. With each thrust, he filled her completely, hitting that sensitive spot inside. The sound of flesh slapping against flesh filled the room, mingling with their heavy breathing.

As Talon pushed deeper, Aurora's body began to convulse around the thick strap-on, twitching and spasming as it stretched around the massive invasion. He wrapped his other hand around her waist, pulling her back onto him harder, making her take more of the thick length.

In a sudden wild frenzy, Talon's grip on her wrist and waist tightened as he began to pound into her with brutal force. The strap-on's thick length filled her completely, reaching places no man ever had, and he mercilessly hammered into those sensitive spots over and over again.

Aurora's body convulsed violently around the thick strap-on as Talon pounded into her without mercy, hitting that sweet spot inside that made her see stars. She was gasping, choking on her own breath, as he filled her completely over and over again. "Tal…on…"

Talon's brutal thrusts became erratic, bordering on animalistic, as he chased his own release and forced Aurora's. He wrapped his arm around her waist, pulling her up onto her knees, allowing him to drive deeper. Aurora's head lolled back onto his shoulder, her eyes glazed over with pleasure. Talon captured her mouth in a searing kiss, swallowing her cries as he continued to pound into her relentlessly. Their tongues danced wildly, mimicking the primal rhythm of their bodies joining.

Talon wrapped his arms around her waist as she sat on his lap, the strap-on buried inside her as she bounced up and down, taking the thick length in and out. His face was buried between her generous breasts, the soft mounds slapping against his face with each bounce.

Talon captured one of her nipples in his mouth, sucking hard as Aurora bounced faster, completely lost in pleasure. The thick strap-on filled her completely with each descent, hitting that spot that made her see stars. Her moans grew louder, more desperate, as she approached her climax.

Aurora suddenly pulled the strap-on out, slick with her arousal, and began grinding her now exposed clit against Talon's muscular thighs. She moved frantically, her juices coating his skin as she chased her impending orgasm. Her breasts bounced wildly with each grind; her nipples hardened peaks begging for attention.

Talon smirked, pulling Aurora's hair as he stood, making her kneel before him. "You've created quite the mess, Aurora," he teased, slapping the slick strap-on against her face. Without warning, he shoved the thick length into her mouth, holding her hair tightly.

Talon gazed down at Aurora, his eyes dark with lust as he gripped her hair tightly, holding her firmly in place. He began to thrust his hips, face-fucking her relentlessly. The thick strap-on plunged in and out of her mouth, bumping against the back of her throat with each stroke.

Talon pulled back sharply, making Aurora choke as the strap-on left her throat. His voice dripped with dominance, "You're a good girl, taking my cock so perfectly…" He wiped a strand of hair from her face, then suddenly shoved the dick back in, fucking her mouth brutally again.

After a few more brutal thrusts, Talon pulled out, breathing heavily. He tossed the strap-on aside and crawled over Aurora's mess-covered body, holding her face gently. "You did so well, my good girl," he praised before pulling her into a deep, passionate kiss.

Talon gently wiped the saliva and tears from Aurora's face, his touch gentle and soothing. He grabbed a warm washcloth and tenderly cleaned her face and throat. "Turn over," he instructed softly, lifting her into his lap.

Talon gently turned Aurora over and began wiping the sweat and arousal from her back and ass. He took special care cleaning her pussy and thighs, his touch now comforting rather than dominant. Pressing a soft kiss to her shoulder, he wrapped a blanket around her trembling body. "You alright, sweetheart?"

Aurora nodded weakly, snuggling into Talon's chest. "I'm okay," she murmured, her voice hoarse from the intense session. Talon held her close, running a soothing hand through her hair as he rocked her gently. "You were perfect, love. So fucking perfect."

Aurora's eyelids grew heavy, and soon, she was fast asleep in Talon's arms. He continued to stare at her adoringly, gently playing with her hair. His heart swelled with affection for the sleeping beauty in his arms. He kissed her forehead softly.

Talon wrapped his heavy black cloak around Aurora's naked body, tucking it tightly around her. He continued to watch her sleep, his expression soft. His rough fingers gently combed through her hair, spreading it messily around her shoulders. "Beautiful," he murmured softly, careful not to wake her.

Talon's fingers lightly brushed over Aurora's skin just to reassure himself she was real. His touch was feather-light, gentle caresses that barely made contact. He marveled at the softness of her skin, the way it flushed pink under his touch.

Chapter 22

Talon's breathing was steady but shallow, his body taut with tension as he sat on the edge of the bed. Aurora stood in front of him, arms crossed as she studied him with a mixture of curiosity and concern. Havoc lay by the door, his sharp eyes flicking between them as if sensing the gravity of the moment.

"This feels different," Aurora said, her voice soft but thoughtful.

"It is," Talon replied, his hands resting on his thighs, his gaze fixed on the floor. "It has to be."

She took a step closer, her brow furrowing slightly as she tried to read his expression. "Are you sure you're ready for this?"

Talon finally looked up at her, and though his gaze was steady, she could see the flicker of uncertainty behind his eyes. "I trust you."

The words landed heavily, their weight lingering in the space between them. He had said them before, but now they felt more deliberate, more intentional. Aurora let the moment settle before reaching for the blindfold he'd placed on the bed. It wasn't about testing boundaries or control this time; it was about something deeper—trust, vulnerability, and letting her see him fully.

Without a word, she stepped behind him, her fingers brushing against his temple as she tied the blindfold in place. His body tensed at the initial touch, but as her hands lingered on his shoulders, she felt him relax slightly beneath her fingertips.

"You can tell me to stop at any time," she said, her tone firm but reassuring.

"I know," he replied, his voice quieter now, almost tentative.

She moved back in front of him, watching the way his chest rose and fell in slow, measured breaths. His hands were still resting on his thighs, his fingers twitching slightly as though resisting the urge to clench into fists. He wasn't used to this—to giving up control, to letting someone else take the reins—but he wasn't fighting it, either.

"This isn't about control," Aurora said softly. "It's about trust."

"I know," Talon said again, though his voice carried the faintest edge of hesitation.

Aurora reached out, her fingers brushing against his hands. He stilled at the contact, his breathing momentarily faltering before evening out again. "You don't have to prove anything to me, Talon."

"I'm not doing this to prove anything to you," he admitted, his tone raw. "I need to prove it to myself."

She nodded, even though he couldn't see her. "Then let me help."

His lips quirked slightly, almost as if he were trying to smile. "You already are."

The silence that followed wasn't heavy or uncomfortable. It was filled with the quiet hum of understanding, the kind that didn't need words. Aurora settled beside him on the bed, her hand resting lightly on his knee as she spoke.

"Tell me what you're feeling," she prompted gently.

Talon hesitated, his jaw tightening as he searched for the right words. "Exposed," he finally said. "But not in a bad way."

Aurora smiled faintly, her thumb brushing against his knee. "You don't have to hide from me, you know. Not anymore."

"That's easier said than done," he replied, his voice tinged with dry humor.

"I'm not saying it'll happen overnight," she said, leaning closer. "But you've already taken the first step."

He let out a quiet breath, his shoulders relaxing slightly as the tension began to ebb. "You make it sound so simple."

"It's not," she admitted. "But it's worth it."

He tilted his head slightly, his blindfolded gaze seeming to search for her even though he couldn't see. "You're really good at this," he said after a moment.

"At what?" she asked, tilting her head.

"Making me feel like I'm not completely broken."

Aurora's chest tightened at the vulnerability in his words, but she didn't let the emotion overwhelm her. Instead, she squeezed his knee gently, her voice steady as she replied. "You're not broken, Talon. You're just rebuilding."

The corners of his lips curved into a faint smile. "You make it sound like I'm a fixer-upper."

"Maybe you are," she teased lightly, her tone warm. "But I've got plenty of tools."

The chuckle he let out was soft but real, the sound breaking some of the tension that had lingered between them. "Lucky me."

"Very lucky," she said, her grin widening.

Aurora shifted slightly, her hand brushing against his arm as she moved closer. The intimacy of the moment wasn't about their proximity; it was about the trust, the way Talon was letting her see him in a way he hadn't before. She reached up, her fingers lightly tracing the line of his jaw, and he didn't pull away.

"You're doing better than you think," she said softly.

"That's because you make it easier," he replied, his voice steady but quiet.

"Good," she said, her hand dropping back to his knee. "Because I'm not going anywhere."

Talon's breathing hitched slightly, but he didn't speak. Aurora could feel the weight of the moment settling over them, the unspoken promise in her words weaving its way into the silence. Havoc let out a low huff from his spot by the door, his tail wagging faintly against the floor as if to remind them he was still there. Aurora laughed quietly, her fingers brushing through the dog's fur.

"Looks like someone approves," she said, glancing back at Talon.

"He always liked you better," Talon muttered, though there was no bitterness in his tone.

"Maybe because he knows I won't let you get away with your bullshit," she teased, her grin widening.

Talon shook his head slightly, his lips quirking into a faint smile. "You're impossible."

"And you're stubborn," she shot back. "But somehow, it works."

The quiet that followed wasn't heavy or awkward. It was peaceful, a kind of stillness they both seemed to need. Aurora reached up to untie the blindfold, her fingers brushing against his hair as she loosened the knot. When the fabric fell away, Talon blinked a few times, his gaze meeting hers. There was something softer in his expression now, something open and unguarded.

"I'm trying," he said simply, his voice steady but low.

Aurora nodded, her smile gentle. "That's enough for now."

They stayed like that for a while, the world outside the safehouse fading into the background. Havoc stretched out at their feet, his tail thumping lazily against the floor, and Aurora leaned against Talon, her head resting on his shoulder.

For the first time in a long time, they weren't fighting. They weren't running. They were just existing together. And for now, that was enough

Aurora shifted slightly, her head still resting on Talon's shoulder. She listened to the steady rhythm of his breathing, her own heart slowing to match its pace. The quiet felt fragile, like a delicate thread that could snap if either of them moved too quickly or spoke too loudly. Havoc stirred at their feet, letting out a contented sigh as he stretched his legs. Aurora smiled faintly, reaching down to scratch behind his ears.

After a long pause, her voice soft, she said, "You know, this is probably the most relaxed I've seen you."

Talon huffed a quiet laugh, the sound low and rough. "Don't get used to it."

Aurora tilted her head to look up at him. "Why not?"

"Because this isn't who I am," he replied, his voice steady but laced with a tinge of regret.

"That's not true," she said, sitting up slightly so she could face him fully. "This is exactly who you are. You just don't let yourself be him often enough."

Talon's gaze dropped, his jaw tightening as he processed her words. "It's not that simple, Aurora."

"It's never simple," she agreed. "But that doesn't mean it's impossible."

He let out a slow breath, his shoulders sagging slightly. "You make it sound easy."

"I didn't say it would be easy," she countered, her tone gentle but firm. "But it's worth it."

Talon didn't respond immediately, his eyes distant as though he were sifting through a lifetime of memories and regrets. Aurora reached out, her fingers brushing against his, grounding him in the present. "You don't have to do this all at once," she said. "One step at a time, remember?"

He glanced at her, his expression softening. "You're too patient for your own good."

"Or maybe I'm just stubborn," she said with a small smile. "Either way, you're stuck with me."

Talon shook his head, but the faint curve of his lips betrayed his amusement. "I guess I don't have much of a choice."

"Exactly," Aurora teased, leaning back against the couch. "Resistance is futile."

Havoc let out another huff, his tail thumping against the floor as if to emphasize her point. Aurora laughed, the sound light and free, and for a moment, Talon allowed himself to bask in the warmth of her presence.

But the moment didn't last. His smile faded, replaced by a shadow of doubt. "What happens when I mess this up?"

Aurora's laughter quieted, her expression turning serious. "Then we deal with it. Together."

"And if I hurt you?" he asked, his voice barely above a whisper.

"You won't," she said firmly. "Because I won't let you. And neither will you."

He met her gaze, his eyes searching hers for reassurance. "You sound so sure."

"Because I am," she replied. "I've seen the worst of you, Talon. And I'm still here."

The weight of her words hung in the air, pressing against the fragile peace they had built. Talon's throat tightened, but he forced himself to speak. "You shouldn't have to deal with the worst of me."

"I don't think I have much of a choice," she said, her tone light but her eyes unwavering. "Resistance is futile, remember?"

Talon's lips twitched into a faint smile, though the emotion in his eyes remained raw. "I don't deserve you, Aurora."

"That's not for you to decide," she replied simply. "And for the record, you deserve more than you think."

He leaned back against the couch, his head resting against the worn fabric as he stared at the ceiling. Aurora watched him, her chest tightening at the vulnerability etched into his features. She wanted to reach out, to pull him closer, but she knew better than to push too hard.

"Do you ever think about what happens after this?" he asked suddenly, his voice breaking the silence.

"After what?" she asked, tilting her head.

"After the fight. After we're done running and chasing and surviving," he said. "What happens then?"

Aurora paused, considering his words. "I think... we figure out what living looks like. Together."

Talon's gaze shifted to her, his eyes soft but uncertain. "You make it sound so simple."

"It's not," she admitted. "But it's worth it."

The quiet stretched between them again, but this time, it felt different—full of possibility rather than hesitation. Havoc shifted closer to Aurora, resting his head on her knee as if offering his own silent support. She smiled, her hand moving to scratch behind his ears.

"We'll figure it out," she said, more to herself than to Talon. "One step at a time."

"Yeah," he said softly, his gaze dropping to her hand where it rested on Havoc. "One step at a time."

They stayed like that for what felt like hours, the weight of their shared burdens easing slightly in the warmth of their quiet connection. The world outside the safehouse felt distant, and for the first time in a long time, Talon allowed himself to believe that maybe, just maybe, there was something waiting for him beyond the fight.

Chapter 23

THE SOFT HUM OF voices and the clatter of cutlery filled the small café, creating an atmosphere so ordinary that it almost felt foreign. Aurora sipped her coffee, the warmth seeping into her hands as she glanced out the window. The streets were busy but calm, sunlight glinting off car hoods and casting long shadows across the pavement. For the first time in weeks, there was no immediate sense of danger, no shadow lurking just out of sight.

Talon sat across from her; his chair tilted back on two legs, and a faint smirk tugged at his lips. He looked more relaxed than she had seen him in a while, though the sharpness in his eyes told her he hadn't let his guard down completely.

"You're staring," he said, his tone teasing.

Aurora rolled her eyes, setting her cup down. "I'm just trying to figure out what's more surprising—that you agreed to this little 'normal' outing or that you haven't complained once."

"I don't complain," he replied, his smirk widening. "I make observations."

"Sure you do," she muttered, but her lips quirked into a smile.

Havoc lay sprawled under the table, his head resting on his paws. He watched the room with quiet vigilance. A few patrons glanced their way, their curiosity piqued by Talon's confident presence and Aurora's quiet strength. She could feel the weight of their stares but tried to ignore it.

Talon didn't. He thrived on it.

When a man at a nearby table let his gaze linger on Aurora for a little too long, Talon's smirk turned into something sharper. He leaned forward slightly, his chair landing on all four legs with a soft thud. His arm draped over the back of Aurora's chair as he gave the man a slow, deliberate once-over. The message was clear: She's with me. Don't even think about it.

The man quickly looked away, muttering something under his breath as he focused on his food. Aurora raised an eyebrow, turning back to Talon. "Was that necessary?"

"Absolutely," Talon replied, his tone smug.

Aurora shook her head, though she couldn't hide her amusement. "You're impossible."

"And you love it," he shot back, his grin downright cocky now.

Before she could respond, Havoc let out a soft growl, his ears perking up as his gaze locked onto something—or someone—near the door. Talon's demeanor shifted instantly, his smirk fading as his hand dropped to his side, where a knife was hidden beneath his jacket.

Aurora followed Havoc's line of sight, her body tensing as she spotted a man lingering near the entrance. He was dressed casually, but there was something about the way he scanned the room that set her on edge. When his gaze landed on their table, Aurora's breath caught. He didn't approach, but the way he lingered sent a clear message: I know who you are.

Talon leaned back in his chair, his posture deceptively relaxed. "Stay calm," he murmured, his voice low enough that only she could hear.

"I'm calm," Aurora replied, though her pulse was racing.

The man didn't move for several long moments, his eyes narrowing slightly before he turned and walked away. Talon watched him go, his sharp gaze following the man until he disappeared from view. Only then did he relax, though his hand remained close to his weapon.

"Friend of yours?" Aurora asked, her tone light but her eyes serious.

"Hardly," Talon replied, his smirk returning, though it didn't reach his eyes. "But he got the message."

Aurora leaned back in her chair, her fingers brushing against Havoc's fur as she tried to steady her breathing. The moment had passed, but the unease lingered, a reminder that their normal life was always teetering on the edge of danger.

"You're enjoying this way too much," she said, glancing at Talon.

He shrugged, his smirk widening. "What can I say? I like keeping people on their toes."

Aurora shook her head, though she couldn't help but smile. "You're ridiculous."

"And you're still here," he pointed out, his tone laced with warmth.

"Someone has to keep you in check," she replied, taking another sip of her coffee.

The tension in the room eased as they fell back into their quiet rhythm. Talon's cockiness was both infuriating and endearing, a reminder that even amidst the chaos, he was still himself. Aurora glanced out the window again, her gaze lingering on the bustling streets. The café felt like a bubble of normalcy, fragile and fleeting, but she held onto it anyway.

Havoc shifted beneath the table, his tail thumping softly against the floor. Aurora reached down to scratch behind his ears, her thoughts drifting. For a moment, she allowed herself to imagine what life could be like if this was their reality—quiet mornings, shared laughter, no threats looming in the shadows. It was a nice thought, even if it felt out of reach.

Talon's voice broke through her reverie. "What are you thinking about?"

"Nothing," she replied, her smile soft. "Just... this."

"This?" he repeated, tilting his head.

"This," she said again, gesturing to the café, the people, the sunlight streaming through the windows. "Normal. Or something close to it."

Talon was quiet for a moment, his gaze searching hers. "You really think this could be our life?"

"I don't know," she admitted. "But I like the idea of it."

He leaned forward, his elbows resting on the table. "Then maybe we make it happen."

Aurora raised an eyebrow. "Talon, when was the last time you did anything normal?"

"Define normal," he said with a grin.

She laughed, the sound light and genuine. "This. Coffee in a café. No ambushes. No running."

"Sounds boring," he teased, though his expression softened. "But for you? I'd give it a shot."

Aurora's heart ached at the sincerity in his voice, but she didn't let it show. Instead, she smiled, her fingers brushing against his. "You're full of surprises."

"And you haven't seen anything yet," he replied, his tone teasing but his eyes warm.

For now, the café was their safe haven, a moment of peace in the storm. Aurora didn't know how long it would last, but she was determined to hold on to it for as long as she could.

Talon leaned back in his chair again, his smirk returning as he twirled a spoon between his fingers with practiced ease. "You know, you're surprisingly good at pretending this is normal," he said, his tone teasing.

Aurora arched an eyebrow. "Maybe because it is normal. You're the one who seems out of place."

"Out of place?" Talon feigned offense, pressing a hand to his chest. "I blend in perfectly."

"You're literally radiating, so don't mess with my energy," she countered. "That guy at the door practically bolted when you looked at him."

"And you're welcome," Talon said with a grin. "You know I enjoy keeping the riffraff away."

Aurora shook her head, though she couldn't help the smile tugging at her lips. Havoc let out a soft huff from beneath the table, his tail thumping against her leg. She reached down to scratch behind his ears, her thoughts briefly drifting to the man who had lingered near the entrance. There was something unsettling about the way he had watched them, even if he hadn't made a move.

"You think he'll come back?" she asked quietly.

Talon's smirk faded, his expression turning serious. "No. Not him, anyway."

"But someone else might," she pressed.

"Always," he said simply. "But that's why we stay ahead."

His confidence was reassuring, but Aurora couldn't shake the unease that lingered at the edges of her thoughts. She glanced out the window again, her gaze sweeping over the bustling street. The world outside seemed so ordinary, so blissfully unaware of the chaos that followed them wherever they went.

"You okay?" Talon asked, his voice softer now.

"Yeah," she said, forcing a smile. "Just... thinking."

"About?"

"Everything," she admitted. "How we ended up here. What comes next."

Talon reached across the table, his fingers brushing against hers. "We'll figure it out."

She met his gaze, her heart aching at the quiet determination in his eyes. "You really believe that?"

"I do," he said firmly. "Because we don't have a choice."

Before she could respond, the bell above the door jingled, drawing their attention. A young couple entered, laughing softly as they found a table near the window. The moment felt so mundane, so completely removed from Aurora's reality, that it almost made her chest ache.

"What?" Talon asked, noticing the shift in her expression.

"Nothing," she said quickly, shaking her head. "It's just... weird."

"What is?"

"Seeing people who don't have to worry about who's watching them or what's waiting around the corner," she said. "I don't even know what that feels like anymore."

Talon was quiet for a moment, his gaze thoughtful. "Maybe you'll get to find out someday."

"Maybe," she said, though she didn't sound convinced.

"You will," he said, his voice firm. "I'll make sure of it."

Aurora smiled faintly, her fingers curling around her coffee cup. "You're awfully confident."

"Comes with the territory," he replied, his smirk returning. "Besides, I've got you and Havoc to keep me in line."

"You're impossible," she said, rolling her eyes.

"And you love it," he shot back, his grin widening.

Havoc let out another soft huff, his gaze flicking toward the door. Aurora followed his line of sight, her muscles tensing slightly out of habit. But it was just another customer—a woman balancing a tray of pastries and coffee cups as she made her way to the counter.

"Relax," Talon murmured, noticing her reaction. "Not everyone's out to get us."

"Force of habit," she muttered, though she tried to let her shoulders relax.

Talon leaned back again, his smirk softening into something more genuine. "You're safe here, Aurora."

"For now," she said, her voice tinged with uncertainty.

"For now," he agreed, his tone lighter. "But that's all any of us ever have, right?"

She didn't answer, but the truth in his words lingered in her mind. The future was uncertain, the past a weight she couldn't fully escape, but the present—this moment, with Talon and Havoc—felt like something worth holding onto.

They finished their coffee in companionable silence, the tension between them easing as the minutes passed. Talon's cocky demeanor was as infuriating as ever, but it was also grounding in a way Aurora couldn't quite explain. He made her feel like they could handle anything, even when the odds were stacked against them.

As they stood to leave, Talon tossed a few bills onto the table and slung his arm around Aurora's shoulders. His touch was casual but protective, a subtle reminder to anyone watching that she wasn't alone. Havoc trotted ahead, his ears perked as he scanned the sidewalk.

"Where to next?" Aurora asked as they stepped outside.

"Back to the safe house," Talon replied, his tone turning serious again. "We've got work to do."

"Of course we do," she said with a sigh. "It was nice while it lasted, though."

Talon glanced at her, his expression softening. "We'll do this again. I promise."

Aurora wasn't sure she believed him, but she nodded anyway. "Okay."

As they walked down the street, the sun warm on their backs, Aurora let herself imagine what a normal life with Talon might look like. Quiet mornings, shared laughter, no shadows lurking around every corner. It was a nice thought, even if it felt like a distant dream.

Talon's hand tightened slightly on her shoulder, pulling her out of her thoughts. She glanced up at him, her heart skipping a beat at the way he was watching her—like she was the only thing that mattered in the world.

"You're staring," she said, echoing his earlier words.

"Maybe I just like the view," he replied, his grin cocky but his tone sincere.

Aurora rolled her eyes, but her smile betrayed her. "You're ridiculous."

"And you're still here," he said, his voice warm.

"Someone has to keep you in check," she shot back.

"Good luck with that," he replied with a laugh.

As they rounded the corner, the safe house came into view. The bubble of normalcy they had shared in the café began to fade, replaced by the familiar weight of responsibility and danger. But as they stepped inside, Havoc trotting ahead of them, Aurora felt a flicker of hope. For now, they were together, and for now, that was enough.

Chapter 24

THE CABIN WAS QUIET, the kind of silence that pressed against Aurora's ears and made her hyper-aware of every creak of the floorboards and rustle of the wind outside in the night. She sat at the edge of the bed, her fingers laced tightly together as she watched Talon pace across the room. Havoc lay near the door, his ears twitching as he tracked Talon's movements.

"We can't keep doing this," Aurora said, her voice breaking the tension-filled silence. Talon stopped mid-step, his head turning sharply toward her. "What do you mean?" he asked.

"I mean running. Hiding. Pretending like we can just disappear and live some normal life," she replied, her tone steady but laced with frustration. "It's not who we are, and it's not working." Talon sighed, raking a hand through his hair as he resumed pacing. "You think I don't know that? You think I don't feel the walls closing in every time we stop moving?"

"Then why are we still pretending?" she demanded, rising to her feet. "Why are we acting like this cabin is anything more than a temporary reprieve?" He stopped pacing, his gaze meeting hers. "Because we need time to figure out our next move," he snapped, his tone sharper than he intended. He immediately softened, his shoulders sagging. "I just wanted to give you a moment to breathe, Aurora. To feel like there's more to life than this fight."

Aurora's chest tightened at his words, but she didn't let the emotion show. "I appreciate that, Talon. I do. But this isn't living—it's waiting. And we both know that the longer we wait, the worse it's going to get." He studied her for a moment, his expression unreadable. "So what do you want to do?"

She took a deep breath, her hands curling into fists at her sides. "I want to fight. I want to take back control instead of letting them dictate every step we take." Talon's jaw tightened as he considered her words. "You're sure about this?" he asked finally. "I've never been more sure," she replied, her voice firm.

Once the decision was made, the tension that had hung over them seemed to lift, replaced by a sense of purpose. Over the next few days, they threw themselves into preparations, their focus shifting from survival to strategy. Talon pored over maps and intel, tracing connections and identifying weak points in their enemies' operations. Aurora worked alongside him, and her sharp mind and keen instincts proved invaluable. One evening, as they studied a hastily sketched diagram of the enemy's known assets, Aurora frowned. "We're outnumbered," she said, her brow furrowing. "Even with surprise on our side, this isn't going to be easy."

"It never is," Talon replied, his tone calm. "But we've done more with less." Havoc let out a soft bark, drawing their attention. The dog stood by the door, his tail wagging as he waited expectantly. "Looks like he's ready," Aurora said with a faint smile. "Are you?" Talon glanced at her, his expression softening. "Always."

"Aurora," Talon's voice was soft, urgent. And Aurora met his gaze. "If this goes wrong-"

"It won't; we'll be fine," Aurora didn't want to think about the possibility of this all falling apart. That everything they worked for, the blood they lost, and the sacrifices would be for nothing.

Talon closed the distance between them and cupped Aurora's cheek in his hand. Aurora couldn't help but lean into his touch, finding comfort in the contact between them.

Without another word, Talon stole a kiss. Not a hungry one like the others. No, this one was deep and gentle. A stark contrast to his otherwise hard shell he held every second. Aurora fell deeper into the feeling his lips brought her.

Aurora wrapped her arms around the man's neck and kissed him back.

As soon as the moment began, Talon ended it by pulling away only by an inch. His eyes were closed, and his brows were cinched as if imagining the worst.

"Talon," Aurora pulled him close. "It's going to be okay."

"And if it's not?"

"Then we figure it out like we always have."

Talon opened his eyes now, slowly. They searched Aurora for something. Answers maybe.

He leaned down and kissed her again, deeper, this time. Aurora's back hit the wall behind her, and she returned the sentiment. Neither wanted to pull away, not now. Not when their entire world was about to be stolen.

Talon's hands traced her curves as if trying to memorize each and every inch of her. And Aurora didn't fight it. She wouldn't, not tonight.

The candles flickered, the only light in the small cabin that had been their refuge. The wind seemed to whisper around the cabin as the two danced in a song of passion.

Neither knew how the next two days would turn out. Neither wanted to know the bloodshed that was promised ahead of them. But they knew they needed each other. Even if it was just for the night, they would lower their walls completely.

Their first move was bold but calculated—a strike against a known supply route used by their enemies. The operation was quick and efficient, a reminder of what they were capable of when they worked together. It wasn't without risks, but the adrenaline that coursed through Aurora's veins as they retreated to safety was a stark contrast to the suffocating helplessness she had felt while hiding. "That went better than expected," she said breathlessly as they reached the edge of the forest.

Talon smirked, his eyes gleaming with satisfaction. "Told you we've done more with less." Aurora rolled her eyes, but her smile betrayed her. "Don't get cocky." "I'm just saying—maybe we're not as outmatched as we thought," he replied, his tone light but his gaze sharp.

The small victories gave them momentum, each one a step closer to reclaiming the sense of control they had lost. But with every success came a reminder of the dangers they faced. Their enemies were relentless, and the more they pushed back, the harder the opposition fought to tighten its grip. One evening, as they sat by the fire, Aurora found herself staring at the pendant that now hung beside Talon's on the chain around her neck. She reached for it, her fingers tracing its edges as she spoke. "Do you think we're making the right choice?" Talon leaned forward, resting his elbows on his knees. "I think the right choice is the one you can live with. And for me, that's fighting." She nodded, her grip tightening on the pendant. "Me too."

By the time they returned to the cabin after another successful raid, the air between them crackled with determination. The cabin was no longer just a refuge; it was a base, a place to regroup and plan their next moves. A sense of clarity had replaced Aurora's earlier doubts—this was who they were, and this was what they were meant to do. As they stood on the porch, watching the sun dip below the horizon, Aurora turned to Talon. "So what's next?"

He smiled faintly, his gaze fixed on the horizon. "We keep going. We make them regret ever coming after us." Aurora smiled, her chest swelling with determination. "Together?" "Always," he said, his voice steady.

The fight wasn't over, but for the first time in a long time, Aurora felt like they were the ones in control. And that made all the difference.

The fight wasn't over, but for the first time in a long time, Aurora felt like they were the ones in control. And that made all the difference.

As the evening deepened, the cool mountain air settled over the cabin. Aurora stood on the porch, her arms crossed, leaning against the wooden railing, gazing out at the tree line. The weight of their decision pressed against her chest—not in a suffocating way but as a constant reminder of what was at stake. Behind her, the door creaked open, and Talon stepped out, his boots scuffing softly against the wood.

"Couldn't sleep?" he asked, his voice low.

Aurora shook her head, her gaze still fixed on the darkened forest. "Too much on my mind."

He leaned against the railing beside her, his shoulder brushing hers. "It's normal to second-guess."

"I'm not second-guessing," she said, glancing at him. "I'm just... trying to see the bigger picture. What happens if we win? What happens if we lose?"

Talon tilted his head slightly, his expression thoughtful. "If we win, we get to decide what happens next. If we lose, at least we went down fighting."

Aurora let out a soft, humorless laugh. "That's oddly comforting."

"It's the truth," he said simply.

They stood in silence for a while, the stillness of the night broken only by the distant rustle of leaves and the occasional hoot of an owl. Havoc lay at their feet, his ears twitching as he dozed. Aurora's thoughts churned with the weight of their past and the uncertainty of their future intertwining in her mind.

"You know," Talon said after a while, "this isn't just about survival anymore."

"What do you mean?" she asked, turning to face him fully.

"This is about taking back what they tried to steal from us—our freedom, our choices," he said, his gaze steady. "It's about making sure no one else has to go through what we did."

Aurora's chest tightened at his words, the fire in his voice igniting something in her. "You're right," she said softly. "It's bigger than us."

"And that's why we can't afford to stop," Talon said, his tone resolute. "Not until we've finished this."

The next morning, they set to work, their focus sharp and unwavering. Talon spread a map across the table, marking key locations with a pencil as he explained their next steps. Aurora listened intently, her mind racing as she absorbed the details.

"We need to disrupt their supply chain further," Talon said, tracing a line across the map. "If we hit here, it'll force them to reroute everything through the northern pass."

"Which will leave them vulnerable," Aurora added, nodding. "But it'll also make them desperate."

"Desperation makes people sloppy," Talon said with a faint smirk. "We can use that."

Aurora studied the map, her fingers tapping lightly against the edge of the table. "And after that?"

"We go for the head of the snake," Talon replied, his expression hardening. "Take out their leadership, and the rest will fall apart."

"It's risky," she said, her brow furrowing. "They'll see us coming."

"That's why we have to be smarter," Talon said. "Faster. And willing to take the hits."

Aurora met his gaze, her resolve hardening. "Then let's make sure we're ready."

Over the next few days, they honed their strategy, refining every detail until there was no room for doubt. Talon trained relentlessly, his movements sharp and precise as he practiced with his knives. Aurora focused on her marksmanship, her aim improving with each passing hour. Havoc seemed to sense the shift in their energy, his usually relaxed demeanor replaced by an almost military focus as he shadowed their every move.

Their first target was a supply convoy traveling along a narrow mountain road. The plan was simple: disable the lead vehicle, neutralize the guards, and seize the cargo. But even simple plans carried risks, and Aurora's heart pounded as they approached the ambush site under the cover of darkness. Talon moved ahead, his steps silent as a shadow, while Aurora covered their rear, her rifle at the ready. Havoc stayed close to her side; his ears perked, and his body tensed.

The convoy came into view, its headlights cutting through the night. Aurora's pulse quickened as Talon signaled for her to take her position. She crouched behind a cluster of rocks, her rifle trained on the lead vehicle. The tension was palpable, every second stretching into an eternity as they waited for the perfect moment to strike.

When Talon gave the signal, everything happened in a blur. The sound of tires screeching, the crack of gunfire, and the shouts of panicked guards filled the air. Aurora's hands were steady as she took out one target after another, her training kicking in like second nature. Beside her, Havoc lunged at a guard who had strayed too close, his growl low and menacing.

By the time the dust settled, the convoy lay immobilized, its cargo secured. Talon emerged from the shadows, his expression grim but triumphant. "Nice work," he said, his voice steady despite the adrenaline coursing through them.

Aurora nodded, her chest heaving as she surveyed the scene. "One down," she said, her voice resolute. "How many more to go?"

"Enough to keep us busy," Talon replied, his smirk returning.

They retreated to the cabin under the cover of night, their victory fueling their determination. As they unloaded the cargo, Aurora couldn't help but feel a flicker of hope. They were making progress—small, measured steps toward dismantling the forces that had hunted them for so long. It wasn't just about survival anymore. It was about reclaiming their lives and carving out a future on their own terms.

That night, as they sat by the fire, Aurora glanced at Talon. "Do you think we're making a difference?" she asked, her voice soft.

Talon met her gaze, his eyes steady. "I know we are," he said. "Because for the first time, they're the ones looking over their shoulders."

Aurora smiled faintly, the weight of their mission tempered by the warmth of his words. "Then let's make sure they never stop."

"Together?" Talon asked, his tone lighter now.

"Always," she replied, her resolve unwavering.

As the fire crackled in the hearth and the shadows danced across the walls, Aurora felt a renewed sense of purpose. The road ahead would be long and fraught with danger, but they weren't running anymore. They were fighting, and they were doing it together. For the first time in a long time, the future didn't feel like an impossibility. It felt like a promise.

Chapter 25

THE CABIN STOOD NESTLED among tall pines, its wooden exterior weathered but sturdy, as though it had endured years of storms without faltering. Smoke curled lazily from the chimney, mingling with the crisp mountain air. Aurora paused at the edge of the clearing, her gaze sweeping over the scene. It was quiet—no hum of traffic, no distant sirens, no shadows lurking around every corner. For the first time in what felt like forever, she could breathe.

"Not bad," Talon said from behind her, his tone casual but carrying a hint of approval.

She glanced back at him, a small smile tugging at her lips. "It's perfect."

Talon stepped past her, pushing open the cabin door with a soft creak. He gestured for her to follow, and she stepped inside, taking in the cozy simplicity of their new home. The single open space was dominated by a stone fireplace, with a small kitchen tucked into one corner and a pair of well-worn armchairs facing a wide window that framed the mountains beyond. Havoc padded in after them, sniffing the floor before settling near the hearth, his tail wagging lazily.

"It's rustic," Talon said, dropping their bags by the door. "But it'll do."

Aurora chuckled as she wandered through the space, running her fingers along the rough-hewn wood of the table. "Rustic is exactly what we need."

As the afternoon wore on, the cabin began to feel like more than just a refuge. Aurora unpacked their sparse belongings, placing them carefully on shelves and counters, while Talon worked on reinforcing the locks and ensuring the surrounding area was secure. The sound of birdsong filled the air, and for the first time in weeks, they weren't constantly looking over their shoulders. By the time the sun dipped below the horizon, the cabin was warm and inviting, the fire crackling softly as it cast a golden glow across the room.

Aurora sat on the floor near the hearth. Havoc sprawled beside her with his head resting on her knee. She watched the flames dance, her thoughts drifting to everything they'd been through to get here. Talon sat in one of the armchairs, his posture relaxed but his eyes sharp, always scanning, always ready. For a moment, she let herself imagine that this was their life now—simple, quiet, safe.

"It feels strange," she said, breaking the silence.

"What does?" Talon asked, his gaze shifting to her.

"Not running," she replied, her voice quieter now. "Not looking over our shoulders."

Talon leaned forward, resting his elbows on his knees. "You'll get used to it."

"Will you?" she asked, tilting her head slightly.

His lips curved into a faint smile. "Probably not."

She laughed softly, the sound blending with the crackle of the fire. Her hand moved to the pendant around her neck, her fingers tracing its edges. It had been with her through everything, a reminder of what she'd lost and what she'd fought for. When Talon's gaze dropped to the pendant, his expression shifted slightly, a flicker of something unreadable crossing his face.

"You still wear that," he said after a moment.

"Of course," Aurora replied, meeting his gaze. "It's a part of me."

Talon was silent for a moment before he reached into his pocket and pulled out a similar pendant. The edges were worn, and the surface was slightly tarnished, but it gleamed faintly in the firelight. He held it out to her, his movements deliberate.

"I kept it," he said simply.

Aurora's breath caught as she reached for the pendant, her fingers brushing against his. "Why?"

"Because it reminded me of you," Talon said, his voice steady but soft. "Of everything we've been through. Everything we survived."

She turned the pendant over in her hands, her vision blurring slightly. The weight of it felt heavier than it should have, laden with memories and meaning she hadn't realized she was carrying. "You don't have to let it go," she said, her voice trembling slightly.

"I'm not letting it go," he replied. "I'm giving it to you. You're better at holding onto hope than I am."

Aurora laughed softly, shaking her head as tears spilled down her cheeks. "You're impossible."

"And you're still here," Talon said with a faint smirk. "Guess I must be doing something right."

She placed the pendant beside hers on the table, the two pieces glinting faintly in the firelight. For a long time, neither of them spoke, the quiet filled with the soft crackle of the fire and the steady breathing of Havoc at their feet. Aurora leaned back against the armchair, her head resting lightly against Talon's knee. His hand drifted to her shoulder, a small, grounding touch that spoke volumes.

"Do you think it's really over?" she asked, her voice barely above a whisper.

Talon's fingers tightened slightly on her shoulder. "Not yet," he admitted. "But this is a start."

Aurora closed her eyes, letting the words sink in. The past still lingered, its shadows long and heavy, but here, in this quiet cabin, she felt something she hadn't in a long time—hope. She didn't know what the future held, but for the first time, she felt like they might have a chance to shape it on their own terms.

The next morning, sunlight streamed through the wide windows, casting golden light across the floor. Aurora woke to the sound of birdsong, a soft, unfamiliar melody that made her smile. She stretched, the warmth of the fire lingering in the air as she glanced toward the bed across the room. Talon was still asleep, his face relaxed in a way she rarely saw. Havoc was sprawled near the door, his ears twitching as he dreamed.

Aurora slipped out of bed, pulling on a sweater, and stepped onto the porch. The air was crisp, carrying the scent of pine and earth. She wrapped her hands around a mug of coffee, savoring the quiet as she gazed out at the mountains. It was beautiful here—untouched, peaceful, and far removed from the chaos of their old lives.

She didn't hear Talon approach until he stepped onto the porch beside her, his presence solid and grounding. "You're up early," he said, his voice rough with sleep.

"I couldn't sleep," she replied, offering him a small smile. "Too much to think about."

"Like what?"

"Like whether this can actually work," she admitted, her gaze distant. "Whether we can leave it all behind."

Talon leaned against the porch railing, his arms crossed as he watched her. "We're not leaving it behind," he said. "We're carrying it with us. But that doesn't mean it has to control us."

Aurora glanced at him, her heart aching at the quiet strength in his voice. "You really believe that?"

"I do," he said simply. "Because I've got you. And Havoc, of course."

She laughed softly, shaking her head. "You're ridiculous."

"And you're still here," he replied, his lips curving into a faint smile.

"Someone has to keep you in line," she teased, nudging him lightly with her shoulder.

"Good luck with that," he said, his tone light but his eyes warm.

They stood in silence for a while, the sunlight filtering through the trees as the world slowly came to life around them. Aurora didn't know what the future held, but in that moment, she let herself believe that they might just have a chance at something better. Together.

They stood in silence for a while, the sunlight filtering through the trees as the world slowly came to life around them. Aurora didn't know what the future held, but in that moment, she let herself believe that they might just have a chance at something better. Together.

The quiet stretched between them, the kind of quiet that didn't demand to be filled. Aurora leaned against the porch railing, letting the cool wood press into her palms. The scent of pine and earth lingered in the crisp air, mingling with the faint smokiness from the cabin's chimney. Havoc padded onto the porch, his ears perked as he surveyed the surroundings with the same vigilance that Talon always carried.

"You think he'll ever relax?" Aurora asked, nodding toward Havoc.

Talon smirked, his gaze following the dog. "Not likely. He takes after me."

Aurora rolled her eyes, though her lips curved into a faint smile. "Of course he does."

Talon tilted his head, studying her with an expression she couldn't quite read. "And what about you?"

"What about me?" she asked, turning to face him fully.

"Do you think you'll ever relax?" he asked, his voice softer now.

Aurora hesitated, her fingers brushing against the pendant that now hung alongside Talon's on the chain around her neck. "I don't know. Maybe. It's hard to let go of the feeling that something's always lurking around the corner."

"You don't have to let it go," Talon said, his tone steady but firm. "You just have to trust that whatever is out there, we'll face it together."

Her chest tightened at the sincerity in his voice. "You make it sound so easy."

"It's not," he admitted. "But it's worth it."

Aurora turned back to the view, her thoughts swirling. The mountains stretched endlessly before them, their peaks catching the early morning light. It was beautiful, untouched, and so unlike the world they had left behind. She wanted to believe they could build a life here, away from the chaos, but the scars of their past still felt too fresh.

Talon stepped closer, his hand brushing against hers as he leaned on the railing beside her. "You don't have to figure it all out right now, you know."

"I know," she said quietly. "But it feels like if I stop thinking about it, I'll lose control."

"You've never lost control," he said, his voice filled with quiet conviction. "Not once."

Aurora glanced at him, her brow furrowing. "How can you be so sure?"

"Because you're still here," he replied simply. "And you're stronger than you think."

She laughed softly, shaking her head. "You're a lot more optimistic than I gave you credit for."

"Don't get used to it," he teased, though his smirk softened into something more genuine. "But for you, I'll try."

Aurora reached up, brushing a strand of hair out of her face as she studied him. Talon wasn't a man who showed his emotions easily, but at that moment, she saw him laid bare—his walls down, his defenses lowered. It was a version of him she hadn't dared hope to see, and it made her heart ache in the best way.

"Do you think we'll be okay?" she asked after a long pause.

"We'll be more than okay," he said. "We'll be unstoppable."

She smiled, leaning into him slightly as Havoc settled at their feet. The warmth of his presence, the solidness of his confidence, eased some of the tension coiled in her chest. For the first time in a long time, she felt like they might actually have a chance.

The sound of rustling leaves broke the quiet, and Aurora tensed instinctively. Talon's hand moved toward the knife at his side, but when a deer stepped out of the trees, its head tilting curiously toward them, they both relaxed. The animal stared at them for a moment before bounding off into the forest, its white tail disappearing among the pines.

"You're jumpy," Talon said, though there was no judgment in his tone.

"Force of habit," she replied, her hand falling away from the pendant.

"It's not a bad habit," he said. "But you're allowed to let your guard down here. Just a little."

Aurora nodded, though she wasn't sure she believed him. Letting her guard down had never come naturally, and after everything they'd been through, it felt even harder to do. But she trusted Talon, and for now, that was enough.

As the morning wore on, they began to settle into the rhythm of the cabin. Aurora cooked breakfast, the scent of eggs and toast filling the small space, while Talon checked the perimeter, ensuring that the area was secure. Havoc followed him dutifully, his nose low to the ground as he sniffed for anything out of place.

When Talon returned, his expression was calm but focused. "It's quiet," he said, sitting at the table as Aurora set down two plates.

"That's a good thing, right?" she asked, sliding into the chair across from him.

"It is," he said. "But it's still weird."

She arched an eyebrow. "Weird, how?"

"We've never had quiet before," he replied, his gaze meeting hers. "It feels... unnatural."

Aurora laughed softly. "Maybe you just need to get used to it."

"Maybe," he said, though his smirk hinted at doubt.

They ate in comfortable silence, the clinking of silverware and the crackle of the fire the only sounds. Havoc lay by the door, his ears twitching occasionally but otherwise relaxed. It was the kind of peace Aurora hadn't thought possible, and she found herself clinging to it, afraid it might slip away.

After breakfast, Talon suggested they explore the area. The woods surrounding the cabin were dense but beautiful, the sunlight filtering through the trees in dappled patterns. Havoc bounded ahead, his tail wagging as he sniffed at everything in sight. Aurora followed Talon down a narrow path, her steps light as she took in the sights and sounds of the forest.

"It's beautiful here," she said, her voice filled with quiet awe.

"It is," Talon agreed, glancing back at her. "And it's ours. For as long as we want it."

Aurora's heart swelled at his words, and for the first time, she allowed herself to believe that this place could be more than just a hiding spot. It could be home. They walked for hours, the tension of their old lives slowly giving way to something lighter, something freer.

When they returned to the cabin, the sun was beginning to set, casting the sky in shades of orange and pink. Aurora stood on the porch, watching as the colors deepened into dusk. Talon joined her, his arm slipping around her waist as he pulled her close.

"We're going to be okay," he said, his voice steady and sure.

Aurora leaned into him, her head resting against his shoulder. "I think we will."

Havoc let out a soft bark, settling at their feet as the first stars began to appear in the sky. For the first time in a long time, the future didn't feel so daunting. Together, they could face whatever came next.

Epilogue

The meadow stretched before them, a sea of green and gold swaying gently in the summer breeze. Wildflowers dotted the landscape, their vibrant hues bursting against the backdrop of rolling hills. Aurora stood at the edge of the field, her hands on her hips as she surveyed the cabin nestled in the distance. It looked different now—more like a home and less like a hideout. The weathered wood had been sanded smooth, the windows now framed with curtains she'd sewn herself. A garden flourished in the sunlight, rows of vegetables and herbs thriving in the rich soil.

She turned when she heard the crunch of footsteps behind her. Talon approached, carrying a basket brimming with freshly picked tomatoes. He wore a faint smirk, but there was a lightness in his step that she hadn't seen before. Havoc trotted beside him, his tail wagging as he carried a stick in his mouth.

"Good haul?" Aurora asked, nodding toward the basket.

"Decent," Talon replied, holding it up for her to inspect. "Though I think the dog's more interested in his stick than the garden."

Aurora laughed, her gaze softening as she reached down to scratch Havoc's ears. "He's earned it. We all have."

Talon set the basket on the porch and leaned against the railing; his arms crossed as he watched her. The sun caught the flecks of gold in his eyes, and for a moment, Aurora was struck by how different he looked. The lines of tension that had once etched his face were softer now, replaced by something she could only describe as peace.

"What?" he asked, catching her stare.

"Nothing," she said, smiling. "You just... look happy."

Talon raised an eyebrow, his smirk widening. "That so hard to believe?"

"It used to be," she admitted, stepping closer to him. "But not anymore."

He reached for her hand, his fingers curling around hers as he pulled her closer. "That's because I've got you," he said simply. "And this."

Aurora leaned against him, her head resting on his shoulder. They stood there in comfortable silence, the breeze carrying the scent of wildflowers and freshly turned earth. Havoc lay down at their feet, gnawing contentedly on his stick. For the first time in what felt like forever, the world around them was still.

"You ever think about what's next?" Aurora asked softly.

"Not really," Talon replied. "I used to spend so much time planning for what might happen that I forgot how to live in the moment. I'm done doing that."

Aurora tilted her head to look up at him. "So you're just going to enjoy this?"

"Yeah," he said, his tone resolute. "Because, for once, I can."

Her heart swelled at his words, the simplicity of them carrying a weight that spoke to how far they had come. Talon wasn't just surviving anymore—he was living, and that was something she'd never thought she'd see.

"Do you miss it?" she asked after a while.

"Miss what?"

"The fight. The adrenaline. Always looking over your shoulder."

Talon shook his head, his expression thoughtful. "I used to think I needed it. That it was the only thing I was good at. But now? I don't miss it. Not even a little."

Aurora smiled, her hand brushing against his chest. "Good."

They moved inside as the sun dipped below the horizon, casting the cabin in a warm, golden light. The fire crackled in the hearth, filling the space with a soft glow as they settled onto the couch. Havoc curled up on the rug, letting out a contented sigh.

Talon rested his arm along the back of the couch, his fingers brushing against Aurora's shoulder as she leaned into him. "You know," he said, his voice low, "I never thought I'd get this."

"This?" Aurora asked, glancing up at him.

"A happy ending," he said. "Someone like me doesn't usually get that."

Aurora's throat tightened, but she forced herself to smile. "Well, maybe it's time you stopped thinking of yourself that way."

"Maybe," he said, his lips curving into a faint smile. "You've got a way of making me believe things I didn't think were possible."

"Like happiness?" she teased.

"Like happiness," he echoed, his tone serious but warm.

They sat in comfortable silence, the firelight dancing across the walls. Outside, the stars began to appear, dotting the sky with their faint, steady glow. Aurora closed her eyes, letting the warmth of the fire and the steady rhythm of Talon's breathing lull her into a state of contentment.

For the first time, there were no plans to make, no enemies to fight, no shadows lurking at the edge of their peace. They had fought for this, bled for this, and now it was theirs. The cabin wasn't just a place to hide—it was a home. Their home.

As Aurora drifted off to sleep, Talon kissed the top of her head. "We made it," he whispered, the words meaning as much to himself as for her. We really made it."

For the first time in his life, Talon allowed himself to believe in a future—a quiet, happy one. And as the fire crackled softly and Havoc snored at their feet, he knew he wouldn't trade it for anything.

For the first time in his life, Talon allowed himself to believe in a future—a quiet, happy one. And as the fire crackled softly and Havoc snored at their feet, he knew he wouldn't trade it for anything.

The early morning sunlight spilled through the cabin's windows, casting soft golden rays across the wooden floor. Talon stirred awake to the faint rustling of fabric and the quiet hum of Aurora moving about the kitchen. He lay still for a moment, letting the warmth of the sunlight and the smell of fresh coffee ground him in this new reality.

When he finally rose, the creak of the floorboards under his weight made Aurora glance over her shoulder. She smiled, holding out a steaming mug toward him. "Good morning, sleepyhead."

Talon chuckled, ruffling his hair as he crossed the room. "What time is it?"

"Time to enjoy another day of doing absolutely nothing," she replied, setting the mug down on the table as he took a seat. "Unless you count weeding the garden as something."

Talon raised an eyebrow as he sipped his coffee. "Weeding counts as torture."

Aurora laughed, sitting across from him. "Maybe for you. For me, it's oddly therapeutic."

"Therapeutic?" he teased. "Since when?"

"Since we started building something worth taking care of," she replied, her voice soft but steady.

Talon's smirk faded into something more thoughtful. He reached out, brushing his fingers against hers. "You're right. It is worth it."

They spent the morning in the garden, Aurora carefully pulling weeds and tending to the vegetables while Talon worked on reinforcing the fence. Havoc lounged nearby, his nose twitching as he watched a pair of squirrels dart through the trees. The peaceful rhythm of the day was interrupted only by the occasional quip from Talon or Aurora's playful scolding when he slacked off.

By the time the sun was high in the sky, they retreated to the shade of the porch. Aurora poured two glasses of iced tea, handing one to Talon as they settled into the chairs. The breeze rustled the leaves of the nearby trees, carrying with it the faint scent of wildflowers.

"You ever think about how far we've come?" Aurora asked, her gaze fixed on the horizon.

"All the time," Talon replied, his voice quieter now. "There were days I didn't think we'd make it."

Aurora nodded, her expression contemplative. "Me too. But here we are."

"Here we are," he echoed, a faint smile tugging at his lips.

They sat in silence for a while, the quiet filled only by the sounds of nature. For Talon, the stillness was a stark contrast to the life he'd known—a life of chaos, danger, and never-ending battles. He realized he didn't miss it. Not even a little.

As the afternoon stretched into evening, Talon grabbed a small box from inside the cabin and carried it out to the porch. Aurora looked up from her book, her curiosity piqued as he set it on the table between them.

"What's this?" she asked, setting her book aside.

Talon hesitated for a moment, rubbing the back of his neck. "Something I've been working on."

He opened the box to reveal a small wooden carving—a delicate figure of Havoc, his tail curled and his ears perked. The details were intricate, each line carefully etched to capture the dog's playful yet vigilant demeanor.

Aurora's breath caught as she picked up the carving, her fingers brushing over the smooth wood. "Talon... this is beautiful."

"I figured we should have something to remember this by," he said, his tone almost shy.

Aurora smiled, her heart swelling. "We don't need a carving to remember this. But it's perfect. Thank you."

She leaned over, pressing a kiss to his cheek. Talon's ears reddened slightly, but he grinned. "Don't get used to me being sentimental."

"Oh, I will," she teased, setting the carving down carefully.

As the sun dipped below the horizon, painting the sky in shades of orange and pink, they stayed on the porch, sharing stories and memories. Aurora laughed until her sides ached as Talon recounted a particularly disastrous raid that ended with Havoc stealing a loaf of bread. It was a simple evening, but it was everything they'd fought for.

Later, as the stars blanketed the sky, Aurora tilted her head back, gazing at the constellations. "It's funny," she said softly. "I used to think I'd never see the stars like this again."

"Me too," Talon admitted, his voice low. "I thought I'd spend the rest of my life looking over my shoulder."

"And now?" she asked, glancing at him.

"Now I look forward," he said, his eyes meeting hers. "Because for the first time, there's something worth looking forward to."

Aurora smiled, her hand finding his. "We've come a long way."

"We have," Talon agreed, his tone filled with quiet pride. "And I'm not going back."

As the fire in the hearth crackled softly and Havoc snored at their feet, Aurora leaned against Talon, her head resting on his shoulder. The cabin was quiet, the kind of silence that spoke of peace rather than tension. It wasn't just a place to hide—it was a place to grow, to dream, to heal.

Talon reached for the pendant that hung around his neck, his fingers brushing against it as he spoke. "You know, I used to think happiness wasn't something I deserved."

"And now?" Aurora asked, her voice barely above a whisper.

"Now I know it's something you fight for," he said. "And when you find it, you hold on to it."

Aurora's throat tightened, but she smiled, her hand squeezing his. "I'm glad you finally figured that out."

He chuckled softly, his lips brushing against her temple. "Took me long enough."

As the night deepened and the stars shone brighter, they drifted into a comfortable silence. There were no plans to make, no enemies to fight, no shadows to fear. For the first time in their lives, they were free.

And as Talon held Aurora close, he allowed himself to believe in the life they had built—a life of peace, love, and hope. It wasn't perfect, but it was theirs. And that was more than enough.

Afterword

PLOT TWIST: YOU FINISHED!

That last page turn feels bittersweet, doesn't it? But hey, thanks for taking this journey with me! I poured my heart into this story, and knowing you embarked on it with me means the world.

Writing this book was a blast, and I truly hope you enjoyed getting lost in its pages. Your support is what keeps the ink flowing, and I can't thank you enough for picking up a copy.

What did you think? Your thoughts and feedback are like gold! They not only fuel my inspiration, but they also help other readers discover the world you just explored. Leave a review or shoot me a message – I'd love to hear from you!

Consider yourself an honorary member of the Darker Than Desire Family!

P.S. Craving more Darker Than Desire awesomeness? Snag some exclusive merch (think shirts, mugs, etc.) at: Lucindawicked.com

P.P.S. Let's stay connected! Follow me on social media for the latest updates and more bookish fun:
Lucindaswickedcorner** (on all platforms)
Lucindawicked.com

P.P.P.S. We now have a monthly newsletter join us at: https://lucinda-wicked.kit.com/382b1abd6d

Happy reading adventures!

Lucinda Wicked

About the Author

Meet Lucinda Wicked – a seasoned cosplayer with over a decade of experience. When she's not rocking epic costumes, Luci's crafting eerie delights for spooky souls. Stickers, sweaters, and more – she's got your macabre cravings covered. Her passion for the spooky is woven into everything she creates.

But Luci is more than a business owner; she's a proud member of the LGBT+, BIPOC, and neurodivergent communities. For her, diversity and uniqueness aren't trends – they're a way of life.

You can find Luci's otherworldly wares at *lucindawicked.com*, where she blends the spooky and supernatural into every design. Need a quick cosmic escape? Check out her TikTok micro-episodes featuring the *Cosmic Requiem Circle*.

In her downtime, Luci's dreaming up magical worlds, embracing the spooky, and spreading cosmic vibes. This is Lucinda Wicked – infusing the supernatural into your everyday life.

Join our new Monthly Newsletter! https://lucinda-wicked.kit.com/382b1abd6d

https://www.lucindawicked.com
https://www.facebook.com/Lucindaswickedcorner
https://www.instagram.com/Lucindaswickedcorner/

Also by Lucinda Wicked

Cosmic Requiem Circle Series

The smartest woman in the world

Death has a full time job beheading evil, organising her boot collection, saving the world and thwarting assassination attempts with a ragtag crew of the most chaotic and most lethal people in the world but for all her insight, Death cannot recognise love when it comes visiting.

Let it marinate for a few thousand years...

Sometimes you don't know what love is till it slaps you across the face and sends you to the other side of the room or in this case, when it sits between you both for a few thousand years. In this universe where there are no absolutes and impossibility is a construct, it takes a few impossibles, near world destruction four times over and a couple of thefts for Misery to realise that she's in love with the most lethal woman in the world.

From oblivion to love...

In this story, we watch Death and Misery along with the rest of the crew evolve from indifference to love

Reader Advisory: 'Cosmic Requiem Circle Series' contains content that may be sensitive or triggering for some individuals.

Whispers Across the Styx

In the sultry shadows of the human world, Charon finds a normal fulfilling life. But in the dark hours of the night when the world is asleep, he dons the cloak of the ferryman, guiding souls to the world below. Bound by his duty to the underworld and his love for the simple human life he's living on earth, he struggles to balance the two worlds, his existence, a delicate dance between the living and the dead. His world comes crashing when his heart becomes entangled and he unknowingly falls in love with a goddess.

Circe is a powerful sorceress under the disguise of an average, typical girl living a simple, satisfying life. Haunted by her mother's ghostly echoes, she sets out on a mission impossible, to cross her back to the afterlife. An action that defies the laws of life and death. And this can only be done by one person, the ferryman.

She finds out the ferryman has been right under her nose the whole time and sets out to free herself from her mum's hold. In a bid to protect herself from her past, Circe dances around the truth and soon, the line between love and deception blurs. Charon defies the laws of death, a daring act of love to help Circe, untangling a series of unfortunate events.

Their fate is tested when the veil lifts and Circe's divine nature is revealed. Torn by forbidden love and divine duty, they make drastic decisions. Was their connection ever real or just a form of manipulation to achieve her ends? Or will their love at the end stand the chaos that threatens to tear them apart?

Reader Advisory: 'Whispers Across the Styx' contains content that may be sensitive or triggering for some individuals.

<u>Serpentine Symphony</u>

In the city's pulsing heart, where every corner holds a surprise, Loki, a silver-tongued charmer, locks eyes with Sigyn, a woman rooted in nature's embrace. But Sigyn isn't one to fall for Loki's usual sleight of hand. She's on her own path, with no room for romantic distractions.

Yet fate has other plans—a chance rendezvous at a café, another among the pages of a bookstore, and even the vibrant buzz of a local community affair. At first, annoyed by Loki's persistent presence, Sigyn glimpses a different side to him, a playful, unexpectedly genuine aspect.

When Loki uncovers Sigyn's passion for the great outdoors, he takes a daring leap, joining her on volunteer days and hikes. As they bond over the wilderness, a subtle connection unfurls between them. Intrigued by Sigyn's independence, Loki is drawn to her resilience which ignites a slow-burning courtship neither anticipated.

As Loki peels back the layers of his charm to unveil vulnerability, Sigyn discovers a depth beyond his facade. Their journey becomes an unconventional courtship, where Loki's charisma collides with sincere efforts to capture Sigyn's heart, and Sigyn learns that, sometimes, love blossoms in the most unexpected of places

Reader Advisory: 'Serpentine Symphony' contains content that may be sensitive or triggering for some individuals.

Hearts of Valor & Elegance

In the castle at the heart of battle-scarred Elysia, Tessa Serafina di Acampora faces her wedding to Duka Yosef. She's spent years building herself into a strategic advisor invaluable to the ailing leader of the nation, becoming a woman the world won't forget. The betrothal should be a boon, a promise of the good life. But she can't stop thinking of the other beautiful ladies of the court...

Prema Nyssa, hero of Elysia who just ended their long war with Ermandi, finds herself dragged to Casteli Valoria to reap the rewards. After the relative freedom of the battlefield, she bucks against the firm constraints of noble life and struggles to find her footing in the wake of all she's lost.

When a sinister conspiracy threatens the stability of the kingdom and forces them together, Serafina and Nyssa must navigate a web of political lies and the sparks between them. Not that either knows whether the sparks come from their clash of personalities or the chemistry they can't acknowledge with the eyes of the court on them. In the end, Serafina and Nyssa must decide if those sparks are worth the ultimate sacrifice. Will love win the day, or will the forces allied against them prevail?

Find echoes of lush Renaissance Italy in this forbidden romance, filled with passionate encounters and tender moments. Hearts of Valor and Elegance is a captivating tale of courage, love, and resilience. Perfect for fans of period dramas and epic romances, this novel will sweep you off your feet and leave you yearning for more. Dive into a world of opulence, intrigue, and unspeakable love.

Veil of Deceit

Noa believed that moving away from home and leaving all the memories of her past would help her start a new life without any form of ties to the event that could totally destroy the life she has built. Her stepmother is however determined to draw her back to the shadows of teenage mistakes that Noa has struggled to leave behind. She is also constantly surrounded by the presence of an unknown protector and predator.

Riley after suffering through a toxic childhood and having to murder her own parents as a child finally gets a job as a private investigator. The job is the perfect cover for her second identity as a masked stalker which comes out only at night. Riley finds the perfect prey for her night identity as a stalker and waits everyday for night time when she can stalk Noa. Her job gets better when she gets the official offer to protect Noa during the day as a private investigator. Her obsession with Noa soon develops into a tornado of feelings she can't control.

The clash from discovering the truth of the dual personalities puts Riley in a place of regret and Noa in a place of heartbreak and betrayal.

Will the truth of Noa's past and the stalker's exposed identity prove to be their end? Or will it be the final reason for their bond to become stronger forever?

Reader Advisory: 'Veil of Deceit' contains content that may be sensitive or triggering for some individuals.

Bound to the Queen

When the gods unite two unlikely wolves, Rosalie Thorne feels as if it's a cruel joke. She is taken from her family and held at Moon's Reach in the teeth of the seemingly venomous queen Soraya Stormrend. As days turn into weeks, a fragile but persistent feeling begins to blossom in Rosalie, for the once thought cruel ruler of Moon's Reach. Just as the two women begin to fully accept their bond, the kingdom is plunged into the grips of death and chaos by the betrayal of an unlikely enemy. Whether a cruel joke or the strings of destiny itself, the two mates must test their fated bond and battle with blood to defend their home.

Will the gods be forgiving with their trials, or have they decided to test their decision between the two mates?

Reader Advisory: 'Bound to the ' contains content that may be sensitive or triggering for some individuals.

A Silent Night, A Dangerous Love: A Dark Sapphic Holiday Romance

Nestled in a quaint town, fiery Mairi is determined to escape the ashes of her scandalous and tumultuous past. When whispers begin to snake through her once peaceful home, Mairi returns to her home in New Orleans to finally put the rumors to rest. Feeling backed into a corner, Mairi hires Charlie, an unapologetic woman who works in the city's underbelly. Mairi hopes to reclaim her life and the peace she's held onto for so long. However, as the chemistry between them ignites, their playful charade spirals into a game of passion and desire, revealing hidden depths neither anticipated.

As Mairi and Charlie dive deeper into their lie, the simmering tension between them becomes impossible to ignore. Late-night whispers and stolen glances turn into unforgettable encounters. Just as Mairi's peace is only a breath away, shadows from her past threaten to unravel everything they've built. Both women must choose to confront their dark pasts if they ever want to break the line they have created between illusion and reality

Reader Advisory: 'A Silent Night, A Dangerous Love' contains content that may be sensitive or triggering for some individuals.

Fallen Justice: A Dark Criminal Romance

Snaking through the bustling streets is an unforgiving disease. One that rips away life like the grim reaper during a plague. The city is tainted with cancer-like greed that has shown no whisper of stopping until now. Declan Voss moves throughout life like a shadow-an unwritten ghost set to collect payment from those who benefit from the ones they hold under their boot.

After his most recent hit, the world was set ablaze. Both fear and rejuvenation swirled hand in hand like twin comets. Declan has never had shaky hands when collecting payment, but this time is different-there's an extra obstacle. Sloane Callahan was known for her skills-prey that had learned how to bare teeth and bite back. And she has caught the scent of Declan. Though she walks a thin line, she dedicates herself to her craft and refuses to let her past repeat itself.

As the newly hired protection for the son of Declan's most recent collection, Sloane doesn't plan on failing this time. But little does she know, Declan doesn't plan on it either.

Reader Advisory: 'Deny Defend Depose' contains content that may be sensitive or triggering for some individuals.

Reckless Passions & Dangerous Alliances

Eva seeks refuge in the city's heart, only to find a captivating enigma named Nikki. A chance encounter ignites a spark, but Nikki's truth electrifies - she leads the Infernos, a notorious biker gang shrouded in mystery.

Forbidden desires simmer as Eva delves deeper. The city whispers of Nikki's power, yet Eva can't resist the pull. Threats rise from the shadows, rivals exploit Nikki's attachment, igniting a war. Nikki shields Eva while tightening her grip on power, forcing Eva to witness both the protector and the predator within her.

Loyalties blur as a bond forms, forged in secrets and trust. But a hidden enemy emerges, a rival plotting Nikki's downfall. The Infernos face a brutal showdown, testing love and empire. Sacrifice reveals truth as Nikki makes a heart-stopping choice, and Eva, transformed by danger, rises to the challenge.

A new order dawns. The city awakens to Eva and Nikki, their love forged in passion and sacrifice. But whispers linger, hinting at a deeper mystery that binds them. Can their love face the darkness beneath the surface?

Reader Advisory: *'Reckless Passions & Dangerous Alliances' contains content that may be sensitive or triggering for some individuals.*

Shadows in the Spotlight

Dancing Through Shadows is a story of passion, resilience, and the transformative power of love—both for the art of dance and for each other.

Isabella and Roni are a powerhouse dance duo, known for their magnetic chemistry and precision on stage. But behind the polished performances lies a partnership strained by relentless pressure and unspoken fears. When their pursuit of perfection leads them to the pinnacle of their careers—a high-stakes competition that could define their futures—the cracks in their relationship begin to widen.

As the demands of the spotlight threaten to tear them apart, Isabella and Roni must confront not only their individual insecurities but also the growing distance between them. With their bond unraveling, they make the bold choice to step back from the competitive world and rediscover the joy and freedom that brought them together in the first place.

In a quiet studio far from the chaos, they embark on a journey of healing and self-discovery. Through laughter, tears, and the unshakable rhythm of dance, Isabella and Roni find their way back to the connection that once felt unbreakable—and uncover something even deeper.

Filled with tender moments, raw vulnerability, and a love that grows stronger in the face of adversity, Dancing Through Shadows is a poignant exploration of what it means to truly let someone in—and the beauty of learning to trust yourself along the way.

Will they find the courage to embrace the imperfections and dance together toward a brighter future? One step at a time, they just might.

Reader Advisory: *'Shadows in the Spotlight' contains content that may be sensitive or triggering for some individuals.*

Stolen By Time (Woven Through Time Book 1)

Excited by a curious archaeological find, Dr. Alexandra Sinclair is called to the National Museum of Scotland to analyze 250-year-old artifacts. Inexplicably drawn to what seems to be a perfectly preserved tartan, she can't help herself. It seems to magically call to her, stealing her professional discipline.

Suddenly she is on a hillside in the Scottish Highlands; mystified not only as to where she ended up, but when.

Lost and alone, Alex is thrown into a world that is hostile and dangerous, and the few amicable people she finds are embroiled in a violent rebellion. She seeks safety with the strong, heroic and unbelievably sexy Eilidh MacAlister, a fierce warrior woman with whom she shares explosive chemistry.

She knows she does not belong here, but the longer she stays, the less she wants to go, even if she knew how to get home.

With unlikely allies, and steamy budding romance, Alex is forced to decide if a forbidden love is worth fighting for, or if it was doomed before it ever began.

Ruthless Hearts

Avery, the gritty bouncer, and Jade, the enigmatic beauty, share a tumultuous connection sparked in the nightlife's dark corners. As public tension simmers, their relentless chase evolves into a thrilling hunt, exploring explicit scenes of BDSM passion.

Praise kinks and emotional depths intensify their dark romance, featuring rough passion and moments that'll make you squirm. In the shadows, Avery and Jade evolve, breaking down walls and discovering unexpected facets, culminating in a resolution that embraces the complexities of desire.

Are you ready to step into the Shadows of Desire? Explore the mystery, passion, and unexpected turns in this dark and thrilling romance.

Reader Advisory: 'Ruthless Hearts' contains content that may be sensitive or triggering for some individuals.

Secrets of the Fae (Veiled Chronicles Book 1)

In *Secrets of the Fae*, the Goddess of Death reigns as the guardian of balance, her powers rooted in the shadows of destruction. But when an ancient evil threatens to shatter the delicate equilibrium of the universe, Death must forge an unlikely alliance with Erebelle—a half-demon fae with a mysterious past and a connection to realms beyond comprehension.

Erebelle, grappling with the truth of their existence and the haunting beauty of Death herself, finds their world unraveling. As they delve deeper into the mysteries of their lineage, Erebelle discovers a half-sister they never knew and unearths secrets about their parents that could alter the fate of the universe.

Together, Death and Erebelle must navigate a labyrinth of treachery, ancient gods, and forbidden love, where every choice could tip the scales of life and death. As they confront their innermost fears and desires, they must decide whether to save the universe or sacrifice it all for the sake of truth and passion.

Reader Advisory: 'Secrets of the Fae' contains content that may be sensitive or triggering for some individuals.

www.ingramcontent.com/pod-product-compliance
Lightning Source LLC
LaVergne TN
LVHW041702060526
838201LV00043B/531